HER
NEW
STORY

Center Point
Large Print

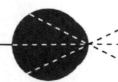

**This Large Print Book carries the
Seal of Approval of N.A.V.H.**

HER
NEW
STORY

Laura Bradford

CENTER POINT LARGE PRINT
THORNDIKE, MAINE

This Center Point Large Print edition
is published in the year 2021 by arrangement with
Kensington Publishing Corp.

The text of this Large Print edition is unabridged.
In other aspects, this book may vary
from the original edition.
Printed in the United States of America
on permanent paper.
Set in 16-point Times New Roman type.

ISBN: 978-1-63808-146-3

The Library of Congress has cataloged this record
under Library of Congress Control Number: 2021944074

For Lynn

Having you, as a friend, has been
one of my true blessings in life

Dear Readers,

Betrayal, particularly at the hands of a loved one, can really change a person. It brings sadness, it brings anger, and, more often than not, it brings with it a reluctance to open one's heart to new people and new opportunities. But it's in this reluctance to forgive ourselves for trusting the wrong people that the greatest pain truly occurs. For when we close ourselves off to new friends and new opportunities, we can't move on, can't heal.

Here, in *Her New Story*, we see how shattered trust at the hands of a loved one affects so many aspects of Tess Baker's life. Because of the betrayal she endures, Tess comes to embrace the common belief that by holding her heart back, she'll avoid future hurt.

But *does* she?

Do we?

Because maybe the best parts of life—the best people and the best moments—are just around the bend if we can only keep our hope and our faith alive.

Happy Reading,
Laura

HER
NEW
STORY

CHAPTER 1

It was happening. It was finally, finally happening. She, Tess Baker, was less than fifteen minutes away from the one dream come true no one could ruin . . . Not her ex-husband . . . Not her once best friend . . . And not their combined betrayal of everything she'd held so near and dear.

Shaking herself off that mental path, she squared her shoulders inside her freshly dry-cleaned navy blazer and reclaimed the smile she'd woken with not more than an hour earlier. *Let them* grab coffee together . . . *Let them* wrap their arms around each other and glide down the sidewalk across from her place every day if they must . . . Because by this time tomorrow, Tess would no longer care. Instead, she'd be nestled in an airplane seat, basking in the rewards of finally believing in no one but herself.

The groan of the restroom door pulled her from her thoughts and sent her gaze scurrying past her own reflection to the sixtysomething woman headed in her direction. Short yet mighty, Debbie Callahan was to the magazine's editorial department what sunlight was to a flower.

"I was hoping I'd catch you before you went into the meeting." Debbie stepped over to the second of the bathroom's two sinks and, after contemplating the nearly empty soap dispenser, turned her full attention to Tess. "Did you manage to get any sleep at all last night?"

"That depends on your definition of *sleep*."

Debbie's left eyebrow rose in amusement. "So that would be a no?"

"No. Well, not exactly. I—" She drew in a breath, held it to a silent count of five, and released it with a *whoosh*. "I got a little. Maybe two or three hours. Maybe a little less."

"I figured as much."

Tess glanced back at the mirror and kneaded at the stubborn shadows beneath her eyes. "It's that obvious, huh?"

"No worries, dear. Your smile is all anyone is going to notice in there, anyway. Especially when it's been such a long time since it's been so genuine, so heartfelt." Debbie leaned against the sink and grinned. "So, have you packed?"

"I have. One suitcase with warm-weather clothes, and one with cold-weather clothes, just like you said."

"Good girl." Reaching out, Debbie guided Tess's fingers away from her face. "Nervous?"

"More like *over the moon*." And it was true. For the first time in far too long, something was about to go her way. The plane ticket and month-long change of scenery it came with were simply the icing on the cake.

"I'm glad. You work every bit as hard as

the so-called"—Debbie lowered her voice—"*veterans.* And you write every bit as well as they do, in my opinion."

Something about the woman's earnestness brought a mistiness to Tess's eyes—a mistiness she hastily blinked away. Sure, it was a nice thing to hear, but just as life had taught her to count on no one but herself, it'd also taught her to place little stock in people's words.

Except, perhaps, Murph's.

Max Murphy—aka Murph—was everything Tess wanted to be as a reporter. A legend in the business, Murph could smell a story halfway across the country. His way with sources, with words, with everyone except, perhaps, his fellow reporters, was, quite literally, award winning. Yet for reasons she still couldn't quite fathom, he'd grudgingly agreed to mentor *her:* a wet-behind-the-ears newbie who'd spent her first month under his tutelage, crying at the drop of a hat. Without him, she'd be hard-pressed to still have a job, let alone poised to be sent out on the kind of assignment normally reserved for those with more than a decade of experience under their belt.

"You okay, Tess?"

Startled back into the moment, she met Debbie's worried brow with an emphatic nod and a reciprocated squeeze. "I'm fine. Really. Just thinking, I guess."

"Then I'll leave you to it." Debbie crossed to the door and tugged it open. "Good luck in there this morning, Tess. I hope you get someplace really fabulous. You deserve it."

"Thanks, Debbie."

Turning back to start, she stared, unseeingly, at her now-lone reflection, her thoughts revisiting the litany of possibilities she'd dreamed up during the wee hours of the night . . .

Would she be paired with a criminal profiler? Travel the back roads of some drug-infested country alongside an undercover agent? Or would she be given something safer this first time—like shadowing a former, yet still beloved, celebrity as he or she searched for their comeback role?

All she could do was guess. For the moment, anyway.

Inhaling deeply, Tess glanced at her watch and then back at the mirror, the smile she found there a perfect reflection of the one she felt clear down to her toes. "It's time. It's really, really time," she whispered.

They were all there, seated around the conference table as if it were any other Monday morning, when she stepped through the open doorway, notebook and pen in hand. Yet, for the first time since joining the magazine's editorial staff the previous year, she didn't scurry toward the end of the table reserved for the junior staff. Instead, she made haste toward the chair Murph motioned her to with his chin and a look she couldn't quite identify.

"I was beginning to wonder if Sam opted to pull you aside first," he murmured as she sank onto the vinyl seat beside him.

She gasped at the thought. "Are you kidding me? I want to get my envelope with all the appropriate fanfare just like I watched you and Russ and Stanley get last year. Giving it to me out in the hallway would ruin half the fun."

Swiveling her chair ever so slightly toward the left, Tess met and held the eyes of the man she both admired and tried to emulate inside the newsroom. To her ignorant and shallow peers, Max Murphy was just some crotchety old man who was set in his ways and would likely die of old age while pecking away at his keyboard in the corner office they all coveted. But to Tess, Max Murphy was everything a veteran news-man should be—sharp, dedicated, and wholly devoted to putting out the magazine's best-ever issue every single time. If he thought an article was well written, he'd say so. If he thought it could have gone a little further, answered a few more questions, he'd mince no words about that fact much to the chagrin of the junior reporters on the team. But what they failed to acknowl-edge—what they failed to step back far enough to see beyond their bruised egos—was something she had come to embrace by the end of her first week on the job: Max Murphy was always right.

He knew the magazine's target market better than anyone else. He knew the kind of stories that spoke to their readers more than any other. And he knew how to tackle them in a way that both educated and intrigued. Anyone who doubted that needed only to look at the byline name on ninety-five percent of the plaques hanging throughout the building.

Yes, the folks in the advertising department were important, their work kept the once-a-month glossy publication thriving financially. And yes, the art department was masterful in its ability to compel people to pick the magazine off the newsstand. But without Murph leading the editorial charge, everything else would be for naught. Period.

Today, though, he looked tired—even a little worn-out. And it unsettled her in a way she hadn't thought anything could in that moment. Glancing quickly toward the owner's still-empty chair, she lowered her voice to a level only Murph could hear. "Are you okay? You look . . . *off.*"

He lifted his pen from the table, poked at his own notepad a few times, but said nothing.

"C'mon, Murph, today is gonna be a great day. For you . . . for Russ . . . for Stanley . . . for"— she sucked back another squeal—"*me!* In just a

16

few hours, you'll be on your way to somewhere supercool, doing what you do best. And when you're done, and it's time to come back, you'll turn all those pages and pages of notes you'll have taken into yet another award-winning story for the magazine, and yet another shiny new plaque for the lobby."

"I don't need another plaque," he said.

"It's not about *needing*, Murph. It's about *earning*. But this time—since I'm part of the mix now—I plan on giving you a run for your money for Story of the Year." Glancing around at their coworkers, she lowered her voice even more. "Just in case you were wondering, that is."

He paused his pen on top of the pad and finally met her eye. "Take it from me. There are other things in life that are more important than a writing award, Tess. Or could be, if you don't narrow your world too much."

"Said the man who has an oft-utilized cot in his office . . ."

"My point, exactly." Dropping his pen onto the table, he glanced from the door, to the wall clock, and back again, an odd sense of discomfort blanketing his very being. "These location assignments aren't always the *be-all that ends all* you seem to think they are, kid. They're really not."

A sense of unease tickled at her spine. "They are to me."

"I know that. But they shouldn't be. Some of the best stories are born in unexpected places— remember that."

"Is there a reason you're saying this stuff, Murph? Is there something I need to know . . . something I—"

"Good morning, everyone! Sorry I'm a few minutes late." Sam Livingston, president and CEO of *In Depth* magazine, blew into the room in his trademark way—shoulders hunched, hair askew, tie in need of straightening, glasses crooked. In his hand, atop his normal meeting notepad, was the stack of envelopes Tess had been imagining for weeks.

"I'm so excited right now I could explode," she whispered to Murph from behind her hand.

Murph, in turn, said nothing as his gaze moved from his feet to their boss.

"We've got a lot to cover in a short amount of time so let's get right to it, shall we?" The wheels of Sam's chair squeaked as he pulled it out from under the table and sank onto its vinyl cushion. "The last issue, with one notable exception, was a good one. Eye-catching pictures . . . thought-provoking interviews . . . and more than a few stories that have prompted some great reader response . . .

"Murph, that piece on the kids' cancer nurse was a real tearjerker that not only resonated on an emotional level but also one that had people

18

reaching into their pockets and donating money to the tune of ten thousand buckaroos in the past week alone. So nice job with that.

"And, Stanley, you've managed to stir up some strong opinions on that piece about the homeless guy and his guitar. So much so, in fact, I'm thinking the subject merits a revisit in an upcoming issue. Surely there are others, like him, with a talent you can showcase."

"You got it, boss." Stanley jotted a few notes on the pad in front of him before returning his attention and, thus, Tess's back to Sam.

"Unfortunately, much of the good I just mentioned was eclipsed by news of an engagement between two of the biggest celebrities of the decade—news our competitor managed to scoop us on even though our very own Tess Baker was in the same park, at the same time it all happened."

Like moths with an open flame, every eye in the room found Tess.

"I . . ." She stopped, blew out a breath, and began again. "I'm sorry, Sam. I just missed it."

Sam held up the competitor's cover picture showing the male half of the powerhouse couple on bended knee. "*Life and Times* didn't."

She dropped her gaze to the table and swallowed.

"C'mon, Sam. Just because Tess was in the same park at the same time doesn't mean she knows what's happening around each and every corner. *Life and Times* got lucky, that's all. End of story," Russ interjected from his spot on the opposite side of Sam. "Look at the picture. Our boy Romeo clearly picked a low traffic area to pop the question. I mean, save for the person on the park bench in the background, it's clear there was no one around other than the photographer with the telephoto lens."

"Oh?" Sam slapped the magazine down on the table in front of Russ. "See anyone *familiar* on that park bench?"

Tess swallowed again, her face hot with embarrassment.

"Whoa," Russ murmured, looking from the picture to Tess and back again. "Wait. You were sitting right there when he asked? How did you miss that, Tess?"

Murph held up his hands as Russ turned the picture for everyone else on staff to see. "What's done is done, right? Harping on it now isn't going to change anything."

Sam's charcoal-colored eyes lit on Murph's before coming to rest on Tess once again. "I believe the more apt summation in this case is what's *not done* is *not* done. But, yes, there's nothing that can be done now except hope we don't lose those readers who put a high value on celebrity news."

A weighted yet deliberate silence hung in the

air for a few moments before Sam grabbed hold of the stack of envelopes at his elbow. "Moving on. It's hard to believe another year has come and gone, but it has. As it always does. But, honestly, this year's crop of assignments is out of this world, if I do say so myself. In fact, these places and subjects have got me itching to be sitting where you are instead of where I am."

The murmuring was back. So, too, was Tess's excitement.

"So, without further ado, here we go." Sam pulled the first envelope off the stack, the name visible to everyone at the table thanks to the large block letters. "Russ, you might want to pack an extra coat for this one, my friend, because it's going to be cold, cold, *cold*."

Russ accepted the envelope from the boss, shook it, felt the right-hand corner with his index finger and thumb, and grinned. "Dare I hope the key I feel in here is for a snowmobile?"

"You can *hope,* sure. But we figured you'd rather have a place to *sleep* seeing as how you'll be gone for a month." Sam moved on to the second envelope. "And, Stanley"—he handed it to the always-rumpled reporter—"*you* don't need a coat of any kind."

Stanley held up his envelope, his gaze meeting and finding Russ's. "Want to switch?"

"Nope. I don't do heat." Russ set his still-unopened envelope on the table in front of him as, once again, all eyes in the room shifted back to Sam.

"I don't know how I'm going to be able to wait to open mine," she whispered to Murph. "Especially when I want to rip *everyone else's* open."

He started to say something but stopped as Sam turned to him. "Murph? I, for one, can't wait to see what you're going to come back with from this one."

Murph leaned in front of Tess, took the envelope with his name on top, and nodded. "I'll do my best."

She knew Murph was still talking—knew he was even exchanging a bit of rapid-fire trash talk with Russ and Stanley—but it was all just an audible blur. She was next . . . She was about to get—

Sam's voice commanded the room once again, causing an immediate flutter in Tess's chest. "Tess?"

She wiped her palms down the sides of her navy blue slacks as he studied the fourth and final envelope in his hand. "Yes, sir?"

"I suggest you move Murph all the way to the top of your holiday shopping list this year. Because, quite frankly, if it wasn't for him, you wouldn't even be going *here*." He thrust the envelope into her trembling hand, waited a beat, and then released her gaze as he stood. "Now while I'd love to stay and watch the reactions to your various locations, I've got a conference call I need to be on in two minutes. That said, if there are any questions your various instructions do not cover, I should be available again in about thirty minutes."

And then he was gone, the echo of his purposeful footsteps quickly drowned out by the repeated chorus of "Open them" from the room's empty-handed.

"Man, Tess, so much for being the rising star," joked Russ as he flipped his envelope over in his hand and slid his index finger beneath the seal. "As for *this?* Drum roll, please. I'm going to— *yes! Alaska!* Finally!"

Pulling out first his plane ticket and then a sheet of paper, Russ silently read the words his eyes raced across. Halfway down the page, he laughed. "So much for a snowmobile . . ."

"Snowshoes?" Stanley quipped.

Russ shook his head.

Murph leaned forward. "Cross-country skis?"

Again Russ shook his head. "Nope. Dogsled."

"Nice," Murph murmured before nudging his chin toward Stanley. "What about you? Where are you going?"

"Let's find out, shall we?" Stanley ripped open his envelope, reached inside, and pulled out his own plane ticket and instructions. "I'm going to . . ." He stopped. Cleared his throat. And, when he felt everyone was properly salivating, turned his ticket around for all to see. "South Africa. To hunt *lion* poachers of all things."

Murph ended his own ensuing silence with a finger snap. "Okay, yes! Poachers are using lion parts to make magic potions! Great assignment!"

Stanley gathered the contents of his envelope in his hand, stuffed them back inside, and then nudged his chin back at Murph. "What'd you get?"

"Let's take a look." Murph pulled a letter opener from his shirt pocket, slid it beneath the seal, and peeked inside, a slow smile making its way across his lips. "I'm shadowing a Special Forces unit in Afghanistan."

"Seriously?" Stanley asked.

Murph pulled out his sheet of paper, unfolded it, and nodded. "I leave tonight."

"Wow! Nice! I'm jealous." Russ nudged his chin at Tess. "And you? What'd you get?"

Looking down at her name written in black Sharpie across the center of the envelope, Tess willed the roar borne on Sam's reprimand to recede from her ears. Twenty minutes earlier, she'd been eagerly anticipating this moment, crazy excited to see where she was going. But now . . . after what Sam had said . . .

She sensed the curiosity building around the room. Felt the table shift as her colleagues seated on the other side leaned forward, waiting. But it was Murph's squeeze on her shoulder that let her know she couldn't stall her way out of opening her envelope.

Drawing in a breath, Tess turned her envelope over in her hand, silently counted to five, and bypassed Murph's offer of his letter opener in favor of her finger.

"Don't be thrown," Murph whispered. "Not here. Not in front of everyone."

Don't be thrown?

Slowly she reached inside the envelope and slid the contents onto the table.

"Is that a *bus* ticket?" Stanley asked, pulling a face of disgust.

She stared down at the ticket, the noted destination making her double-check her name on the envelope. When she found no suitable explanation, she unfolded the accompanying letter and—

No . . .

No . . .

Please, God, no . . .

Glancing at Murph, she saw the confirmation she didn't want yet couldn't ignore away.

"C'mon, Tess, we don't have all day," Russ said, standing. "Where are you going?"

She looked down at the paper a second time, hoping and praying she'd read it wrong the first go-round. But as her eyes fell on the destination printed across the top, and the description of her assignment outlined succinctly below it, there was no mistake to be made. "I-I'm going to Pennsylvania."

Stanley's booming voice cut short a snort of amusement from one of her peers. "Coal mine assignment?"

She shook her head.

"Fracking?" Russ paused en route toward the door. "Because that could actually be a pretty interesting assignment. Especially in the areas where people are starting to realize the environmental risks outweigh the economic benefits."

Stanley, too, stood. "Russ is right. Some of the protests going on in those areas are getting pretty heated."

"I-I'm not going for fracking, or for coal mines," she whispered on the heels of a hard swallow. "I'm going to . . ." She squeezed her eyes closed. "I'm going to Amish country."

CHAPTER 2

The second the conference door clicked closed with Murph's deliberate guidance, Tess pushed back from the now-empty table and gave voice to the frustration she could no longer contain. "Amish country?" she echoed. *"Amish country?"*

"Keep your voice down, Tess. You don't want—"

"Don't want *what?* To reinforce what everyone—including Sam—knows is true?"

Murph crossed his arms in front of his chest and leaned back against the door. "What is this truth, exactly?"

She stared at her mentor, her jaw slacking. "You can't be serious . . ."

"Humor me."

Tess stood and made her way around the back side of the table, her feelings if not her destination crystal clear. "I've earned way better than some throwaway assignment to-to Amish country of all places! I mean, *Amish country? Really?*" She stopped beside their boss's vacant seat and, after staring at it for a moment, lifted her eyes to Murph's. "Wait. Are Sam and Celia having issues again? Because now that I think about it, the last time their marriage was on the skids, his brain sort of disengaged from anything resembling common sense."

"Sam and Celia are fine as far as I know."

She considered his words, another thought dawning on their heels. "Could he be sick? I know he had some sort of doctor visit a week or so ago . . . Maybe there's an issue or something?"

"It was a dentist appointment—routine teeth cleaning. He's fine."

"Then why on earth did he give me this?" Tess waved the assignment sheet in the air. "I'm better than this."

"You saw the cover of *Life and Times*, Tess. That was a huge miss on your part, kid. Huge."

"Okay, so I missed a story. One. Story."

"One too many," he countered. "But in reality there's been a lot more than just that one missed story. You know this."

She stared at him. "What are you talking about?"

"Tess, let's not do this right now."

"No. Please. Let's. What else have I supposedly missed? Because I can't think of a single . . ." The rest of her protest fell away as her thoughts traveled back to the layout meeting she'd missed, a phone call she'd forgotten to make, a—

"Face it, kid, the stuff with Brian and your friend has affected you whether you want to admit it or not."

She dropped the paper onto the desk. "It hasn't. I-I'm over that—over *all* of that. I swear."

"If that's true, why do I see you staring at the phone sometimes when it's ringing? Why do I see you disappear into the restroom for upwards of thirty minutes some days only to come out with your eyes all red and puffy? And why is Brian's picture still the first thing I see when I open your top desk drawer?"

"Why are you opening my desk drawer?"

"I was out of paper clips, but that's not the point here. Everything I just mentioned says you're not even close to being over what happened. And it's understandable, Tess. It is. You got blindsided, kid. In the worst way possible. But you're not going to be able to truly move on until you deal with it head-on."

She looked up at the ceiling, gathered her breath, and released it in a long, drawn-out sigh. "I *have* moved on, Murph. I'm fine."

"You're not fine," he argued, his voice gentle. "Missing that story? That was colossal. In this day and age when everyone is getting their news online, we've gotta do everything better than the other guy. You know this. We've talked about this countless times. And if even *one* of the *Life and Times'* staffers notices that it's you on that bench in the background and blows you—and *In Depth*—up on social media, it won't be good. For any of us."

"I know. It-it was a mistake. That's all. I just wasn't paying attention. It could've happened to anyone."

"Not to a reporter of your caliber." Consulting his watch, Murph yanked the closest chair away from the table and took a seat. "You might not want to hear this, but I'm gonna say it anyway. Sam had already pulled you out of the lineup when I saw him last night. In fact, when I stuck my head in his office on my way out for dinner, he'd just gotten finished canceling your original itinerary. I convinced him to give you a chance with something different—something easy, where no balls can be dropped."

She felt herself squirming under his watchful eye. "Where was I supposed to go?" she asked.

"It doesn't matter."

"It does to me."

"You really want to know?" he asked.

"Yes."

"You were going to Belize. To cover the efforts being made to transplant living coral to those places where it's dying off."

She blinked against the tears borne on his words—at a reality that was supposed to be but now wasn't. "So instead I'm going to *Amish country?*" she asked, her voice raspy. "How is that fair? They couldn't be more night and day from each other."

"You're right. They couldn't be."

Closing her eyes against the image of marine biologists and the stories waiting to be told, she forced herself to breathe, to steady her voice. "Do you think it's too late to still go there instead?"

"Yes, Tess. It's too late. Trust me."

"But *Amish country?* There's no juice—no splash—to be had there. And there's most definitely nothing that'll get my name on a plaque out in the lobby."

"Maybe juice isn't always what's needed. Maybe, just maybe, there's a group of readers who will find that lack of juice refreshing. People need light and good, too, Tess. And the Amish"—he pulled her assignment sheet in front of him and silently perused the details—"could be an interesting counterpoint to life as we know it today if you opt to go that route."

"Do you really believe that?"

He pushed the paper back in her direction and shrugged. "It doesn't matter what I believe. Or what you believe, either. Because unless you've got another job offer, or a trust fund stashed away somewhere, this assignment in Amish country is what you've got."

"But—"

"Do you remember your first day on the job? How you asked me what it took to move up the ladder with Sam?"

She nodded.

"Do you remember what I told you?"

"You mean after you asked me if I wanted a career or just a job?" At his nod, she repeated the short but oh-so-accurate list that had proven to be invaluable over the past year. "Take on the assignments no one else wants. Never under-

31

estimate the power of a picture. Never shirk a story because it's too close to deadline. Quadruple-check every word in every story, always. And write something that gets us noticed, either by an increase in newsstand sales or an award of some kind that Sam can use to woo more advertising dollars."

Murph tented his fingers beneath his chin. "And do you remember what I told you when you asked what angers him most?"

"Of course. Getting scooped on a . . ." The rest of her sentence drifted away as the reality behind her current state of affairs made her stagger back against the wall.

"You were *in the background* of the photo, Tess. Which means you were in full-detail proximity when the biggest couple-of-the-moment got engaged. Yet we didn't have it on our cover—or even anywhere inside the issue, for that matter—because you were somewhere other than on that park bench that day."

She held up her hands. "Look, I get it. I really, really do. I missed a story—a big one. But I've also *uncovered* a lot of big ones since I've been here, too. Doesn't that count for anything?"

"He gave you an envelope, didn't he?" Murph countered. "Look, I won't lie. He was a tough sell. But Sam Livingston is nothing if not fair."

She didn't mean to snicker. She really didn't. But neither could she hold it back.

"You disagree?" he said, eyeing her across the top of his fingertips.

"*Fair* isn't the first word that comes to mind when we're talking about being given a location assignment to Amish country, P-A," she murmured.

"Okay. Then what is?"

"Torture . . . pathetic . . . embarrassing . . . Take your pick."

"You blew a story, Tess. The *alternative* to Amish country was either your desk chair *here*"—he pulled his hands apart to gesture at their surroundings—"or the unemployment line."

"But—"

"I know you can prove him wrong, kid. It's why I fought for you to get this assignment."

Her mouth grew dry. "Meaning?"

"Meaning, in Sam's eyes, your little oversight at the park will likely have a certain segment of our readership looking to our competition for entertainment news. And if they start looking elsewhere for *that,* they might start looking elsewhere for other stories, too." Murph looked again at his watch, compared it to the wall clock behind Tess, and then pushed back in his chair. "So you might want to start looking at the gift he gave you as something other than torture, pathetic, and *what else* did you say?"

"Embarrassing."

"Yeah. That. Because this could be your chance

33

to earn us some new readers and maybe even some of those plaque-mounted accolades Sam likes so much."

"But *Amish country?* Really? What's to investigate there? Someone driving their horse and buggy out on the main road?"

He crossed to the door but stopped short of actually opening it. "They *all* ride on the main road, Tess."

"Okay, then what? Someone buys a stick of butter instead of using the family churn?" She forced a quick, dramatic inhale. "Ooooh, how very *edge of your seat.*"

"You've seen my portfolio, Tess. Some of the best stories I've ever written weren't of the edge-of-your-seat variety. Instead, they grabbed readers on an entirely different level. So find that level and knock it out of the ballpark like I know you can. Appealing to new readers is the name of the game these days." Murph tucked his envelope into his back pocket. "You want to go to Belize next year? Then you've got to get yourself back in Sam's good graces. And the only way that's going to happen is if you find the magazine some new readers and give Sam a reason to puff out his chest in pride. *Do that*—and lose the bitterness—and you'll be okay."

"I'm not bitter," she managed past the rising lump in her throat.

He raised his eyebrow. "Did you not hear yourself just now? Making assumptions about an assignment before you're even there? You know better than that."

Blinking against her eyes' renewed misting, Tess wandered over to the door and Murph, her heart heavy. "When do you have to leave?"

"Tonight."

"Any chance we'll be able to talk while you're over there at all?"

"I can't say for certain until I'm there, but I would imagine I'll have the occasional down-time."

In lieu of the words she couldn't muster lest she start to cry, she nodded.

Murph, in turn, released his hold on the doorknob for a moment and waited until she met his gaze. "The Amish live at a much slower pace than we do."

"Yeah, I've got that," she said.

"That doesn't have to be a bad thing, Tess." At her humorless laugh, he continued, "It might actually end up being what you need most."

"I *need* this job. I *need* to be the best I can be. That's it."

"You can be, and you will be. But even more than that, you need your life back."

Her answering laugh was wooden, even to her own ears. "I don't *want* my life back. Ever."

"You don't want Brian and Mandy *in* your life. That's different. But you need to get back

35

to *living* your life." The crustiness he wore like a favorite cloak dimmed with a softness he didn't often show. "I may not have much of a life outside this building, but that doesn't mean I don't know what one is or what it's supposed to be. Likewise, I know that having it ripped away like you did could take anyone to the edge."

"I'm not—"

He stopped her words with a splayed palm. "I'm worried about you, kid. Have been for a while now. That's why I gave you the card for that therapist friend of mine last month. But you never called her, did you?"

"I don't *need* a therapist, Murph. I've told you that a million times. I'm fine—truly! Because, when it comes right down to it, Brian and Mandy did me a favor."

"A favor?"

"Yes! They showed me exactly who I can count on in life—and that's *me*. As long as I know that, and never let myself think otherwise again, I'm fine."

"Then why are you always turning down invites to go out with the rest of the crew after work? It'd be good for you."

"You don't go, either," she protested.

"Apples and oranges, kid. Apples and oranges."

"No, it's not apples and oranges, Murph! You've gotten where you are by working hard, not by running out the door at five o'clock to belly up to some bar and talk trash about all the coworkers who aren't there."

"They do that, huh?"

She rolled her eyes. "I told you at the end of my first week on this job that I wanted to *be you* one day."

He laughed. "You might want to aim a little higher in life, because this ain't what you think it is. Trust me on that."

"Fine. But I need *you* to trust *me* when I tell you I've got nothing to work through"—she swept her hand toward her abandoned envelope— "present situation excluded, of course."

"I suspect a place like that could be very healing if you give it a chance."

"I don't need to *heal,* Murph," she said through gritted teeth. "How many different ways can I say that?"

"You can *say* it all you want. But that smile of yours? The one that's been essentially missing since you walked in on them in your apartment that day? That—or, rather, the lack of it—says otherwise."

"I smile!" She forced her lips into the most convincing example she could muster. "See?"

His left eyebrow rose.

"Okay, so I'm not a smiler," she argued, abandoning her efforts. "Big deal. Neither are you, now that we're on the subject. But that doesn't mean you need to see a therapist, does it? Or that you need to go live with people who prefer to bump into furniture at night rather than flip on the big, bad, evil light switch, right?"

Momentary amusement lifted his right eyebrow in line with his left. "Okay, okay . . . Just give it a chance, will you? That's all I'm saying."

"You say that like I actually have a choice in the matter."

"Because you do," he said, pausing with his hand on the doorknob. "Remember that."

CHAPTER 3

Tess was mere steps from the same coffeehouse she could see from her apartment's living room window when she heard the melodic laugh that had been as much a part of her daily life as the deep rumbly voice that followed. But instead of the joy both had once brought, there was only dread—teeth-clenching, palm-sweating, pulse-thudding dread.

And, just like that, she was standing outside her apartment door once again, grinning like the naïve idiot she'd been as she slid her key into the lock and stepped inside her once-perfect world. Even now, nearly a year after that life-changing day, she could still hear the echo of her own gasp as her gaze fell on her best friend—unclothed—and the man she'd exchanged vows with in front of God and their respective families less than six months earlier. Call it shock, call it stupidity, but in the actual moment her thoughts had raced about in search of an innocent explanation: Mandy's clothes had gotten wet in the rain that wasn't falling, or she'd spilled something greasy on her work clothes that required an immediate washing lest they be ruined . . . But as Brian's face had grown beet red and he'd shifted from foot to foot, clutching a pillow in front of his own unclothed body, reality had come crashing in around her like a tsunami.

Her best friend since high school was having an affair with the very same man who'd promised to love and cherish Tess all the days of his life and—

Shaking the rawness of the memory from her mind's eye, Tess took in her immediate surroundings, spied a dumpster midway down the narrow alley to her left, and ducked behind it, her heart pounding wildly inside her chest. Yes, in some dark recess of her brain, she knew she wasn't the one who should be hiding, but the heart these same two people had shattered into a million pieces was a long way from beating normally let alone being able to stand on anything resembling principle.

She tried to close her eyes to save herself the added pain of watching her ex-husband and her ex-best friend walk by without so much as a backward glance in her direction, but like a career rubbernecker at the scene of a fatal accident, she couldn't. Instead, as the laugh—and the voice that sparked it—grew louder, Tess peeked around the edge of the dumpster just in time to see her life walk by without her.

Like a punch to the gut, the fleeting moment buckled her knees and threatened to drop her where she stood. But as she lurched forward to steady herself against the metal container, her satchel gaped open just enough to send its contents skittering across the concrete. Glancing back toward the sidewalk, Tess held her breath as the clatter of pens and coins—some against the dumpster itself—seemed to ricochet its way toward the sidewalk.

Would they turn around?

Would they step into the alley, looking for the source of the sound?

Would they see her peeking out from behind the trash container—hands shaking, cheeks flaming, tears brimming?

Please, God, no . . .

Seconds turned to minutes as she waited, the now-silent alleyway giving up no further sounds beyond her own shallow breaths. When those, too, subsided, she collected the items she'd dropped, stuffed them back into her bag, and made haste across the street to her apartment building.

Inside, she avoided the eyes of her neighbors as she maneuvered around them to her mailbox. After nearly twelve months, she recognized everyone who lived in the three-story building even if she didn't know their names. There was the tall, lanky redhead on the third floor who, like Tess, seemed content to keep to himself . . . There was the elderly gentleman who lived on the first floor, his penchant for playing along with television game shows audible to anyone who happened by his closed door between the

41

hours of ten and twelve on any given week-day . . . And there was, of course, the single mom and her rambunctious seven-year-old son who lived across the hall from the redhead and directly above Tess . . . All nice people. All happy to trade a smile on the way in or out of the building without any sort of expectation for the kind of friendship she didn't want.

Even Mrs. Appleton, the one tenant she knew by name, kept a respectful-enough distance, provided Tess gave the sweet-natured gossip something fairly innocuous to chew on every once in a—

A *tsk-tsk* sound just over her shoulder pulled her attention from the bills she was procuring from her box, and fixed it, instead, on the eightysomething woman eyeing her from behind wire-rimmed bifocals.

"Mrs. Appleton, hello. I didn't know you were there," Tess said as she closed and locked her mailbox door.

"How could you? Your mind was a million miles away just now. And judging by the expression on your face, I'm guessing it wasn't visiting a particularly happy place."

"You're right. It wasn't."

"He didn't deserve you, dear. Not one little bit. Remember that."

She stared at the woman. *"He?"*

"The one who broke your heart."

42

"H-how did you know?"

"My first clue was your ring finger," Mrs. Appleton said, lifting her own as an example. "The tan line you had when you first moved in stopped where a wedding ring would have been."

Tess swallowed.

"The second clue was the trash receptacle in those first few days and weeks."

"The trash receptacle?"

Pursing her lips, Mrs. Appleton nodded, knowingly. "There were at least four-dozen photographs that had been ripped down the center with the same young man's face in all of them."

Tess dropped her gaze to the ground.

"And third? The nighttime crying."

She felt her face flush at the accuracy of the woman's words. More than anything, she wanted to object, to blame a too-loud television program for the sounds that had clearly seeped through the vents in Tess's bedroom floor. But the denial required to do so took more energy than she had at the moment. Instead, she pulled the stack of mail to her chest and concentrated on keeping her voice as steady as possible. "I-I didn't know. I'm sorry if I've kept you awake a time or two."

"There are no apologies needed, dear. Except, perhaps, *from me.* I've often thought of knocking on your door and offering you a shoulder to cry on, but my arthritis makes the steps up to your place a bit difficult even on the best of days."

"I'm fine. Really." Tess tucked her mail into her satchel and squared her shoulders. "That's all behind me now."

"Good girl, my dear! Keep telling yourself that until it's finally true."

"It *is* true," she countered.

Mrs. Appleton rested a wrinkly, age-spotted hand on Tess's forearm. "When the crying stops once and for all, it'll be true."

"It—"

"Now tell me, dear, did you get your assignment?"

She drew back. "My assignment?"

"The one you've been talking to yourself about for days."

Making a mental note to find some sort of cover for her floor vents, Tess embraced the conversational shift. "Oh. Yes. That . . . Yes, I got it. Unfortunately."

"I take that to mean it wasn't what you'd hoped?"

She didn't mean to laugh, nor could she not. What she'd wanted and what she'd gotten were as far from each other on the hope spectrum as humanly possible. "Definitely not what I'd hoped."

"I'm sorry to hear that, dear. But it's still somewhere different, right?"

"Oh, it's different, all right. In every sense of the word."

44

"That's good."

"Good?" she echoed, only to shake off the woman's summation completely. "Yeah, no . . . This is most definitely *not* a good different."

Slipping her mailbox key into the front pocket of her flowered housecoat, Mrs. Appleton motioned for Tess to follow her into the hallway. When they reached the spot where Tess would turn toward the stairs, the woman stopped, her large owlish eyes lifting to meet Tess's. "When you've lived as long as I have, young lady, you find that you've learned many things—some right on time, and some a bit later than you might have liked. But all are worthwhile in the grand scheme of things."

"Okay . . ."

"One of my favorites is one I suspect you're about to learn, and, boy, is it a good one."

"Oh?" Tess asked. "And what is that?"

"That sometimes the biggest blessings in life come from the places we least expect."

Tess sat on the edge of her bed and stared at the two suitcases she'd meticulously packed roughly twenty-four hours earlier. The tan one on the left held all of her winter clothes—her sweaters, her warmest jacket, her jeans and corduroys, two hats, two sets of fleece-lined gloves, and the pair of winter boots she'd found online the previous week. The outer compartment held a pair of earmuffs and an extra-wide wool scarf. The black one on the right catered to the opposite end of the weather spectrum—shorts, a few simple skirts, a dozen comfortable shirts in a variety of colors, hiking boots, sneakers, sandals, and the pack of cooling neckbands she'd added to her boot order at the last minute.

"Ready no matter what I get," she murmured. "Yeah, what a joke."

Dropping onto her back, she blocked her view of the ceiling with her arm. If she were Russ, the tan suitcase would have been perfect. If she'd been Stanley, the black would've worked just fine. If she were Murph, some combination of the two with a quick stop at the army-navy store on the way to the airport would have sufficed. And if she was the version of herself that wouldn't have missed a celebrity engagement happening mere feet away, she'd be tossing a handful of swimsuits into the black suitcase in the event she might be invited along on a few dives around the reef . . .

"But hey, who wants to go to Belize when they can go to *Amish country, P-A*." She threw her arm back onto the bed and let loose a groan so loud she quickly followed it with an apology in the direction of the floor vent.

Seconds turned to minutes as her gaze moved from one end of the ceiling to the other, her mind's eye replacing the bubbling paint and occasional water stain from the super's failed attempt to *make things nice* with a veritable slide-show of images.

Russ on a dogsled, shouting *Mush* again and again . . .

Stanley sitting shotgun in a topless Jeep while the driver raced across the open tundra in pursuit of a poacher . . .

Murph, dressed in camouflage, trekking across mountains and through a labyrinth of underground tunnels behind five stealthy warriors determined to—

A persistent buzz brought the parade of scenes to a merciful end and Tess to her feet in time to catch Murph's name on her phone's illuminated screen. Drawing in a steadying breath, she took the call.

"Hey, Murph. Are you at the airport?"

"I am." A quick crunch in her ear was followed by an audible sip of what was surely the Murph Special—black coffee, large. "So, what time are you rolling out?"

She closed her eyes against the image of the bus ticket she wished she could banish from her reality yet couldn't. "One p.m."

"Ready to go?"

This time, when her mind wandered, it wasn't to Alaska with Russ, or Africa with Stanley, or even Afghanistan with Murph. No, this time it was to the lab she wouldn't get to explore and the scuba tank she wouldn't be able to don because—

"Tess? You still there?"

"Unfortunately."

"Have you packed yet?"

"I did . . . last night . . . for both extremes. But now, neither is right." She heard the emotion building in her voice and tried to hold it at bay, but that was better than giving heed to the tears she felt waiting in the wings. "I mean, I'm supposed to be living among these people, aren't I? So what does that mean in terms of packing? Do I leave all of my socks and shoes behind? And where on earth am I going to find a bonnet this late in the game?"

Murph's answering laugh gave way to first a cough and then a string of PG-rated expletives she'd all but memorized.

"You're wearing half your coffee, aren't you?" she asked.

"No . . ."

"Liar."

"Wait . . . Hold on a minute . . ." She knew from the sudden absence of any sound in her ear that he'd either set the phone down or covered it with his hand. Soon, though, his two-pack-a-day voice was back. "Looks like we've gotta wrap this up, kid. They're starting to board my flight, and I probably should hit the head before they call my group number."

The emotion was back. So, too, was the promise

of tears. "Check in as soon as you're able, okay? A call, a text, an email, whatever."

"Will do." A change in his cadence suggested he'd stood, maybe even grabbed his bag. "You've got this, Tess. You really do. But two things before I go, okay?"

"What's that?"

"First, the Amish wear shoes *and* socks."

"Are you sure?" she asked, only half kidding.

"Yes."

She returned her gaze to the pair of suitcases. "And the second thing?"

"That thing the Amish women wear on their heads? It's called a prayer kapp, and you don't need one. You're English."

"Wait. How do you know that's what it's called? Were you Amish at some point along the way?"

Again he laughed. And again it gave way to a string of gibberish in which only every third or fourth word was even the slightest bit coherent.

"Here's hoping your camo is coffee colored," she quipped while simultaneously willing herself up and onto her feet.

"Ha . . . ha . . . ha . . . Funny." And then, "Pack your bag, kid. You'll be staying in a cottage on a working Amish farm. Jeans, shirts, *and sneakers* should be fine."

"Should I bring my milking stool, too?"

"Nah, you should probably leave that at home.

And while you're at it, you might want to leave that bitterness we talked about behind, too. It doesn't become you."

Tightening her grip on the phone, Tess made herself cross to the pair of suitcases flanking her dresser. "C'mon, Murph. If you were me, you'd be dreading this assignment every bit as much as I am."

"Actually, kid, if I were you, I'd just be glad I still had a job."

CHAPTER 4

Ever since Tess was little, the steady speed and rhythmic pace that came with highway travel had been an instant sleep tonic. As long as the car or, in this case, the bus moved with consistency, point A and point B were always next-door neighbors in her book regardless of whatever mileage may have separated them on a map. But the moment the movement began to change, her eyes would snap open and the fog of sleep would lift as quickly as it had come, depositing her at the park . . . the beach . . . the city . . . the mountains . . . or—

"Did you have a good rest, dear?"

Rubbing her eyes, Tess abandoned her view of a working windmill in favor of her seatmate. Roughly in her seventies, the woman who'd introduced herself as Mildred within seconds of sitting down followed her warm, grandmotherly smile with a chuckle Tess needed no help to decipher.

"I fell asleep while we were talking, didn't I?"

"Right in the middle of a sentence."

"It wasn't the company, I promise. Rather it was more about being unable to keep my eyes open at highway speeds." Swinging her focus back to the window, Tess took in the seemingly endless patchwork of lush green land to her right and gave into the sigh she couldn't hold back. "But, clearly, anything resembling speed is over now."

"In more ways than one."

She glanced at her seatmate. "Meaning?"

"There's nothing about being here that's speedy. Not the people, not the pace, not anything." The woman nudged Tess's gaze back to the window. "How long are you here for?"

"*Thirty* days." Tess reached up and kneaded at the hint of a headache scrambling into position near her temples. "As in thirty days too—"

The audible hitch of Mildred's breath stole the rest of her words and replaced them with Mildred's. "Thirty days? Really? How wonderful!"

"You call that wonderful?"

A flash of surprise traded places with an emphatic nod. "Of course. I would love to spend that kind of time here."

Tess drew back. "Why?"

"It's the only place I know that can put some much-needed distance between myself and stress."

"What about the beach?"

"No."

"The mountains?"

"No."

"What about . . ." She cast about for another possibility. "A spa?"

The woman's laugh earned them a few looks

from across the aisle, looks the woman didn't seem to see as her own gaze gravitated back to the window. "No. Those sorts of places might be peaceful for some, but not for me. This? *This* is *my* happy place."

Not sure what to say, Tess opted to say nothing lest she hurt the woman's feelings.

"Do you have family here?" Mildred asked. "Is that why you're here so long?"

"No, it's just a work thing."

"I see . . . Are you staying at one of the hotels or a bed-and-breakfast?"

She resisted the urge to roll her eyes and, instead, let her frustration power a second, longer sigh. "Neither, unfortunately. I'm apparently staying with an Amish family on their farm."

Mildred's fingers squeezed Tess's forearm, only to pull back in conjunction with a quick apology. "You're actually *staying* with an *Amish family? In their house?*"

"I think so. I-I'm not sure, exactly."

"Oh I would love to do that. Absolutely love it. To live the way they do even for a few days would be such a treat."

Tess stared at the woman. "*Seriously?* Don't they live as if they're stuck in another century or something?"

"In many ways, yes."

"You find that appealing?"

Mildred lowered her hand to her lap and

quietly pointed Tess's attention to a mother and daughter in a neighboring seat, their eyes cast downward at individual phones. "Do you see that? That doesn't happen in an Amish home. The Amish see to that by the way they choose to live, by voiding their world of things they see as damaging to their relationship with God and their families. I admire that. I—oh, look . . . There's a young family coming back from church right now."

Tess turned back to the window as the bus driver swung wide to avoid an open-top buggy with four little ones seated across a bench seat behind two people who were clearly their mother and father. The children looked up at the bus, with the youngest returning Mildred's wave. "See? Everything about them reminds me of a simpler time—a time when the right things were the only things that mattered."

"You make them sound as if they can do no wrong," she mused, her intrigue growing.

Shrugging, Mildred liberated an overflowing tote bag from beneath the seat in front of her and set it on her lap. "My husband says that, too. He thinks I'm a little over-the-top in my feelings for these people and this area. But I know what I know. And I know that being here—even for a few days—brings me a kind of peace I rarely find anywhere else. And these days? I'll take that feeling anywhere I can get it. You'll see . . . This place will get under your skin, too. Trust me."

She opened her mouth to challenge the woman's words but closed it as she felt the bus come to a stop. Turning back to the window, she drank in the sight of the small bus terminal to her right, and the line of cars waiting to pick up arriving passengers just beyond the open-air structure. A second, more thorough sweep of the line yielded nothing resembling a taxi or a shuttle bus.

Movement out of the corner of her eye stole her attention back to Mildred in time to see the woman stand, tug the tote bag into place on her shoulder, and ready herself to fall into line behind their fellow passengers making haste down the aisle toward the door. "Are they picking you up here or are you going to them?"

"Them?"

"The Amish family you're staying with."

The thought stalled her hands atop her own travel bag as her gaze gravitated back to the line of cars. "I would imagine my job has a car waiting for me. They handled all of the planning."

"Lucky you."

She didn't need a mirror to know her answering smile had been hijacked by a grimace. She could feel it just as surely as she could dread's return in the pit of her stomach. *Lucky* would have had her exiting a plane not a bus . . . Lucky would have had her staring at a *Welcome to Belize* sign rather than one for Amish country . . . *Lucky* would have her inhaling a potpourri of ocean scents rather than dirt and livestock and God knew what else.

At the base of the steps, she plucked her suitcase from beside the bus, wheeled it over to a shady spot beneath a young maple tree, and pulled out her wrinkled itinerary.

"Excuse me, are you Tess Baker?"

Startled, she looked up to find a thirtysomething Amish woman peering back at her with wide-set hazel eyes and a smattering of freckles beneath a hint of honey-blond hair just visible along the front edge of the white gauzy head covering Murph had called a prayer kapp. Swallowing, Tess lowered the assignment sheet to her side and nodded. "I am."

The woman's trim yet sturdy shoulders rose and fell in relief. "I guessed correctly. That is good."

"And you are?" Tess prodded.

"I am Naomi. Naomi King."

She waited for more, but when no further explanation was offered, she unfolded her paper and skimmed the details. "Naomi King . . . Okay, yes, here it is. You and your husband own the farm where I will be staying."

"Yah."

"I didn't know you would be here to meet me."

Naomi's full lips spread wide with a smile. "I didn't want you to have to walk so far with a suitcase. Once you are settled on the farm, Isaiah

56

has a bike for you to use. It will help you get wherever you must go."

"I don't think this assignment comes with any *must go* destinations. Unfortunately." At Naomi's raised eyebrow, Tess pulled up her suitcase's handle and swept her hand toward the road. "I'm sorry you had to walk all the way here only to have to walk all the way back now with me."

"We will not walk."

"Then how . . ." The rest of her question faded away as she followed Naomi's gaze to a gunmetal-gray buggy and a chestnut-colored mare parked beneath a tree on the far side of the parking lot. "Wait. We're riding in *that?*"

"Yah."

Tess looked from the buggy to her suitcase and back again, her internal wheel turning faster than her thoughts seemed able to keep up. "Is-is there room?"

"Yah. There is much room. Come. You will see."

With nary another word, the Amish woman turned and headed in the direction of the buggy, her plain, black lace-up boots making a soft patter on the macadam. For a moment, Tess remained in place, her mind's eye following the Amish woman across the parking lot while noting the absence of bare feet. Next came the dress—a simple navy blue affair that reached past the knee and was topped with a white, almost apron-like, covering. At the halfway point to the buggy, a flash of movement propelled her gaze beyond her hostess to a young boy standing beside the horse, the straw hat atop his head making it difficult to see whether he was looking at Naomi or Tess. She decided it was her when his hand popped up in a quick yet friendly wave.

Naomi glanced back at Tess. "Come. Marta will not bite, and she will get us where we need to go."

"Marta?"

"My husband's buggy horse."

"Right. Sorry. I'm coming." She wheeled the suitcase across the lot, stopping just shy of the buggy and the boy. "Hi. I'm Tess . . . Who are you?"

"This is Aaron, my son."

"I didn't know you had a child. My boss didn't mention that."

"I have four sons, three daughters, and"— Naomi touched a quick hand to her abdomen— "another one on the way."

"Eight children?" she echoed, drawing back. "How *old* are—" Her words circled around to her ears in time to stop the rest of her question, if not the shame that warmed her face. "I'm so sorry. I didn't mean to be so rude."

"I am thirty-six." Then, without another word, Naomi took control of Tess's suitcase, wheeled it around to the other side of the buggy, and—

"Whoa, whoa. You're pregnant. I can lift that," Tess said, scurrying over only to stop as Naomi hoisted the suitcase into the buggy and instructed her son to climb in beside it. "I could've done that, you know."

"Yah. But so can I. Being with child doesn't mean I can't lift such things."

"Still, you should've let me get it."

"You can get it out when we get to the farm if you would like." Gesturing Tess to follow, Naomi unhitched the mare from a simple metal post, said something to the animal in what sounded like a cross between gibberish and a foreign language, and then directed Tess onto the single narrow bench that served as both the driver and front passenger's seat. Once they were settled in place, Naomi again said something Tess didn't recognize, and the horse began a slow, steady trot toward the exit sign and out onto the road.

Tess tried to drink it all in—the *clip-clop* of the horse's hooves on the road, the warmth of the late-evening sun on her face, and the sudden pounding of her heart as the same bus she'd been on passed them by mere inches, its size and speed shaking their buggy seat as it did. Soon, though, they were on a quieter country road that meandered alongside a field of cattle on their left and crops to their right. "I feel like I've stepped into a different universe," she murmured.

"Are you from the big city?"

"If you're referring to New York City, I live on the outskirts, yes." When Naomi remained silent, she swung her attention off the passing scenery and onto the woman. "Have you ever even *seen* a city?"

"Yah. Many. I have seen Philadelphia, Baltimore, and Tampa. They were all very big."

"So you can actually *leave* this place then?" she asked, motioning to their surroundings.

Naomi's lips twitched with restrained amusement. "Yah. We can leave."

She considered the woman's answer only to find it unleashed even more questions. "How long did it take to get to Tampa in a buggy?"

Amusement gave way to a laugh. "You can't take a horse and buggy that far, Tess."

"A bike?"

"No, not a bike. We went in a car."

"A car? I thought you couldn't drive cars."

"We don't, but we can ride in them." At the end of the road, Naomi guided the horse to go left onto another country road. "Isaiah hires an Englisher to drive us when it is too far to go with the buggy."

"An Englisher? That's what you call people like me, right? Someone who isn't Amish?"

"Yah."

"So Murph—my friend from work—was right about that, too."

"Too?"

"I thought you went barefoot everywhere. He said you didn't."

The amusement was back. So, too, was another odd command directed at the horse.

"Is that Pennsylvania Dutch you're speaking?" Tess asked.

"It is. But it's really just Deutsch, or German. It is what we speak in our home most days, and it is what the children learn before they go off to school. But don't worry. We will speak English with you."

"You do the one-room schoolhouse thing, right?"

"Yah. Through the eighth grade. It is there, like everyone else, that we learn how to read and write, how to add and subtract, and how to do many other things that are useful in our daily life, both at home and in business."

"I want to be a furniture maker when I am big like Dat," Aaron said, sticking his head into the front half of the buggy. "I can make footstools and simple chairs, and I am almost finished with my first table."

"Your first *table?*" Tess echoed. "How old are you?"

"I am eight. Mark and Mervin are nine, and they want to farm like Dat."

"Mark and Mervin are twins," Naomi said, slowing the horse.

"You had twin one-year-olds when this one"—

she hooked her thumb toward the smiling face behind her—"came along?" At Naomi's answering nod, Tess shook her head in awe. "Wow. I can't even imagine that."

Naomi turned onto a sparsely graveled road, her gaze moving from the horse to Tess's hand and back again. "You are not married?"

Just like that, the distraction that was her new surroundings, disappeared. "I . . ." Aware of the wobble in her voice, she took a moment to breathe through it and then course-corrected her way to the only answer necessary. "No. I'm not married."

She could feel Naomi's eyes searching her face for more, but she kept her own on the two-story farmhouse growing ever closer in front of them. Being on assignment was about getting away, about shedding the old Tess in favor of a new one, and about proving to Murph and Sam and everyone else that the days of Brian and Mandy affecting her life were truly over. Because they were, had been for—

Turning her head to the right, Tess used the momentary break from Naomi's visual inquisition to swipe away the wetness gathering in the corners of her eyes.

"That's Dat's barn right there."

Grateful for the distraction for both herself and Naomi, Tess followed the path forged by Aaron's finger to a large, weathered structure open wide to the evening air. To its right were stacks of baled hay, and to its left were a pair of cats who'd wandered out onto the grass just long enough to stop, stare, and then scurry back inside as the buggy drew closer.

"And that's where we live," Aaron said, directing her gaze back to the farmhouse in front of them.

The house was simple with white clapboard siding, a wide front porch with a trio of rocking chairs to the side of the door, and dark green shades open to the midway point in all of the second-floor windows. To the left of the house, not much more than twenty feet away, was an empty clothesline. To the right of the house and secured inside the kind of metal rack Tess remembered from her elementary school days was a series of bicycles, in various sizes and colors. A closer look yielded a lack of seats and a foot shelf that more closely resembled that of a scooter.

Beyond the bike rack was a second, smaller structure that appeared, from her vantage point inside the buggy, to be attached to the main house.

"You will stay there, in the Grossdawdy Haus."

"What is a Grossdawdy Haus?" Tess asked.

"It is where Isaiah's mamm and dat lived before they passed last spring. It is small but cozy, and the girls have helped ready it for your visit."

Naomi brought the buggy to a stop beneath a tall oak tree. "Mr. Livingston said you would like to live as we live while you are here, yah? He said you will rise when we rise, eat when we eat, work as we work, and visit when we visit."

She stifled the urge to groan and, instead, nodded. Slowly. "That's generally the way these assignments work. Full immersion and all that."

"The only thing Isaiah would not allow is church. Since the sermon and songs are sung in German, you would not be able to follow along, anyway."

"That's fine. I can fit in extra time at my computer while you're gone."

"There is no electricity in the Grossdawdy Haus." Naomi tucked the reins on the buggy floor, gave permission to Aaron to join his father in the barn, and then climbed out with the same efficiency she'd driven the buggy.

"Whoa, whoa. Wait up!" Jumping down, Tess hurried to catch up with Naomi. "I get that you don't use lights and stuff like that, but I'm a reporter. Writing is my job. That's why I'm here—to write."

"Yah. That is why there is a notebook and a pen in the Grossdawdy Haus."

She knew she should be lifting her own suitcase out of the buggy, but in that moment she was so busy trying to wrap her head around what she was hearing, all else faded. "It's just one computer—a laptop, actually. And because the screen is lit, I don't even really need a light of any kind while I'm using it. Surely it'll be okay to plug in that one thing, right? If I keep it to a minimum?"

"We are Amish. We do not have electricity in our homes."

Tess glanced toward the eaves, noted the absence of electrical wires, and staggered back a step. "Please tell me you have underground wires?"

"We don't have any wires."

"But I'm not a longhand writer. I write straight into my computer!"

"I am sorry, Tess. It is the Amish way."

"Then I'll need to call my boss real quick and let him know about this little wrinkle. Since I'm here on a work assignment, he'll want to make arrangements for me at one of the hotels in town."

"Mr. Livingston knows. It was he who asked me to have a notebook and pen waiting for you when you arrived." Lifting her face to the sky, Naomi drew in an audible breath. "It will rain soon. We should get you settled inside before it falls. Come, let me show you where you will stay."

CHAPTER 5

As she followed Naomi from the sparsely fur-
nished living room into the small but ample
kitchen, Tess strained to pick out any sort of
sound—a laugh or the rapid shutter of a camera—
that would prove she was the butt of some sort
of twisted joke. But try as she might, reality won
out over any and all mental pleading.

"Do you like to cook?"

Stopping at the simple wooden table, Tess sank
onto the first of its two sturdy benches. "Cook?
Me? No, not really. Not anymore. Not since"—
she sat up tall, swallowed back the rest of an
answer she didn't want to give, and hurriedly
crafted a better, more palatable one to offer in its
place. "With the hours I put in at work, it's just
easier to grab takeout most days."

"I'll start you with bread then. It was my
mamm's recipe. And how about quilting or
sewing? Do you do that?"

Her gaze snapped to the woman now opening
and closing cabinets as if searching for something. "Quilting? Sewing? No . . . Why?"

"I bought a bolt of fabric to make into shirts for
Isaiah and the boys."

She was waving her hands before Naomi was
even done. "I might be able to figure out how

to replace a button with time, but making actual shirts that people will wear? I don't know about—"

"I will teach you." Naomi opened and closed the last cabinet in the kitchen, and when everything was to her satisfaction, she joined Tess at the table. "Since it's your first day and you'll want to get settled in, I think it'll be best to start tomorrow morning. Rita can meet you in the barn and show you how to gather the eggs."

"Rita is your daughter?"

"Yah. She is twelve."

"How will I know what time to meet her?" Tess asked.

"The rooster will tell you."

She glanced toward the front window and its view of the barn, her thoughts traveling beyond the rooster that likely dwelled inside its walls to the assignment she'd almost had—*should've* had if she hadn't been lost in her head at exactly the wrong time. It had become the story of her life this past year with thoughts of Brian and Mandy and their betrayal not much different from a violent storm that had stalled atop her life, ever widening its casualty zone to include not only her confidence and sense of self-worth but also her boss's trust in her ability to do her job.

"Tess?"

Shaking her thoughts back into the room, she

forced a stilted smile. "Sorry. I guess I was a million miles away there for a moment. Did I miss something about the rooster?"

"Just that he's loud and tends to wake us a little *before* dawn."

"Loud. Before dawn. Got it. Anything else?"

"This is your notebook and pen." Naomi slid a spiral-bound notepad and pen across the table. "If your pen runs dry, Isaiah has more in his desk."

She traced her finger across the tan cover and willed her thoughts to stay focused, to remain in the room rather than revisiting the two people who—

"Tess? Are you okay? You look so sad all of a sudden."

It was on the tip of her tongue to correct the woman's use of the word *sudden,* but, thankfully, she stopped herself in the nick of time. "I-I'm fine. Really. Just tired from the bus ride, I guess."

"Then I will let you get settled." Naomi stood and crossed to the door. "I'll send Aaron to get you when it is time to eat."

It was dusk by the time she let herself back into the Grossdawdy Haus after dinner, her thoughts already revisiting her time with Naomi's family. From the moment the screen door had banged closed behind her as she'd trailed Aaron into the main house, she'd felt . . .

Well, she wasn't entirely sure *how* she'd felt.

In some ways her evening with the Amish family was everything she'd expected when she'd opened Sam's envelope in the conference room the previous day. But in other ways—ways she couldn't quite wrap her head around—it was nothing like she imagined, either.

Back at the magazine, when she felt a little unsettled about a story, she'd talk it through with Murph, knowing that, eventually, the right angle would present itself. Sometimes it came quickly, as if it had been there all along yet needed to be spoken aloud first. Other times it took some hair tugging and a few *I give ups* before Murph called a time-out and basically plied her with leading questions until she figured it out.

But now? With Tess in Pennsylvania and Murph in—

Plucking her phone from the back pocket of her dress slacks, Tess pressed her way into the message center. There, after a quick glance at the time, she began to type, her thumbs practically flying across the tiny keyboard, backspacing and retyping to avoid angering her mentor with anything less than complete sentences of fully spelled words.

> Hi Murph! I'm here. In PA. By my calculations, it's morning where you are. Any chance you have a few minutes to text with me?

She paused, checked her battery-life icon, and then pressed Send, the *whooshing* sound almost deafening in the otherwise silent and now almost pitch-black room. With the help of her phone's still-lit screen, she searched the wall to the left of the front door for the light switch she just as quickly knew she wouldn't find. Instead, she sought out the first of the three drawers to the left of the refrigerator for the box of matches Naomi had shown her earlier in the evening. With them, she lit the large candle in the center of the kitchen table, another, slightly smaller one on the countertop beside the propane powered stove, and still another atop the dresser in the bedroom.

For a moment, her gaze lingered on the flame as it reached upward from the narrow black wick, its shadow dancing and shimmying on the wall. When had she last lit a candle? During some brief power outage she couldn't quite remember? When she surprised Murph at work with a plate of cupcakes for his birthday a few months ago? No, it couldn't be. He'd refused the very notion of candles before she'd even pulled them out of her bag. Was it—

And then she knew.

It had been that last evening with Brian. She'd taken extra care with dinner that night—trying a new recipe, buying a good wine, using their best plates and glasses, and lighting the two candles she'd set between them on the table.

She closed her eyes against the memory of his hand as he'd reached across the linen tablecloth she'd painstakingly ironed and entwined their fingers.

Why had he done that? How could he have looked at her with such tenderness when he knew what he was about to do and—as she'd come to realize—had been doing for quite some time?

It made no sense. None.

"I will always care about you, Tess. Always. But this thing with Mandy? It's like nothing I can explain or pretend away."

Even now, nearly twelve months later, his words, his explanation, *his voice* were as clear and sharp as if he were standing wherever she was at that particular moment—the shower, the car, church, staring at the television, sitting in on a meeting at work, interviewing someone for a story, or standing in an Amish bedroom with her hands pressed against her ears. In some ways, it reminded her of one of her parents' old records, that moment akin to a scratch on the vinyl—one where the same lyric kept playing over and over again until someone got up and moved the needle.

But no matter how often she moved the needle, her thoughts returned to the same scratch, the same lyric again and again.

"Give it a rest, Tess," she hissed, dropping her hands to her sides. "Focus on the now. Focus on this lame assign—"

The telltale buzz of an incoming call set her in a run toward the kitchen. The name on the screen had her pressing Accept on the video call and sinking onto the closest bench in relief as Murph's stubbled face sprang into view. "Murph! You're calling! How are you?"

"About the same as I was when we last talked."

"So you arrived at your destination safely?"

Murph's hand disappeared from view, only to appear again with a coffee cup in tow. "I did. And it's a good thing I got some shut-eye on the flight because I haven't even seen where I'm bunking yet. I basically stepped right off that plane and into a *here's how it's going to be* welcome talk designed specifically for me."

"Think you'll see some cool stuff?"

"I do, but that's all I can say while I'm here." He took a sip of what she knew was black coffee, glanced beyond the phone's camera lens for a moment, and then leaned forward, his attention all hers once again. "So how about you? You settled in your spot?"

She nodded.

"What's that weird flickering on the cabinet behind you?" he asked.

"That's the shadow from one of the candles I had to light to be able to see two feet in front of my face."

"Oh. Right. I forgot."

"Lucky you," she murmured, before pushing

back from the table and switching the phone's view outward. "Actually, why don't I give you a tour of my accommodations? I'm staying in what's called a Grossdawdy Haus on Isaiah and Naomi King's farm. It's really just a cottage that's attached to the main house, but I have my own entrance. It's where Isaiah's parents lived until their passing, which means I've got my own kitchen, see?"

Slowly, she turned the camera so he could see the table, the refrigerator, the cabinets and stove, and, finally, the wall. "These people take the notion of simplicity to a whole new level. Though, I have to admit, the mixer they have is more elaborate than I expected. It's one of those ones that cost a couple hundred bucks."

"I didn't know those were battery-operated."

"They're not. The refrigerator, the stove, the mixer—they all run on propane somehow."

"Interesting . . ."

"A little, I guess." She crossed into the small sitting area and, again, gave her mentor a slow yet thorough look at the room. "Again, no frills. Just a place to sit, a Bible on the end table, an old clock on a shelf, a framed cross-stitch showing the names of Isaiah and his siblings. And this weird lamp-cabinet thingy right here."

With a quick push of her foot, she scooted the cabinet toward the kitchen. "See? It's on wheels. But there's no way to power it on seeing as how there's no power cord and no electricity."

"What's *in* the cabinet?"

"I don't know. I didn't look."

"So look."

"Are you condoning illegal searches now?" she quipped.

"Just open the cabinet, kid."

"Fine." Tess switched the phone to her left hand, pushed the cabinet into the candlelight, and tugged open the single door. "Oh. Okay. There's a propane tank in here. Only instead of powering an outdoor grill like it does in the real world, it can apparently run what looks to be a fairly standard sixty-watt light bulb for the Amish."

"So now you've got a real lamp you can use at night."

She set him down atop a nearby rocking chair, fiddled with the tank, and, with a turn of the lamp, bathed the once shadowy room in full light. Pushing the lamp back into place, she retrieved Murph from the chair and held her gaze on the lamp. "Putting wheels on that thing is actually pretty clever. Lets you move it from room to room as needed."

"I see that. Certainly shores up what I've always heard about the Amish."

"Which is what?"

"That they're extremely smart people."

She mulled his description for a moment and then lowered herself onto the rocking chair. "Do

74

you know they only go to school through the eighth grade?"

"I may have heard that fact along the way."

"Don't you think that's weird? Like they're intentionally trying to keep everyone ignorant?"

"Can't say." Murph set down his coffee cup and cracked his fingers. "So, what do you think of this couple you're staying with?"

Resting her head against the seatback, she stared up at the ceiling. "Naomi, the wife, is only thirty-six. They're expecting their eighth kid in a few months."

"Their *eighth?*"

"I know, right? Anyway, I ate dinner with them tonight."

"And was it sheer craziness?"

She thought back over her evening and shook her head. "Actually, it wasn't. There were seven kids under the age of twelve, and there was no fighting, no throwing of food, no bratty behavior, no temper tantrums, and no whining about having to eat vegetables or wanting something different. And you know what? Now that I think about it, that's kind of a little weird, don't you think?"

"It shouldn't be."

In her head, she made her way around every face at Naomi's table, her thoughts plugging in a name for each one. As she came to the last little face, she couldn't help but smile. "This one little boy—Reuben? He's four years old and such a little character. Super, *super* adorable."

Tilting his chin to the side, Murph smacked his ear a few times with the palm of his hand. After a second, maybe two, he righted his head and locked eyes with Tess. "Nope. Hearing is fine."

"What are you doing?"

"Just making sure I heard you correctly just now."

"You mean about the kids?" she asked, confused.

"Nah, it was more your tone."

She stopped the gentle rock of her chair and studied her friend, the significant time-zone change evident in the dark circles beneath his eyes. "My *tone—what* tone?"

"The one that suggests you might have actually enjoyed yourself tonight."

The chair creaked as she stood. "The food was good. The kids were cute. That's it. It's no big deal, Murph."

"Relax, kid. It was just an observation. And one I'm glad for, by the way. I was hoping you'd enjoy yourself."

"I'm not here to enjoy myself. I'm here to knock this second-rate assignment out of the ballpark the way you told me to, remember?" Without waiting for a response, she carried Murph over to the window while she looked out into the dark night. "And, honestly, now that I'm here? Seeing what these people live like? The fact they don't go to high school? That their kids are a little too well behaved? That they seemingly have money one wouldn't expect them to have? Maybe I really can find a story worth writing here."

"Stop."

She dropped the edge of the shade back against the window and stared at the face looking back at her from the screen. "Did you tell me to stop?"

"Yes."

"Stop what?"

"You're looking for the wrong kind of story, Tess. It's not there."

"How do you know? Maybe it is. Maybe it's even a big one."

"There are all sorts of stories to be told. You know that. You also know your job is to find and tell just the right one." A muffled voice in the background of the call brought Murph to his feet for the goodbye she dreaded. "Find *that* one, kid. Tell *that* one."

CHAPTER 6

Rolling onto her side, Tess threw her hand off the front edge of her mattress and felt around in the dark, straining to make out the hard plastic rectangular shape of her alarm clock, the cylinder shape of her drinking glass, or even the soft, embossed cover of her latest mass-market paperback purchase. But there was nothing. Moving her hand a half inch to the left, she tried again, her fruitless search leading her up and onto her elbow in time to hear an encore of the *cock-a-doodle-doo* that had found its way into her dreams.

"What on earth?" she murmured, rubbing her eyes.

And then she remembered.

She was in Amish country. Sleeping in a bed in a guest cottage on Naomi and Isaiah King's farm. And the noise that had delivered her, albeit briefly, to a vividly real petting zoo in her head was actually the one Naomi had warned her about. But a glance at the shade she'd lowered prior to climbing in bed showed not so much as a sliver of daylight around its edges.

Shaking the moment away, she lowered herself back onto her pillow and closed her—

Cock-a-doodle-doo.

"Seriously?" Again, she struggled up onto her

elbow. This time, though, she reached over the edge of the bed to the floor, her hand finding and retrieving her phone in short order. A check of the screen had her groaning along with a third, slightly less strident but no less obnoxious *cock-a-doodle-doo.*

5:45 a.m.

She gave some thought to ignoring the birds, but when a fourth and then a fifth greeting filled the air, she knew claiming ignorance wasn't going to work. Instead, she flung her legs over the edge of the bed, slipped her feet into her waiting slippers, and stood as the faintest hint of light made its way around the shade and turned the darkened blobs around her into more-concrete shapes.

There was the line of wooden dowels that jutted from the wall on which she'd hung her windbreaker . . .

There was the washbasin and pitcher she'd wrongly assumed had met its demise after the Colonial period . . .

There was the long, narrow dresser with the drawers she'd filled after her phone call with Murph . . .

Wandering over to the window, Tess pulled back the edge of the dark green shade and peeked out at the dirt driveway and the large barn that stood sentry on the opposite side. Even with the limited light afforded by the sun's initial rise, she could make out Isaiah's tall form making haste toward the barn. Behind him, running to catch up, was a smaller version of the family patriarch in everything from the black pants and suspenders to the tan shirt and straw, brimmed hat. Silently, she ran through the names and ages of the children as they'd introduced themselves to her at the table the previous evening, the name Mark emerging as the likely front-runner. Then again, seeing as how Mervin was the boy's identical twin, it was possible—

Movement in her peripheral vision delivered the missing twin as he hastily clambered down the front steps of the main house to fall in step behind his father and brother. Seconds later, another boy, one she recognized as Aaron, emerged from the same direction as the second of the twins, his boot-clad feet moving with purpose. She took a moment to imagine what they were heading into the barn to do. Maybe milk a cow or two? Hitch Marta to the buggy? Clean a stall?

A soft yet persistent knocking broke through her still-sleepy thoughts, summoning her away from the window to her robe and, finally, across the kitchen to the front door. Seeing nothing through the thin curtain that covered the top half of the door, she cracked it open, glanced down, and felt the instant smile spawned by the sight of the little boy looking back at her from underneath the brim of his own straw hat.

"Well good morning, Reuben," she said,

looking from the child to the main house, and back again. The four-year-old was a miniature version of every male member of his family she'd just spotted. But even in the limited morning light, she knew that unlike his father and four brothers, Ruben's eyes were hazel—a color he shared with one of his sisters and Naomi. "Is there something I can help you with?"

"Yah." Pulling his hand from behind his back, he brandished a basket in the space between them. "Mamm said you would like to help me gather the chicken eggs."

"Oh she did, did she?" Tess asked, toeing the door open a few additional inches.

"Yah. She said it is something I can teach you."

Again, her gaze left the little boy, this time traveling toward the open barn door and the occasional sound seeping beyond its confines. "I'm not dressed for the day yet."

"Didn't you hear Dat's roosters? The day has started."

"Oh, I heard them. Several times, in fact. But I'm not dressed for the day."

Reuben's little shoulders rose and fell beneath his suspenders just before he dropped into a seated position with the empty basket nestled in his small lap. "Mamm says I should wait for you to get ready."

She opened her mouth to protest but closed it as the boy continued. "You want to hurry. Mamm is making pancakes for breakfast and they are very yummy. She says you can sit next to me again if you would like!"

"I'd love to sit next to you again, kiddo, but I'm not a big breakfast eater."

His smile faded and then disappeared completely as he fidgeted with the basket handle between his chubby hands. "You do not like Mamm's pancakes?" he asked, injury hanging on his every word.

"It's not that I don't like them—I've never had them."

"You will like them. I know you will!"

Oh, how she wanted to send him on his way, but the anticipation on his face, coupled with the fact he was practically staging a sit-in on her front porch, made her continued protests seem all the more futile. "Okay. You won. Let me throw on some clothes and—wait! I thought your mom said *Ruth* would be showing me how to gather eggs."

"Ruth is helping Mamm in the kitchen. And I am big enough to show you."

"Ahhh, right. Okay. I'll be right out."

Leaving the door slightly ajar, she crossed back to her room, swapped her pajamas for jeans and a top, and her slippers for socks and sneakers, and then returned to the door and Reuben. "Okay, kiddo, let's go get those eggs."

"You can hold the basket," he said, standing. "Ruth made it."

She took the basket from the little boy and trailed him down the stairs, her thoughts returning to his parents' dinner table and the three little girls who'd helped their mom with everything from setting the table to passing out the food to cleaning up afterward with nary a complaint or eye roll. "Ruth—she's the oldest girl, right?"

"Yah! She reads stories to me every night!"

"That's nice. I bet you like that." Tess sped up her pace to match Reuben's, while her gaze skipped still farther ahead to a long, narrow wooden house that appeared to be their destination. "I take it that's the chicken house?"

"It's new. Mark and Mervin built it when the old chicken house fell down in a storm!" As they drew closer, a trio of chickens raced down a ramp and into the driveway, prompting Reuben to slow down just long enough to greet each one by name. When all had been acknowledged, he led her to the first of three open doors at the top of narrow ramps.

"Put the eggs in the basket one at a time." Pointing inside, he scrunched his face tight. "If you put in two at a time, they might break."

"I take it that's happened to you before?" she asked, grinning.

Shame drove his bright hazel eyes down to his feet. A long, slow nod inched them back to Tess's. "I don't do that anymore."

"Sounds like you learned a lesson. And that's good."

She watched his little hand shoot inside the opening closest to him and reemerge with an egg for her basket. When it was safely inside, he reached through the opening again and felt around. "Did you learn that lesson when you were little, too?" he asked.

"That same lesson? No. But that's because I didn't grow up on a farm like this. I didn't have to gather eggs before breakfast each morning."

"What kind of lessons did you learn?" Reuben placed a second and then a third egg in the basket and then moved on to the next opening.

"Oh, I don't know. Stuff like looking both ways before I crossed the road . . . Putting my bike in the garage so it wouldn't get all wet if it rained . . . Picking my toys up off the ground so someone didn't step on them and get hurt . . . The usual stuff."

"Mamm says big people learn lessons, too. About all sorts of stuff."

She felt her smile falter. "That's true, we do."

"Like what?" he asked, retrieving four more eggs—one at a time.

Glancing down at the eggs now lining the bottom of the basket, she shrugged. "Well, I just learned that I should only put one egg into the basket at a time."

Reuben's chin tilted upward until his eyes were

back on Tess. "You learned that from me!"

"You're right, I did. So thank you for that."

His answering smile was triumphant and stole her breath. "Now it's your turn," he said, pointing her toward the third and final opening.

"I'm fine just holding the basket, little one. You do it."

"Mamm says I should let you try."

With equal parts nervousness and care, Tess squatted down so the opening was at eye level, and immediately spotted an egg not far from a chicken. "I see one, only there's a chicken who might not like me taking it away."

"Just shoo her with your hand and she will move."

Tess eyed the chicken. "I don't know about this, kiddo. She looks a little protective of it."

"I will show you." Stepping in next to Tess, Reuben reached inside, waved the chicken away, and then nudged his chin and Tess's hand toward the waiting egg. "Now you can put it in the basket."

With a quick hand and a wary eye, Tess plucked the egg from the straw and set it gently on top of the others. "I got it. Let's go."

"You have to get all of them," he said, shaking his head.

"I did."

Again, he shook his head, his finger directing her attention back inside the chicken house. "There are two more, see?"

When the last two eggs were safely in the basket alongside the others, she tapped Reuben on the nose and smiled. "Thanks for teaching me how to do that."

"Teach *me* something," he said, hopping from foot to foot. "Like I taught you about the eggs!"

Standing, she handed him the basket and lifted her chin to the warmth of the morning sun. "What do you want to learn?"

"A big-person lesson!"

"Okay, how about always eat your vegetables?"

"I know that one."

"Then you're good."

"I want one I don't know," he said. "A big one!"

"Okay, here's one . . ." She closed her eyes and willed the sun to stop the chill suddenly inching up her spine. "Stay small. You'll save yourself a lot of heartache, if you do."

"But Dat says everybody grows!"

"And sadly he's right."

A tug on her now-empty hand brought her eyes back to Reuben. "Isn't it good to grow big?"

"I thought it was," she whispered. "I wanted it to be . . . But—actually wait . . . I've got a lesson for you. An important one I wish I'd been told along the way."

He stared up at her, waiting.

"Trust no one completely except yourself. If you can remember that, you'll save yourself a whole lot of hurt and pain in the long run."

Confusion etched tiny furrows in his otherwise baby-smooth forehead. "Mamm says we are to trust God. Always."

Unsure of what to say in light of everything she knew she *shouldn't* say, Tess, instead, pointed at the house. "You know what? We should probably get these eggs into your mom before she calls out a search party."

She was almost finished wiping down the table, ridding it of any residual breakfast crumbs, when Naomi reentered the kitchen with a heavy, almost-reticent step, her brow knit with worry lines.

"Is it true? What Reuben says?" Naomi asked, shifting her pregnant form across her simple yet sturdy shoes. "That you do not trust in God?"

Tess stilled the cloth, mid-wipe. "I didn't *say* that, no. I just said that, as he grows, he can really only ever trust himself completely."

"So he is right. You do not trust in God."

"I trust *me*. Infer from that what you will." She finished wiping the last corner and carried the cloth to the sink. "If I overstepped in sharing that with Reuben, I'm sorry. He was excited when he taught me how important it is to gather the eggs one at a time, as opposed to grabbing two or three with one reach."

A knowing smile tugged at the corners of

Naomi's full lips only to disappear as Tess continued. "When I thanked him for sharing that lesson with me, he asked me to share one that I have learned. And so I did. I'm sorry if the one I chose to share upset you. It was not my intention."

"Who taught you such a lesson?" With a hand on her back, Naomi lowered herself into the same spot at the table she'd inhabited during breakfast not more than ten minutes earlier. Only this time, the same quiet joy that had been so prevalent in the woman's face while surrounded by her family was missing, replaced, instead, by resignation and . . . *fear?*

Tossing the cloth into the sink, Tess leaned against the countertop. "It's clear that I over-stepped. For that, I am sorry. Truly."

"Who taught you such a lesson?" Naomi repeated, her voice not unkind.

"*Life* taught it to me in what might best be described as a one-two punch."

Naomi seemed to consider Tess's answer, turning it over behind eyes that were both tired yet also strangely alert. "You have been hurt."

It was a statement, not a question, and as a result, Tess said nothing, opting, instead, to venture over to the window and its view of the family's farm. To her left, hidden largely by the corner of the house, she could see just the very end of the clothesline. To her right stood a small flower garden. Straight ahead, as far as her eye could see, were rows and rows of what she now knew was barley.

"Does Isaiah take the children to school in the buggy?" she finally asked, breaking the weighted silence.

"Some days they walk, some they take their bikes. Today, they took their bikes."

"And Reuben? Where is he?"

"Helping Isaiah in the barn."

Pressing her forehead against the glass, she allowed herself a long, deep breath. "He really is a sweet little boy. Very happy, and very open. I'm sorry if what I said upset the two of you."

"Do you have a friend to talk to?" Naomi asked.

She turned, confused by the shift in conversation. "To talk to about what?"

"The hurt that makes it so you do not trust God. Miss Lottie says the shoulders of many make burdens lighter."

"I don't need a friend for that. I have myself. That was the whole point in what I said to Reuben. If I count on myself for everything, I can't be disappointed or blindsided or hurt. Period."

"A friend doesn't do those things, Tess."

Her answering laugh seemed to bounce off the walls of the large sun-infused kitchen. "I thought that once, too. Believed it with everything I was. But I was wrong."

"I don't understand."

"Didn't you just say a friend doesn't do those things?"

"Yah."

"Well, I'm here to tell you that you're wrong. Just like I was. The difference is I found out too late—*after* the disappointment, *after* the blindside, *after* the hurt."

"This person who did these things does not sound like a friend," Naomi mused.

"In hindsight, you're right, she doesn't. But I *thought* she was. Thought she was my best friend, actually. She knew everything there was to know about me, and I thought I knew everything there was to know about her. She was even there when I first laid eyes on Brian, and she was there, as my maid of honor, when I married him," Tess said, squeezing her eyes closed at the memory.

"You said you weren't married!"

"Because I'm not." Working to steady her breath and her growing anger at herself for divulging more than she'd intended, Tess parted her long lashes to find Naomi staring back, waiting. "I was, at one time. But now I'm not. And that's because of that friend—the one I thought I knew."

Bracing her hands on the table, Naomi rose onto her feet, her gaze never leaving Tess's. "That is why you trust only yourself now?"

Aware of the sob climbing up her throat, she

opted to nod rather than speak, and to send up a silent prayer of thanks that Murph was not there to see her on the verge of falling apart—again.

At the feel of Naomi's hand on her arm, she tensed. "Not everyone is a friend like that, Tess."

"If *she* could be like that, *anyone* could. Trust me."

Naomi paused. "Would *you* be that kind of friend—one who does the things you said?"

"Never." She swiped at the tears before they spilled down her face. "I-I couldn't live with myself if I did."

"Then do not let one cloud darken *your* sky."

CHAPTER 7

Tess was sitting on the back step of her cottage, staring out at the many oranges, rich yellows, and dark violets streaking the sky, when she felt the quick yet distinctive vibration of an incoming text. Reaching into her back pocket, she pulled out her phone, and, at the sight of Murph's name, pressed her way into the message.

> I forgot to ask. You didn't bring the milking stool, right?

Laughing, she typed in her answer.

> No. But I should've packed a step stool so I could reach the clothesline better.

The immediate appearance of three dancing dots on the bottom left-hand side of the screen let her know he was typing a reply. With one last peek at the sky, she stood and made her way back inside the house.

> Sorry I had to cut our last chat short. Duty called. So how was today? Still enjoying the family? Do any Amish-y things today?

Her thumbs flew across the tiny keyboard.

> Today was about hanging the wash, tending to the flower garden, and helping Isaiah with—brace yourself—the website he's wanting to put together for the wooden toy chests he makes when he's not farming. Family is kind. Warmer than I expected, I guess.

Pulling her finger away from the Send button without pushing it, she continued to type instead.

> Oh, and I gathered eggs from a chicken coop for the first time in my life. I bet you can't say the same about your day?

She took advantage of the dancing dots to put on a pot of water for the hot chocolate she'd been thinking about off and on since returning from dinner at the main house.

> I can't.

"Okay . . ." she murmured as her fingers returned to the tiny keypad.

> What CAN you say?

The dots letting her know a reply was on the

horizon were back, but they didn't last long.

> Nothing. Sorry. Will share more when I can. Taking notes for your story yet?

Plucking a simple mug from the cabinet to the right of the stove, she set it on the countertop, filled it with the powdered mix Naomi had graciously given her as she'd left the main house, and returned her full attention to the conversation at hand.

> Nothing to take notes about yet. See above re: clothesline and the garden.

When the mug was full, she carried it and the phone to the table.

> In terms of the acts themselves, maybe.

She took a quick sip and then typed her reply.

> Meaning?

The dots appeared for a moment, disappeared for longer, and then, just as she was resigning herself to the fact their window to chat had apparently come to an end, they appeared again.

> I know my impressions of things here will

change as time goes on. It's inevitable. Taking notes now will help me see that change. Not a bad thing to record.

She considered his comment, weighed its validity. Before she could respond, the phone vibrated in her hand again.

You were surprised by warmth? Why?

Shrugging, she took another sip of the hot liquid.

They're Amish. They shun all things modern. I'm modern. Though, honestly, the whole website thing surprised me, you know?

The momentary absence of dots allowed her a longer sip.

Look at that.

She reached for her mug but, at the last minute, pulled her still-empty notebook and pen into writing range as her thoughts began to swirl.

You're thinking from a hypocrisy standpoint, right? Pretending to shun the modern world yet using business as an excuse to embrace it?

Again, there was a lull in dots. But, as before, they finally appeared in advance of his reply.

I suppose . . .

"You suppose?" she murmured. "What else is—"

Sorry, kid. Gotta go. Duty calls. Write it out. You'll see it when you do.

"*See* it? See *what?*" She hurried her fingers across the keypad . . .

Wait. What am I missing?

Her gaze moved from the Send button to the screen, but the dots she prayed to see never came. Sighing, she wrapped her left hand around the mug and scrolled back to the start of their conversation with her right, her eyes revisiting every word they'd exchanged.

"What did I say, Murph? Or should I say, What did you *hear?*"

Confused, she swapped her mug for the notepad Naomi had left her, swung open the cover, and looked between the empty page and her phone.

I know my impressions of things here will change as time goes on. It's inevitable.

Taking notes now will help me see that change. Not a bad thing to record.

And so she wrote.

About waking up in the dark to the unfamiliar sound of a rooster . . .

About Reuben's sweet face peering up at her from beneath his brimmed hat . . .

About seeing the sun rise in the sky . . .

About the feel of the straw beneath her fingers as she retrieved her first egg from some place other than a white Styrofoam container . . .

About the quiet peace that had surrounded her as she was cleaning up after breakfast and Naomi was seeing six of her seven children off to school . . .

About the crisp snap of the laundry on the line once it was dry . . .

About the feel of the dirt on her hands as she weeded and planted . . .

About Isaiah's rapt interest as she made suggestions for the website he was teaching himself how to build . . .

About that moment, just before the kids came home from school, when she'd spotted that tender look between husband and—

She stilled her pen mid-word and shook her head. What on earth was she doing? She wasn't there to keep a diary. She was there to find a real story, to prove to Sam she had what it took to be sent to places like Belize or Afghanistan.

A fluff piece about life on an Amish farm wouldn't fit that bill. But something deeper? More explosive? Something that created a buzz? Got people talking? Tweeting? Debating across social media and news programs? *That* could be her ticket out of the doghouse and, maybe even, to being noticed by the powers that be at other publications . . .

Her mind made up, Tess flipped to a new page, her brain firing off questions faster than her pen could record them.

CHAPTER 8

Scanning the vacant seat cushion to her left, Tess mentally calculated the number of times she'd needed the seam ripper in just the thirty or so minutes since Naomi had declared her ready to start quilting, and it wasn't pretty. Yet, despite her lack of ability, Naomi's ongoing slew of encouragement and willingness to demonstrate the proper technique showed no sign of diminishing.

"I think it's time we face facts here," Tess said, stretching her arms above her head and exhaling away the last of her determination. "I'm not getting this. Not even a little."

"You will learn. You just need to keep trying." Naomi shifted the pastel-colored fabric squares into the open space between them and smiled at Tess. "Perhaps a cookie and something to drink will help."

"While I won't turn down the snack, I'm serious about quilting not being my thing. I'm all thumbs."

"You will learn, if you keep at it," Naomi repeated, leading the way into the kitchen. "But you won't, if you quit."

Tess crossed to the cabinet where the glasses were kept, retrieved two, and, at Naomi's nod, filled each with lemonade and set them on the table. "I get that. But right now it's not looking all that promising, and that's okay. I'm not really a sit-and-do kind of person. I'd rather be up and moving."

"You sit when you write, don't you?"

"I do. But that's only after I've gone out and gotten my story."

"How did you learn to do that?" Naomi asked.

"You mean how did I learn to write stories?" At Naomi's nod, she lowered herself onto the long, wooden bench. "College taught me some of what I needed to know. Murph, my mentor at the magazine, taught me a lot more. But mostly it came down to just doing it. The more I wrote, the better I got."

"It is that way with a quilt, Tess."

"Touché." Resting her elbows on the table, she traded smiles with the woman now seated on the other side. "I'll give it a go another day, I promise. In the meantime, though, everything about the way you live is new to me, so learning *anything* about your day-to-day life and/or your belief system is helpful to why I'm here.

"Like, for instance, do you ever think of leaving?" she asked, tugging her notebook from her tote bag and helping herself to an oatmeal cookie from the plate Naomi set between them.

"Leaving Blue Ball?" Naomi asked, drawing back on her bench. "No. This is our farm. One day it will be Reuben's or"—she rested her hand on the mound beneath her dress—"this one's if he is a boy."

"It wouldn't go to your oldest son?"

Naomi took a cookie, shaking her head as she did. "No. When one of the older boys marry, Reuben and this baby will still be at home with Isaiah and me and the others."

"Ahhh, okay, that makes sense." She flipped her notebook open to the page of questions she'd come up with, and pointed at it with her pen. "You're okay with me taking notes, right?"

"Yah."

She found the correlating question halfway down the page and jotted the answer as Naomi had explained it. When she was done, she redirected the conversation toward the path she'd originally intended. "Do you ever think of leaving the Amish and living a life more like"— she motioned to herself with the pen—*"mine?"*

"Alone?" Naomi asked.

"No, of course not. I meant with Isaiah and the children, of course. So you could pursue a career, and the children could go to school longer and figure out their own path in life."

"We would be put under the ban if we did such a thing."

"The ban?"

"Yah. Our community could not speak to us anymore."

Tightening her grip on the pen, Tess leaned forward, waited as Naomi took a bite of oatmeal cookie and then chased it down with a gulp of lemonade. "How long would this ban of everyone last?"

"It wouldn't be for the children as they have not been baptized yet. But for Isaiah and me, the ban would be forever."

Tess shrugged. "Okay, so? People move away from places they've lived their whole lives all the time. It might be hard to never see a favorite neighbor or two again, but it's life. It happens."

"It's not just neighbors who couldn't speak to us. It's family, too."

Tess stared at Naomi. "Family?"

"Yah."

"As in . . ."

"My parents, my brothers and sisters, Isaiah's brothers and sisters, aunts, uncles, even our own children if they were baptized."

She let the words and their meaning sink in while she continued to study the woman seated opposite her at the table. "So that's how they get you to stay? How they keep this"—she waved her pen around the room, toward the window, and finally at Naomi's kapp and dress—"culture going? By *scaring you* into staying?"

Naomi lowered her remaining piece of cookie onto the table, her eyes wide. "I could have chosen not to be Amish. Isaiah could have done the same. But the time to do that was before baptism, not after."

"What would that have changed?"

"I could still see my family."

Tess made a few notes on the appropriate lines, but the follow-up questions filling her head made it difficult to concentrate on anything but Naomi. "So baptism is, essentially, the do-or-die moment in terms of the Amish?"

"Do-or-die moment?" Naomi echoed. "That is an expression I'm not familiar with."

She waved aside the woman's confusion and continued on, her mouth moving faster than her brain could process. "When does baptism happen? Meaning at what age?"

"When one is ready—usually somewhere between eighteen and twenty."

"And does anyone actually choose to leave before that?"

Naomi's gaze dropped to the table. "Yah. Some."

"And that's really okay?"

"It is not what parents want for their children, but they do not want vows to be made and then broken."

"Because then they'd lose them from their lives completely," she said aloud as she wrote. When she was done, she glanced back up at Naomi. "Do you know of any people who have left before baptism and after baptism? Personally, I mean?"

"Yah. My friend Katie's sister left before baptism. She lives in the big city now."

"You mean *New York?*"

"Yah."

Tess leaned forward, her curiosity piqued. "Wow. That had to be some serious culture shock for her, yes?"

"I don't know."

"Why did she leave? Do you know?"

"I know only that she left." Naomi guided the cookie plate closer to Tess and stood. "The children should be along soon, and I still have chores that must be done."

"I'll help but . . ." She grabbed a cookie and then glanced between her notes and Naomi, the hint of a story beginning to rear its head. "One last question, first? Your friend's sister . . . the one who left before baptism? Does she ever come back here to see her family?"

"Yah. Hannah visits often."

"Would you happen to know how I could reach this *Hannah* person? Maybe a phone number or even an address for her in New York?"

"No. But you do not need such a thing when Hannah is here in Blue Ball, visiting her sister."

The wobble of the bench beneath her provided the audio for her surprise. "Wait. You mean she's *here*—in Blue Ball? *Today?*"

"Yah. Katie said Hannah is here for the week, staying with her and Abram."

Rising, Tess closed her notebook and slid it back into her pocket. "Can you tell me how I can find Katie's place from here? Is it walkable?"

"There is no need to walk. I can take you in the buggy. Tomorrow."

CHAPTER 9

They'd been riding for about ten minutes when Naomi released her gentle hold on the buggy reins and pointed Tess's eyes toward a simple white mailbox up ahead. The box, itself, was no different from the half-dozen or so they'd passed so far, but the post on which it sat was barely visible thanks to the climbing vines and purple blooms of the most vividly beautiful morning glory she'd ever seen. Glancing up at the post-noon sun and then back at the flowers, Tess shifted in her spot atop the buggy seat.

"I've never seen a morning glory still open and thriving at this time of day and in that kind of sun." She leaned closer to the buggy's front window, her gaze riveted on the purple blooms. "Are they using some sort of special Amish plant food or something?"

Naomi's soft laugh filled the space between them, hijacking Tess's attention onto the woman quietly urging the horse to move to the right in advance of an approaching car. "They do not need special food."

"Then how . . ." The rest of her words fell away as the horse's quickened pace brought reality into focus. "Ahhhh, yes, I see it now . . . Wow."

"Katie Zook likes to paint."

"I see that, and she's amazing," Tess mused as the buggy, now side by side with the post, provided a close-up of the woman's detailed work. "I honestly thought they were real from back there. And even now? Knowing they're painted on? I'm still half expecting that if I touched them, they'd be soft like real flowers instead of hard like the painted wood my eyes now know them to be."

"Yah."

Just beyond the mailbox, Naomi steered the horse to turn right, the animal's sturdy legs expertly navigating ruts left behind by what Naomi explained as hard spring rains. Ahead, and to the right, was a pretty white two-story farmhouse with a wide front porch cut in two by a trio of steps bookended by freshly painted handrails. Beyond the house and slightly off to the left was what she'd come to learn from Naomi and Isaiah to be a German-style bank barn. Built into the ground on one side, the two-story structure afforded ground-level access to the second story on one side of the building, and ground-level access to the first floor on the opposite side. On the clothesline that stretched between the two structures was a single pair of blue jeans amid a sea of Amish clothing—men's, women's, and that of a small male child.

"Is Hannah older or younger than Katie?" Tess asked as Naomi stopped the buggy in front of the farmhouse.

"You will see." Naomi stepped down onto the dirt driveway and motioned for Tess to follow. "Come."

Plucking her notebook and pen off her lap, Tess stepped down off the buggy seat, Naomi's pointed gaze quickly leading hers to the top of the porch steps and the two mid-twentysomethings making haste to greet them.

The woman on the left was head-to-toe Amish: dark green dress, black lace-up boots, white gauzy prayer kapp over soft brown hair, and striking cheekbones lifting still higher in a warm, welcoming smile.

The woman on the right was head-to-toe English: formfitting denim jeans topped with a thin brown leather belt, simple white T-shirt, brown leather sandals with freshly pedicured toes peeking out, soft brown hair cascading over narrow shoulders, and thick lashes surrounding the same amber-flecked eyes as the woman on the left.

"You're *twins*," Tess murmured, stepping forward. "*Identical* twins."

"Technically, yes. But I have a scar here"— the English version of the two tapped her chin— "that Katie doesn't have."

"One of us preferred not to climb everything we found," quipped the other.

Rolling her eyes in defiance of her own grin, the English woman bounded down the steps to the driveway. "Hi. I'm Hannah—Hannah Beiler. The *fun* twin."

The Amish version of the pair made her way down the stairs, her own full lips stretching wide in a smile. "And I'm Katie—Katie Zook. The one who is not clumsy. My husband, Abram, would be here to welcome you, too, but a horse that is not ours was in our field this morning, and Abram went off to find the owner."

"You're Katie?" Tess asked, stepping forward. "I-I thought those flowers on your mailbox post were real for a good thirty feet or so. And once I realized they were actually painted on, I still found myself wanting to touch them just to be sure."

"That, I can't do." Hannah tucked her hands into the front pockets of her jeans and cocked her head in the direction of her twin. "My twin gets that one all for herself, don't you, Katie?"

"You could do it if you tried, Hannah. It just takes practice."

Hiking her thumb toward the road, Tess stepped closer. "Practice helps a lot of things, but that out there? That's talent."

Something that looked a lot like shame drove Katie's gaze to the ground. Naomi's strident voice brought it back to Tess.

"This is Tess Baker. She is staying on the farm for the month. She is to learn about our ways for her job."

"What is your job?" Hannah asked.

"I'm a writer."

Hannah's perfectly shaped eyebrows lifted with intrigue. "Of books?"

"No. For a magazine. Every year, my boss sends a few of the staff writers out on location assignments. I got sent here, to Amish country."

"Does your magazine write many articles about the Amish?"

"No. This will be a first to the best of my knowledge."

"Hannah likes to ask questions, as you can see." Katie said, looking from Tess to Naomi and back again. "But would you like to come in out of the sun and sit? Hannah and I made one of our mamm's blueberry pies this morning, and this will give us an excuse to see if we finally got it right."

"We've tried many times since Mamm died, but we can never seem to get it quite right," Hannah said, nodding. "But this time I have a good feeling."

Katie's laugh accompanied them up the stairs and into the house. "You said that last time you visited, Hannah, and we'd forgotten the blueberries!"

"It had everything else!" Hannah countered.

Shooing her sister toward the waiting pie, Katie waited for Tess and Naomi to get settled at the table and then returned with plates, forks, glasses, and a pitcher of milk. "What will your article be about, Tess?" Katie asked.

"I'm not sure yet." Tess took the plate and fork Naomi passed her and set them both down at her spot. "I'm still trying to figure that out."

"Do you *enjoy* writing?"

Hannah carried the pie, now expertly cut into wedges, over to the table and began transferring pieces onto plates, her lips twitching with yet another smile. "And my sister says I am the one who likes to ask questions . . ."

Katie's cheeks flamed red. "It is just *one* question."

"Actually, that's your second. But"—Hannah rolled the pie spatula—"it's one I would've asked, too. So, yes, do you enjoy writing, Tess?"

She liked Katie and Hannah, liked their light-hearted banter and the way they made Tess and Naomi feel as if they, too, were part of the fun. "Actually, yes, very much. It's all I've ever wanted to do besides . . ." She waved the rest of her sentence aside. "Anyway, my mom said I was always following people around, asking them questions. And when I got answers I thought were interesting, I'd scurry off to my room and write stories about what they'd told me."

"Katie was like that about her top secret drawings. But I found out about them, didn't I, Katie?"

"Shhhh, Hannah. There is no need to speak of that—"

"Her top secret drawings?" Tess asked, abandoning her first forkful of pie in favor of the intrigue borne on Katie's sudden discomfort at Hannah's reveal.

Katie locked eyes with Hannah, her displeasure over the topic at hand palpable. But Hannah was undeterred. "Drawing the kind of pictures Katie drew isn't allowed."

"What do you mean by *not allowed?*"

"Katie can draw faces the way a camera takes pictures. With her pencil you could see a person's worry or joy or fear or excitement or pain or uncertainty."

Looking between the sisters, Tess waited for more. When it didn't come readily, she prodded it along. "So why can't Katie draw that stuff? And who says she can't?"

"Because to draw faces of loved ones is to create a graven image."

When Katie grew silent, Tess turned her focus on Hannah, waiting.

"Creating a graven image is wrong in the eyes of the Amish. It's why they won't pose for pictures, and why they don't hang them in their homes." Hannah swept her hand toward the largely barren kitchen walls, stopping on a hanging calendar depicting a field of sunflowers. "Scenery is okay. Just not faces."

Lifting her gaze from her lap, Katie sent a nervous glance toward the only other Amish woman at the table. "I no longer draw such things."

Naomi's nod was quick, her *Yah* little more than a whisper as she, too, looked down.

"I don't understand," Tess said, leaning forward in an effort to get Katie's attention. "Hannah just said you had talent. That you could infuse emotion on the faces of the people you drew. How could you just give that up?"

"I did not give up. I still draw. I still paint. I painted those flowers on the post that you saw."

"And they're beautiful, as I said. But—"

Hannah wiped her lips free of any blueberry stains and dropped her napkin onto the table beside her plate, her voice void of the strain lacing her twin sister's. "In the end, after talking with Miss Lottie, Katie chose our family and the Amish way over the life I lead. She can still draw and paint, but now she does it without showing faces."

"*Your family* didn't approve of your drawing, either?" Tess asked.

Katie set her forkful of pie on her plate and pushed both off to the side. "It is as Hannah said. My drawings were not the Amish way. I could not live in both worlds."

"But isn't that what *you're* doing?" Tess asked, pointing at Hannah.

"It is. But I was not baptized. Katie was."

She looked from one woman to the other, waiting for them to counteract what she thought she was hearing, but they didn't. Instead, they all merely nodded as if their belief, their way of life was somehow normal. "So what are you saying, exactly? That choosing to be baptized means giving up anything resembling a personal dream or passion?"

"When we are young, we are not truly Amish. We are being *raised* Amish. It is why our kin came to the United States. We do not believe in childhood baptism. We believe it should be a choice—a choice an infant is too young to make." Katie wrapped her long, slender fingers around her milk glass but stopped short of actually raising it to her lips. "Hannah chose not to be baptized, not to be Amish. I chose to stay, and to be baptized. That means I made a promise to live my life the Amish way. If I do not do things as I should—like, perhaps, I tell lies about someone in the community—I might be shunned at church. To be shunned that way means backs would be turned to me in church and at home until I changed my ways. And I would, if I were to do such a thing."

Hannah cracked a grin. "Trust me when I say that Katie would never be shunned that way."

But," Katie continued, "if I chose to *leave the Amish after* baptism—after I vowed to live an Amish life—my community and my family would no longer speak to me."

Tess took in Katie's answer, mulled it from every side. "But what happens if you have to get away? Like if something unexpected happens to change the direction of your life?"

"The Amish can visit family and friends in other areas. That is not the same as leaving the Amish ways after baptism."

She chewed on that for a while, too, turning it over in her head and her heart. "So unlike the shunning at church you mentioned a minute ago in regards to more minor transgressions, the Amish resort to scare tactics to keep people like you from pursuing a dream?"

"I like to draw and to paint, but my family is what I love most."

"Don't you think you should be able to have both?"

Katie looked down into her glass, her face void of anything resembling sadness or anger. "I could have had both if I'd left before baptism as Hannah did."

"Okay, but very few people have their lives mapped out at twenty years old, Katie," Tess said.

"I made a choice."

"Mamm was sick," Hannah interjected, quietly. "Katie took care of her, and she took care of our brothers and sisters."

Katie shot a hard look at her sister. "I made *a choice,* Hannah."

She followed the various story threads building off Katie's words and felt her own excitement mounting. Maybe this was it. Maybe this was the story she was looking for . . .

"Do you ever regret your decision?" she asked, catching Katie's eye once again.

"No. Never. This is where I belong. With Abram."

It was an answer she wasn't sure she, herself, could've given in the same circumstance, but from Katie, it felt true. Still, she found herself wondering about Katie's husband Abram and what he might one day do in the future to make the young Amish woman eat those same words.

"I don't regret my decision, either."

At Hannah's words, Tess looked up from her pie plate. "You don't miss your life here at all?"

"I didn't say that. I said I don't regret my decision," Hannah rushed to clarify. "I enjoy my English life, and the things I am learning to do."

"Such as?"

"My sister is taking a class to do English hair," Katie said, smiling. "See? She can make her hair look the way it looks in the English magazines they sell at the grocery store."

Hannah's face glowed with pleasure. "I like to do my own hair, but I'm really hoping to do it for others as a job one day. Maybe even on a television or movie set! I saw that once, in Central Park. They were filming something for a TV show or a movie. My friends were excited to try and see the actors and actresses, but I was more excited to watch the people who were doing their hair."

"One day you will do that, Hannah," Katie said. "If it is God's will."

For a few moments, Tess allowed herself to fade out of the conversation in favor of observing, of processing. With the exception of the scar on Hannah's chin, the only real visual difference between the sisters came down to their clothes. They had the same eyes, the same shade of hair, the same facial structure, the same laugh. But unlike twins who simply opted to dress differently to exude a little individuality, the decision to dress differently in this case went far beyond color or style choices. It represented a different life, a different set of beliefs, a different future.

"Were you close growing up?" Tess finally asked.

Hannah and Katie nodded in unison.

"Was it hard when you went in such separate ways like you did?"

Katie took a quick sip of her milk, her eyes taking on a misty sheen. "Having Hannah leave when she did was very hard. For many reasons. But it is okay. We write letters to each other once a week and—"

"Sometimes twice a week," Hannah corrected.

"Yah. Sometimes twice a week. And Hannah comes for a visit when she is able."

"Is it weird to see her looking so"—Tess jerked her chin toward Hannah—"different?"

Katie shrugged. "It was. At first. But it is Miss Lottie who told me clothes do not change a person. And she is right. Hannah is still my twin sister."

"That's right," Hannah teased. "I'm still fun and funny and—"

"Bossy. Very, very bossy," Katie retorted, her grin widening.

Hannah pulled a face, only to laugh it away just as quickly. "I should argue that, but it is no use. I *am* bossy. But if I hadn't been bossy, Katie would never have tried the things she tried when we were growing up. She would have stayed on the ground instead of climbing trees. She would never have jumped into Dat's hay bales."

"Which means I would not have hurt my arm the way I did," Katie murmured, her eyes sparkling.

"It healed, didn't it?" Setting her elbows on the table, Hannah dropped her chin into her hands. "But Katie taught me things, too. Things that have helped me in my new life."

"Such as?" Tess prodded.

"To listen. To not always do before I think. To go after what makes me happy."

Tess marveled, silently, at the irony of Hannah's last sentence, even as her thoughts led her in a completely different direction. For now.

118

"What's it like for you when you come back here, Hannah?" Tess asked. "Is it . . . *weird,* in any way?"

"It is home."

She drew back at Hannah's answer. "How long have you been in New York, living an English life?"

"About three years now."

She sat with that for a moment, her thoughts racing back to an earlier point. "You corrected me earlier when I thought you didn't miss your life here. I imagine you wanted me to know that you miss seeing Katie and the rest of your family on a daily basis?"

"That is some of what I miss, sure. There are times when something happens in my class, or with the little boy I take care of, that I just want to tell Katie or my father about right then and there. But I can't. I have to write it in a letter and then wait until they get it and write back."

"So are you really *missing,* or maybe just wishing things were different?" Tess asked.

"I wish it was different *because* I miss them, but that is not all that I miss. I miss the Amish ways."

The opening creak and closing bang of the front screen door turned all eyes in the direction of the hallway and the Amish man making haste into the kitchen.

"Abram?" Katie asked, rising quickly. "Is everything okay?"

"The Troyers' barn burned to the ground last night!"

Naomi traded glances with Katie as she, too, stood. "Ernie? Martha? The children?" Katie listed aloud. "Are they okay?"

"Everyone is fine, Katie," Abram shared. "No one was hurt."

"And the horses?"

Abram rested a comforting hand atop his wife's. "Ernie managed to set them all free."

"So the mare you found this morning? It was Ernie's?"

"Yah. It was his buggy horse. I found two of his field mules on the way, too."

Nodding, Katie crossed to the refrigerator, her words, if not her entire focus, on her husband. "I will be ready in just a few minutes."

"I will let Isaiah know, and we will meet you there." Naomi started toward the hallway and stopped. "Tess, we must go."

Hannah, too, stood. "Naomi, you go ahead. I'll bring Tess."

"Bring me where?" she asked, grabbing her notebook and pen and rising.

"To the Troyers'. So you can see, with your own two eyes, what I miss most about being Amish."

CHAPTER 10

Everywhere Tess looked, it was a veritable sea of Amish. Men, clad in dark trousers, long-sleeved shirts, suspenders, and hats, moved about, measuring, cutting wood, and discussing plans. Younger boys, dressed like their fathers and grandfathers, dumped wheelbarrows of dirt on everything and anything still smoldering where the old barn once stood. Off to the left, along the stretch of grass in front of the Troyers' farmhouse, were the women and girls, their aproned dresses swishing against their shins as they offered plates of food to any of the workers needing a momentary break, and then cleaning up after them in preparation for a new round.

She tried to get a count of the men and boys, women and girls actively moving about on land that still carried the pungent odor of a much-too-recent fire. But every time she thought she had a decent-enough guess in her head, another slew of buggies and open-topped wagons would turn into the driveway, depositing another dozen or so neighbors looking to help right a misfortune with tools and supplies in tow. Conservatively, she knew she was looking at a hundred people—everyone bustling about with a purpose that didn't have to be discussed or dissected or noticed by anyone else. Realistically, she knew it was closer to one hundred fifty. Easy.

A glance to her left yielded row after row of parked buggies and wagons, their accompanying horses tethered to a border of trees along the northern edge of the property. A handful of boys Tess guessed to be preteens checked in on the animals from time to time, making sure the feed in the metal troughs was still adequate.

From there, her eyes traveled back to the men and the pieces of wood they were nailing together on the ground, each person intent on a specific task. A few voices floated through the air, but, for the most part, the only real noise came from the activity taking place—hammers striking wood, the occasional squeak of a wheelbarrow's wheel, the quiet whinny of a horse, the smack of boots against dry earth.

Even now, after what had to be close to thirty minutes of out-and-out gawking, she still couldn't quite believe her eyes. Nor could she make herself abandon her viewing spot beneath the oak tree. She knew Hannah was likely inside the house, preparing plates of food alongside Katie and Naomi, but every time she so much as thought about checking to see if she was right, the spectacle that was happening around her made all other thoughts fade away.

"I figured you were still here."

Startled, she turned to find Hannah eyeing

her from the other side of the tree. "Oh. Hey. Yeah . . . Sorry . . . I'd intended to follow you inside but"—Tess swept her hand toward the scene playing out in front of them—"I got sidetracked."

Hannah picked her way around the protruding roots to lean against the trunk of the tree. "And? What do you think?"

"What do I *think?*" Tess echoed, her gaze following Hannah's back to the sea of Amish men and the framed wall they were pulling upright atop the earth. "I've never seen anything like this before. I mean, this fire happened last night, right? Yet here we are, less than eighteen hours later, and they already have an entire wall framed for what will be a brand-new barn."

"A brand-new barn that will be standing and finished by this time tomorrow."

She stared at Hannah. "You can't be serious."

"I can, and I am."

"A new barn . . . Done . . . In twenty-four hours . . ."

Shielding her eyes from the glare of the sun, Hannah nodded. "Sometimes it takes closer to two days, but with this many people, it'll go faster."

"So this is normal?" Tess split her attention between the wall being righted in front of her and the woman standing beside her. "People just show up after a fire like this?"

"After a fire, a death, an accident—take your

pick. If one of their own falls on hard times, the Amish are there, ready to do whatever needs to be done."

"But there's so many. And that's not counting the women."

Again, Hannah nodded as she raised up on the tips of her sandals as if searching for something or someone. "Many hands make light work."

"I get that, but where did they all come from? How did they find out if phones are frowned upon?"

"They come from inside our church district and outside it, too. And as to how they found out, word spreads fast among the Amish." Hannah looked toward the horses, smiled and returned the wave of a boy adding feed to the trough, and then shrugged, her gaze traveling back to Tess's. "You saw the way Katie and Naomi sprang into action when Abram told them what happened, right? The way Katie started gathering food, and Naomi headed home to tell Isaiah? When the Amish hear about a fire like this, or a death, they just go. If it is a fire, they clean up the debris and help rebuild what was lost. If it is a death, the men will help tend the animals and the farm, and the women will help with the cooking or the children or whatever is needed."

"Is it some sort of Amish *rule?* Is that why they all come?"

"They come because it is right. Because the

124

apostle Paul said that to fulfill the law of Christ, brethren must bear one another's burdens."

A momentary lull in hammering drew Tess's attention back to the wall in time to see a half-dozen men right a second section of wall and place it perpendicular to the first. "It's like they don't even have to speak to one another to know what must be done. And from what I've been able to gather from standing here watching, there arc no egos getting in the way, no *one* guy trying to call all the shots or weigh in on the work of another. Likewise, I haven't spotted a single person wandering off looking to escape the heavy lifting by hiding out behind a buggy or a tree until all the work is done."

For a long moment Hannah said nothing, her focus intent on the construction of the Troyers' new barn. When she did finally speak, her words, and the emotion with which she said them, had Tess wishing for the notebook and pen currently sitting on the passenger seat in the woman's car. "There were many things about an Amish life I knew I wouldn't miss when I was making my way toward New York City. I knew I wouldn't miss the clothes. I knew I wouldn't miss the prayer kapps. I knew I wouldn't miss being woken by roosters who were always a good ten minutes too early in their greeting of each new day. I knew I wouldn't miss sitting on those hard benches for three and a half hours every other

Sunday, especially in July. I knew I wouldn't miss cold baths. I knew I wouldn't miss having to walk a half mile down the road to find a phone. And I knew I wouldn't miss getting caught out in the rain or wind with a good half mile or so still to walk."

"Makes sense to me," Tess said. "I wouldn't miss those things, either."

Hannah's chin tilted upward, her focus abandoning the men diligently working with hammers and nails in hand. "Strangely enough, I was wrong. I didn't see it at first, but eventually, when the newness of the city began to wear off, it started keeping me up at night and stealing my thoughts when I was supposed to be doing other things."

"You lost me . . ."

"All the things I was so sure I wouldn't miss actually became things I *did* miss in one form or another."

"You miss the *cold baths?*" Tess countered. "The *rooster?*"

Hannah's laugh silenced the closest hammers for a second, maybe two. "Not the cold baths, no. But the rooster and everything else? Believe it or not, yes . . . Most days I wanted to tie a piece of straw around that rooster's beak, but without him, I don't really see sunrises anymore. I used to daydream about wearing clothes like *this*"— Hannah pointed at her brushed jeans and pretty

126

eyelet shirt—"but every now and again, I miss wearing something my mamm made for me from the same bolt of fabric she used to make things for everyone in my family.

"And my hair? I love styling it in a different way every morning. I love being able to let it hang down my back in waves, or pull it up high in a swishy ponytail. But still, there are days I miss racing Katie to see who could pin theirs up and under their kapp fastest."

Pushing off the tree with her foot, Hannah took a few steps forward, the expression on her face difficult to read. "Those hard benches I hated sitting on for so long on Sunday mornings? They really weren't that awful. I mean, yes, they got uncomfortable after a while, but at least I got to sit on them with Katie. And she was always there with a ready elbow if I started to fall asleep."

Tess tried, unsuccessfully, to nibble back her answering grin. "You fell asleep in church?"

"No, Katie's elbow is very pointy." Rubbing her side at the memory, Hannah continued. "As for walking home from the store in heavy rain or strong winds, I still don't miss that. But every once in a while, when I'm waiting on a crowded subway platform or to cross a busy street along-side a dozen other people, I find myself missing quiet walks along these roads with the sun on my face and the only sound I hear being the wind moving through Dat's wheat."

"Are you sure you don't regret leaving?" Tess asked, trailing Hannah to a nearby fence with an uninhibited view of the barn raising. "Because it sounds like maybe you do."

"No, I made the best decision for me. I know this. But that doesn't mean I can't still see the beautiful parts of my old life—of the place that will always be my *heart's* home." Hannah nudged her chin in the direction of the men swarming the barn grounds like ants at a picnic, their mission clear. "This right here, though, is what I miss the most . . . This coming together to help one another overcome a hardship. It's something I wish everyone could know, and everyone could have."

CHAPTER 11

Tess was sitting on the windowsill, looking out at the vast darkness, when a sudden glow against the wall pulled her out of her head and onto her feet. Crossing the tiny sitting room, she reached past the single candle she'd opted to use rather than the propane-powered lamp, and smiled down at the name staring back at her from the screen.

"Do you actually *work* where you are?" she asked by way of greeting as she sank onto a cushioned rocker. "Because it seems like you're doing a lot of texting and calling . . ."

"It's morning where I am, kid, and I've got a window. And, since it won't be long before your phone is dead, I figured I should take advantage now and make sure you're still alive."

"Still alive, and holding at about fifty percent charge. For now." Tess waited through Murph's quick inhale and subsequent exhale. "I take it I'm officially part of your smoke break?"

"You are."

"I'm honored."

"You should be," Murph retorted.

"Oh, I am. Trust me."

"So, all good with you?"

She tried to imagine Murph at that moment,

cigarette in hand, lingering outside a large, dark green tent as the sun ascended behind a distant mountain. She could even imagine the dirt on which he was likely standing and the sporadic static of radio transmissions happening around him. "Quick. What do you see right now?" she asked.

"I can't really answer that."

"Oh, c'mon, Murph. Play along."

"I see my cigarette. And I see a whole lot of cigarette butts underneath my boots. You?"

Rolling her eyes, she stood and then wandered back to the window. "Fine. I'll show you how this game is played. When you called, I was sitting at the window in my little living area, looking out at what pretty much amounts to total darkness, save for the occasional solar- or propane-powered light in some barn somewhere."

"Sounds peaceful."

"I suppose. In that *nothing is going on at all* way."

"Doesn't have to be a bad thing," Murph said on the heels of another drag of his cigarette.

"You'd be climbing out of your skin if you were here, Murph."

Another drag was followed by first a cough and then a grunt. "Sorry, kid."

"Yeah. Me, too." She lowered herself back onto the windowsill, her eyes drifting in the direction she and Hannah had driven earlier that day, the memory of what she'd seen and learned finding its way back into her thoughts. "There was a fire overnight, in a barn. Not too far from here."

"Pictures?"

"Of the actual fire? No. I didn't even know about it until this afternoon. But I got to see the early stages of a barn raising."

Murph's next inhale ceased in her ear. "Seriously? I've heard that's quite the sight."

"It was. There had to be over a hundred and fifty people there, easy. The guys were building, and the women were keeping them fed. Everyone had a job to do, and everyone did it. Without egos, without issues. It was"—she pulled in a breath—"pretty incredible, actually. And Hannah says the whole thing will likely be done by this time tomorrow night. Next day, worst case."

"You get any pictures of *that?*"

"Actually, yeah, a few. Even though Hannah stuck her hand in front of my camera just as I was getting ready to take a picture of this one Amish guy standing on top of a framed-out wall."

"Oh. Right. The picture thing. I forgot."

"No worries. I got an even better angle when she went off to help her sister with the food again. And I'm telling you, Murph, it's a killer shot. The only thing that would have made it better is if I'd had the work camera with me. Even without that, though, I think it might be a worthy contest submission."

She heard what sounded like the final drag of his cigarette. "Doesn't sound like a very good way to make friends with these people, kid."

"You mean my taking the picture of the Amish guy when Hannah wasn't around to stop me?"

"Yup."

"I'm not here to *make friends,* Murph. I'm here to *knock it out of the ballpark,* remember?"

"But, still, you're a guest in this woman's home."

"Actually, I'm not. I'm staying at Naomi and Isaiah King's place. Hannah is someone I just met earlier today. She's not Amish—not anymore, anyway. She escaped, for lack of a better word. Though I'm not sure *she* sees it that way."

"Interesting. And she was allowed to be there?"

"Yes. Apparently, the breaking point for the Amish is baptism. If you leave before you're baptized, you're fine. They'll still talk to you. But if you leave after baptism, it's *Goodbye, don't let the door hit you on the way out* kind of stuff."

The answering silence left her to revisit her statement along with everything she'd learned that day. "You know, it's kind of *strange* how a group of people can be so giving and so helpful to their neighbors during times of hardship yet so unyielding and unforgiving of their own."

"Meaning?" Murph prodded.

"This girl—Hannah. She has a twin sister. Katie. Hannah left before baptism, as I said. A year or so later, Katie gave some thought to doing the same. But if she'd left, she'd have been excommunicated from her entire family. Forever. Which is nuts, right?"

"She knew that from the start, though, right?"

Tess pressed her forehead against the cool glass pane. "Yes."

"Rules are rules in some cultures, kid. Which isn't necessarily a bad thing."

Rearing back, she returned to her feet. "But this girl had to give up a passion—*a talent,* Murph! That's a lot to ask someone to walk away from."

"Maybe. But you know what they say. Life ain't easy. Not for me. Not for you. Not for the guys on the ground here. And—"

"And where *is* that ground, exactly?" she prodded.

"Not for the Amish," he continued, undaunted. "Not for anybody. But at least we've got choices."

Her answering laugh was stiff, humorless. "That's like saying my being *here* was a choice."

"Because it was."

She paused en route to the kitchen, spun back toward the window, and tightened her grasp on the phone. "C'mon, Murph. You know that's not true."

"You didn't have to take the assignment."

"Of course I did." She tried to relax her jaw, but it was no use. She was worked up, and getting more and more worked up with each passing second. "If I hadn't come here, I'd have either been relegated to reading everyone else's copy or I'd have been standing in the line at Unemployment."

"So you made a choice."

"A forced decision isn't the same as a choice, Murph."

"Were you hog-tied and forced to use that bus ticket?"

She sighed into the phone. "Technically, no. But—"

"Then you made a choice."

"You mean like the one I made when I turned around and walked out the door after finding my husband and my best—" Shaking away the rest of her sentence, she willed herself to breathe, to dial down the anger that had white spots dancing in front of her eyes.

"Yup, kid. Just like that."

Even in the absence of any real light, Tess could just make out the outline of the dresser opposite the bed, the ceramic pitcher and bowl housed on top of it, the wooden dowels that protruded from the wall on which her windbreaker and tote bag hung, and the bedroom door she'd flung closed after hanging up on Murph. She wondered, briefly, if her prone position across Naomi's homemade quilt was detectible but dismissed the question with a labored groan. What difference

134

did it make if she could be seen in the dark or not? She was alone. In the room . . . in the cottage . . . in Amish country . . . in life . . .

Rolling onto her back, she hooked her arm across her still-damp eyelashes, her thoughts traveling back to the words that had led her to hanging up on the only lifeline she had in Amish country. Getting on the bus to come there *hadn't* been a choice. By the very definition of the word, there would have been another viable option on the table. Amish country or the unemployment line wasn't a choice. The choice had been Sam's. Not hers. And as for that fateful night when she turned and walked out of her apartment? She wasn't given a choice. The *choice* had been Brian's and Mandy's. Why Murph couldn't see that was incomprehensible and—

"Enough," she hissed at herself, her breath warm against her upper arm. "You don't owe anyone an explanation for anything."

No, the only one she owed any sort of accountability or explanation to from this point forward was herself. That's it. She knew this. Believed it. She just needed to take the reins of her life once and for all. With no exceptions, no apologies.

Her mind made up, she dropped her hand onto the quilt-topped mattress and hoisted herself upright. If she had to take a guess, she'd put the time at about ten o'clock, maybe eleven—too late to do much of anything.

Or was it?

With haste, Tess pushed herself off the bed, opened the door separating the bedroom from the rest of the cottage, and headed straight for the candle still flickering its determined light across the small sitting room. There, on the rocking chair where she'd tossed it, was her phone, and on the footstool that doubled as an ottoman were her notebook and pen. She carried them into the kitchen, set them on the table, and lit another candle, the wick's immediate and answering flame bathing the room in a muted but still-workable glow.

Next came a mug of coffee, the two cookies Naomi had sent home with her the previous evening, and a spot on the table-side wooden bench. Yet now that she was there, notebook open and pen in hand, she was at a loss. How could she write her way back into Sam's good graces and land a plaque with her name on it in the magazine's front lobby if she had nothing worthy of making herself sit up in excitement, let alone readers?

Trading her pen for her phone, she pressed her way into her album and gazed down at the picture she'd taken after Hannah had headed back inside the Troyers' farmhouse. The man she'd chosen to capture had taken a seconds-long break to look up at the vivid blue sky. His deep brown eyes telegraphed nothing but determination as a bead of sweat rolled down his chiseled cheek.

Tess knew, from bits and pieces she'd picked up since arriving in Amish country, that the length of the man's beard meant he was a relative newlywed. His straw hat, suspenders, pale blue shirt, and simple black pants made his Amish designation a slam dunk for the viewer. Behind him but slightly less clear were the faces of others who shared his same determination, his same goal: to help another person in a time of need.

Scrolling left through a series of pictures, she stopped again when she reached the shots she'd taken of the women. They, like the men, did what needed to be done. Some, in the picture, were cleaning up the remnants of meals that had already been eaten. Others were making sure the latest round of workers had everything they needed to stay fueled.

She used her fingers to enlarge the picture in different places as her mind's eye registered prayer kapps, a variety of solid color dresses, and faces that seemed neither happy nor sad. Slowly she made her way around the image until a familiar face had her fingers holding steady.

Katie Beiler was pretty. Her delicate features and makeup-free face told that story. But underneath the shy smile and the pleasant personality, there had to a whole lot of bitterness and anger. There had to be. Because regardless of what

Murph might say on the subject, Katie hadn't really had a choice in the whole leave-or-stay thing.

After all, just as the prospect of being unemployed had resulted in Tess being where she was at that moment, the knowledge that Katie would never see her family again if she pursued her dreams had made it so the young woman had to stay. *That* wasn't a choice. It was—

"Emotional blackmail," she whispered, sitting up tall.

Slowly, and then with increasing speed, Tess scrolled her way through each and every picture a second and third time. The obvious story, of course, was the barn raising. But maybe there was another story to be told—a much, much *bigger* story than a barn raising and the way the Amish came to help . . .

Aware of the excitement bubbling up inside her chest, Tess set the phone down and reached for her notebook.

CHAPTER 12

Despite sitting at the kitchen table jotting notes and pondering questions until well after midnight, Tess was awake and dressed before the most strident of Isaiah King's roosters saw fit to announce the start of yet another new day. Maybe it was because she was listening for it, or maybe it was because she was already halfway into her second mug of coffee, but the sound she'd found so jarring the previous day wasn't as bad as she remembered. In fact, if she was honest with herself, there was something almost appealing about being woken by nature rather than a man-made object.

Unfortunately, the whole rooster-waking thing was on account of her being a guest on an Amish farm. And being a guest on an Amish farm came complete with a list of morning chores that had to be done before breakfast could be eaten and her real day—her *true workday*—could finally begin.

A soft knock hijacked her attention toward the front door and the single panel of fabric that served as a visual divider between herself and the sweet yet curious face she knew she'd find on the other side. Smiling to herself, Tess set her coffee mug down on the table, pulled her lightweight cardigan more tightly against her body, and then tugged the door open.

"Good morning, Reuben."

The hatted boy, standing just shy of her threshold, rose up on bare toes and flashed a ready smile over the handle of his basket. "Mamm said you are to collect *all* of the eggs today."

"Oh no, I don't need to do that. You already showed me how so we're all good in that department. I can officially check off that box thanks to you."

The four-year-old's freckles disappeared in the answering scrunch of his nose. "I didn't bring a box. I brought a basket—see?" He lifted the basket up, momentarily blocking his view of Tess with the handwoven base. "Mamm says it is easier to hold."

"I didn't mean a *box* box. I meant . . ." She waved away the rest of her words in favor of her mug and another sip of the still-warm liquid. "Anyway, we're good on the egg chore. So what's next? Sweeping? Brushing a horse? What?"

Again, he held out the basket, his large hazel eyes solemn as they locked on hers in confusion. "Mamm said you are to collect all of the eggs before you fill the trough."

"Before *I* fill the trough?" she echoed.

"Yah. Mamm said I am to let you do *all* of my chores before breakfast today."

Memories of standing in the pigpen the previous morning as the little boy turned over the bedding on which the animals had—

She shook the image away. "What about hanging the laundry? Doesn't that need to be done?"

"My sisters help Mamm with those chores. *I* muck."

"I see." Drawing in the deepest, most fortifying breath she could muster, Tess squared her shoulders and took the basket from the child's hand. "Lead the way."

Tess leaned back against the wall, the sense of success over her first two completed chores rapidly fading as she willed herself to remember everything Reuben had said before he headed inside with the eggs. She knew he'd be back— he'd said he would, but she also knew she hadn't done much more than mold her fingers to the handle of the pitchfork and stare into the empty horse stall since he left.

"You do realize that manure isn't going to remove itself, right?"

Startled, she pushed off the wall with her foot and turned to find a man, about her own age, splitting his attention between her and the stall that normally housed Isaiah and Naomi King's buggy horse, Marta, according to the hand-whittled sign above the opening. He was taller than she was by at least six inches and was dressed in a pair of acid-washed denim jeans, a white short-sleeved shirt that showcased the kind of muscled arms that weren't manufactured in a gym, and scuffed work boots that had seen better days. Lifting her gaze to start, she noted the day-old stubble along his jawline, the close-cropped dark hair atop an uncovered head, the brightest blue eyes she'd ever seen, and a mocking grin aimed squarely on . . . *her?*

"Can I help you with something?"

Crossing his arms in front of his chest, he shrugged. "I'm thinking I should be the one asking that question, not you."

"Oh? Why's that?"

"Because you haven't done a thing the whole time you've been standing there."

"Clearly you haven't been standing there long or else you'd have seen me filling water troughs and collecting eggs while you've been"—the pitchfork dinged against the wall as she stood up straight. "Actually, hold that thought. First things first . . . Who are you and what are you doing in this barn—this *Amish* barn?"

His laugh rivaled his smirk in the annoying department. "Last I checked, a barn is a physical structure. Meaning, it's completely incapable of being Amish. That said, in the interest of moving this conversation along, I'm Jack—Jack Cloverton."

"And the rest of my question?"

His gaze dropped to his outstretched yet deliberately ignored hand before returning to Tess with a second yet equally annoying shrug. "I was looking for Isaiah. Have you seen him?"

"No."

"Well, all righty then . . . Thanks for the help." He started to walk away, only to stop and retrace his steps. "And you are?"

She stared at him. "Excuse me?"

"Your name—what's your name?"

"I don't really see how that's any of your—"

"Tess! Tess!" The sound of feet thudding against the barn's hay-strewn ground grew closer, bringing with it a declaration Reuben King was anxious to proclaim if the smile spreading across his face was any indication. "Mamm said you are good at gathering eggs!"

"What did I tell you?" She bent at the waist, tapped the child on the nose, and followed it up with a wink. "You're a good teacher, kiddo."

The child did his best to squash the pride she saw in his eyes, but even so, the tiny grin he couldn't hold back faded to nothing as he looked beyond Tess and into the stall. "You didn't start mucking."

"Nope, she sure didn't, did she?"

Lifting her eyes to the man still hovering nearby, she readied the biting response she was ultimately forced to swallow as Reuben did a little hop in place. "I know! I didn't get the manure cart! I'll get that now!"

And just like that, Reuben disappeared again, the sound of his bare feet against the barn floor fading to a silence she knew wouldn't last. Still, it was long enough . . .

"As you can surely tell by now, *Mr. Cloverton,* Isaiah isn't in the barn." She switched the pitchfork to her free hand in an attempt to give her palm a break from the sharpness of her nails, but it was no use. As long as the man standing in front of her remained in her universe, her fists would be clenched, pitchfork or not. "So, it seems you no longer have a reason for still being here from what I can see."

Light flooded into the barn again as Reuben returned with a cart. "I found it, see?" Then, as he rolled it to a stop in front of Marta's empty stall, he looked up at Jack. "I told Dat you are here."

Jack, in turn, locked eyes with Tess. "Guess I've got that reason you mentioned."

It took every ounce of restraint she had to keep from using the pitchfork in a manner in which it was not intended, but reined in her impulse at the sight of Reuben's earnest expression. "You can put the manure in the cart now, Tess. You just pick it up and put it in."

"The pee, too," Jack interjected, straight-faced. "Marta doesn't want to be stepping on that when Reuben puts her back."

Lifting the pitchfork off the ground, she stared

144

at Jack a moment, the answering glint in his eye intensifying her irritation tenfold. Still, she knew the best way to be rid of him once and for all was to do what needed to be done, as quickly as possible.

Armed with the motivation she needed, Tess stepped into the stall and scooped up the first pile of manure she spotted.

"Don't forget the manure buried underneath the shavings. Marta doesn't want to be in here with that, either, does she, Reuben?"

"No."

The glare she leveled across the child's head reignited Jack's glint. "If it's buried enough that I can't see it, I'm betting Marta can't see it, either."

"Maybe, maybe not. But she'll *know* it's there, and we can't have that."

At Reuben's nod of agreement, Tess turned back, shifted the tines of the pitchfork through the shavings, and sagged in defeat. "There's no way I'm going to be able to get all of this."

"Scoop and roll," Jack said. "That's the trick."

She closed her eyes. Sighed. "Scoop and roll? What on earth does that mean?"

"Scoop up a section and kind of roll your wrist as you heave it—at an angle—against the base of the wall. The shavings will pile up for reuse when you're done, and the stray pieces of manure will roll down the pile in a way that makes it easier to get them up off the ground and into the cart." He stepped in beside her and liberated the pitchfork from her hand. "Watch me for a few seconds. This technique makes mucking a whole lot easier, and it works really well."

"Mamm said *Tess* is to muck the barn," Reuben protested, shyly. "Not anyone else."

"Oh. Right. Sorry, little man. My bad." Jack stopped short his second demonstration and turned back to Tess, his dalliance with something resembling decency gone as fast as it had come. "Your pitchfork, madame."

With nary a word lest she get thrown off the King farm for corrupting a minor, Tess grabbed the pitchfork and set to work, scooping and rolling her way across the stall until all that was left was the pile of shavings. At Reuben's instruction, she raked it all back into place, and, when she was done, sagged against the wall as the four-year-old went off to search for the stall's resident.

"I did it," she said between tired breaths. "It's done. *I'm* done."

"Until breakfast is over."

With great effort, she lifted her chin and her gaze to Jack. "You're still here . . ."

"Still waiting on Isaiah."

"Well, have fun with that." She parted company with the wall and headed out of the stall. "I'm out."

She was almost at the door when the sound of

146

her name coming from between his lips startled her to a stop.

"I think it's safe to say you're not Amish," he said, closing the gap between them with a few quick strides. "So now it's my turn. What are *you* doing here? If you don't mind me asking, of course."

Something about the change in lighting at the front of the barn further electrified the blue of his eyes as they settled on hers, waiting. Before Brian, those eyes might have quickened her pulse . . . Before Brian, that smile might have stirred a flush in her cheeks . . . Before Brian, the obvious ploy to prolong their contact would have made her giddy . . .

But this wasn't before Brian, and that genie could never be put back in the bottle.

"I'm leaving, that's what."

CHAPTER 13

Lifting her face to the gentle breeze making its way through the buggy, Tess allowed herself a moment to breathe in the sun-drenched fields, the smell of earth and livestock, and the hypnotic sway of the buggy. After a busy morning of chores and the encounter in the barn she'd just as soon forget, there was no denying how good it felt to sit, to bask in the afternoon's brightest rays, and to let the clip-clop of Marta's hooves against the country road calm her from the outside in.

"I am glad that you decided to come with me to Emma's house."

She traded her view of the countryside for the woman behind the reins and returned the smile she found waiting. "Trust me, it feels mighty good not to have to move for a little while."

"If I have asked you to do too much, please say so and—"

"No," she said, holding up her hands. "I'm doing what my boss wants me to do while I'm here. It's just that—I don't know. It doesn't matter."

"If it is something you want to say, you should say it, Tess."

She gazed out at the passing landscape. "I

never really knew what living like this actually meant. Technology has really spoiled us non-Amish types with things like washers and dryers. What takes you most of the day to do takes me a mere fraction of that same time to accomplish. And while the machines are doing the work, I'm able to do something else."

"What do you do?" Naomi asked.

"If I'm doing it during the day, I either call contacts for whatever story I'm working on or jump on the computer and write. If it's at night, and it's too late to make calls, I'll cull through old newspapers and magazines, looking for something I think our readers would like to learn more about in a different way. It gives me something to throw out during our Monday-morning staff meetings."

"You don't wash dishes?"

"Nope. I have a dishwasher for that."

"You don't go outside and plant flowers?"

"There is no outside when you live in an apartment—not in terms of planting, anyway."

"Do you cook dinner or bake bread?"

She started to nod but stopped before Naomi noticed. "No. I tend to just eat things I can heat up in the microwave."

"When do you think about things that are not work?"

She cleared her throat of its sudden lump. "Work is enough. For me."

Naomi seemed to weigh Tess's answers as she slowed the horse for a turn. "I would miss that time."

"What do you mean?" she asked, swinging her attention back to Naomi. "You're *always* working, from what I can see."

"With my hands, yah. But not always with my thoughts."

"Meaning?"

"When I am hanging clothes, I am thinking about the sun on my face or listening to Reuben as he feeds the chickens. If the older children are at school and I am washing dishes, I am watching Isaiah in the field. When I am planting flowers, I am thinking about how pretty they will look when they grow. When I am baking bread or cookies, I am thinking about the way the children will soon come around smelling the air and wondering when there will be something to put in their stomachs." With a click of her tongue and a gentle tug of the reins, Naomi directed Marta onto a paved driveway on their right. "We are here."

Tess looked across the top of Marta's head and felt the answering hitch of her breath at the sight of the gabled eaves, the bay windows, the flower boxes bursting with color, and the wraparound porch with what she imagined was a picturesque view of the pond she could see at the base of a small hill. "I-I thought Emma was Amish," she murmured.

"Emma *is* Amish."

"But"—she took in the house again—"this doesn't look like all of the other houses around here. It looks a lot more like the kind of home you'd see in a regular neighborhood."

Naomi tucked the reins on the floor at her feet and then stepped down onto the pavement. "Emma's father is English. He built this home for her and for Levi."

"Her father is—wait!" She, too, exited the buggy and ran around to join Naomi. "I didn't know someone who was born English could become Amish. Does that happen a lot?"

"Emma was raised Amish."

"But then how—"

A flash of movement to her right stole her attention in the direction of a barn she hadn't noticed until that moment. The barn, like the house, seemed different from the normal Amish fare but the specifics as to how were hard to pinpoint as her gaze narrowed in on the Amish man walking toward them with long, purposeful strides.

"Good afternoon, Levi," Naomi called. "Isaiah asked me to bring by a clock you were asking after this morning. He had one more thing to do to it, and now it is done."

The Amish man Tess guessed to be in his midtwenties, with a beard that barely scraped the base of his neck, stopped a few feet from

151

them, his smile wide. "I see you have brought a friend?"

"Yah. This is Tess. She is staying in the Grossdawdy Haus for the next few weeks."

Levi smiled and nodded at Tess before reengaging eye contact with Naomi. "I will get the clock out of the buggy while you go inside. Emma will be pleased to know you have come for a visit, and I will be pleased to have you eat some of the cookies she has been baking. I keep telling her I will get too big to climb ladders with her father with so many cookies, but still she keeps baking."

"Is Harp awake?"

"I don't think so."

And with that, Levi made his way to the back of the buggy, leaving Naomi to direct Tess toward the house.

"Who is Harp?" Tess whispered as they stepped onto the front porch.

"That is Levi and Emma's little boy."

"Harp isn't a very Amish-sounding name."

"It's his grandfather's name."

"The Englisher?"

"Yah."

Before she could ask any more questions, Naomi knocked on the door. Seconds later, a pretty young woman with dark blond hair parted in the middle and covered with a prayer kapp appeared around an interior wall toward the back of the house. Spying Naomi and Tess looking back at her through the screen, she strode toward them with a warm and welcoming smile that reached all the way to her sky-blue eyes. "Naomi! What a blessing it is to see you. Come in . . . come in . . ."

"I have brought a friend I would like you to meet. Emma, this is Tess. She is staying out at the farm for a few weeks."

"It's very nice to meet you, Tess. Welcome." Pushing open the door, Emma waved Naomi and Tess inside and then led them down the hall and into a large country kitchen bathed in sunlight.

"Oh, Emma, this room is beautiful," Tess murmured as her gaze moved between the window and the center island, the window and the cabinets, and, finally, the window and the large handmade wooden table flanked by two benches and a single wooden high chair. "The view of your land is breathtaking."

"Thank you. It's my favorite room in the whole house," Emma said. "It is where I like to be when Harp is sleeping."

Tess followed Emma's gaze to a hand-carved cradle positioned just below the windowsill. A peek inside revealed a sleeping baby with the same high cheekbones as Emma's, and the same dark hair she'd spotted around the edges of Levi's straw hat. Across his nose a tiny smattering of freckles paid homage to Emma, as well. "When my mother dreamed of this kitchen, she imagined me sleeping here, in front of the windows. Now, instead, it is my son who sleeps here."

With one last look at the baby, Emma swept her hand toward the table and the cookie plate in the center. "Would you both like to stay and visit with me for a while? I have lemonade in the refrigerator and fresh cookies from the oven."

"Won't that wake the baby?" Tess asked.

"He will sleep if he is to sleep." Emma crossed to the refrigerator for the pitcher of lemonade and returned to the table with three full glasses. When everyone had a glass and a plate for their cookies, she took a seat and addressed Naomi. "My father says a customer of his wanted one of Isaiah's clocks over the fireplace in their new home."

"Yah. That is why I am here. To bring the clock to Levi. It was not ready when the Englisher stopped by this morning."

Tess felt her ears perk. "Do you mean the guy that was in the barn this morning? Jack something?"

"Jack Cloverton," Emma supplied, nodding. "He works with my father at Harper Construction."

"Harper?" she echoed.

Emma's lips twitched with a shy smile. "Yah, that is right. Like my son. Levi and I call him Harp, but his given name is Ervin Harper."

She helped herself to a cookie. "And so your father owns the construction company?"

"Yah. My birth father, Brad Harper." Emma, too, helped herself to a cookie and a sip of lemonade. "My birth mother was Amish. She died in childbirth with me."

"And so he raised you Amish? Wow, that's kind of cool." She took a long sip of her own drink, only to stop and set the glass back down at the momentary cloud that skittered across Emma's features. "I'm sorry, did I say something wrong?"

"No. I was not raised by my birth father. I was raised by my mamm and dat. Mamm was my birth mother's sister."

"And your birth father was okay with that?"

The faintest sound from the vicinity of the cradle propelled Emma up and onto her feet. "He did not know."

"How could he not know you were being raised Amish?" she asked, drawing back.

"He thought I died along with my birth mother." Squatting down beside the cradle, Emma ran a gentle finger along the edge of her son's face, igniting a flurry of happy leg kicks in return. "But it is okay. He is in my life now, and in Levi's and Harp's, too."

"I still don't—"

A quick yet steady knock sent their collective attention toward the back doorway and the familiar face emerging through it with a wide smile. "Hello? Emma? Are you—" The blue eyes Tess remembered from the barn that morning moved from Naomi . . . to Emma . . . to Tess, and, finally, somewhat reluctantly back to Emma. "Hey. I'm sorry to interrupt, but your dad wanted me to tell you he'll be by closer to six. A new client came in today and threw off the schedule a little, but he won't let it go too long."

"That is good to know. Thank you, Jack." Nudging her chin toward the table, Emma reached inside the cradle and lifted her son into her arms. "Would you like a cookie and some lemonade before you head back to the office? There is plenty."

Jack's answering laugh filled the room. "Levi mentioned something about an overabundance of cookies."

"I'm sure he did. Levi thinks I make too many."

"There's no such thing as too many in my book." Jack crossed to the table, scooped up three cookies, and fixed his gaze on Tess, his expression unreadable. "I didn't expect to see *you* here."

Tess shifted in her spot on the bench. "Nor I, you."

"Isaiah finished the clock that was not ready for you this morning." Naomi finished her drink and rose. "He asked that I bring it to Levi."

Jack nodded, his gaze finding its way back to Tess once again. "And you came along because"—he snapped—"that's right, you never got around to telling me why you're here, in Amish country, did you?"

"Tess is here to learn about our ways." Naomi gathered up the glasses on the table and carried them to the sink. "She is staying out at the farm—in the Grossdawdy Haus."

"Oh? Are you a teacher?" he asked.

Naomi returned to the table with a washcloth. "Tess is a writer. For a magazine."

He crossed his arms in front of his chest and tipped back on the heels of his boots. "A writer . . . I wouldn't have guessed that."

"No? What would you have guessed?" Tess asked, only to silently berate herself for the question. What difference did it make what he thought?

"I pegged you more for something like a motor vehicle department employee. You know, based on all that friendliness you exude."

She didn't need a mirror to know the anger he incited in her was spilling onto her face. Fortunately for Naomi and Emma, though, a glance at both showed Emma focused on Harp, and Naomi on the table she was cleaning. Still, he wasn't worth the response she was itching to give. Instead, she pulled her phone from her pocket, hit the side button to check the time, and felt the fight drain out of her body at the sight of the low-battery icon.

"Problem?"

"Yeah. I've got almost no charge left and . . ." She shook her head. "Forget it. It doesn't matter."

"Then why does everything about you right now say otherwise?"

She glanced down at her phone again, closed her eyes briefly. "It doesn't. I'm fine. When in Rome, right?" She stopped, steadied the wobble in her throat, and, after a short but needed inhale, slipped the phone back into her pocket and lifted her gaze back to Jack's. "So can we be done now? You got your answer. I'm here to write about the Amish."

"You can charge your phone in my car if you'd like."

His offer caught her off guard. So, too, did her inability to process any sort of cohesive thought let alone an actual reply.

"I could hook it up for a few minutes and get it out of the danger zone. Or, if I drive you back to Naomi's, maybe we could get it even closer to full power." At her answering silence, he took another cookie from the plate on the table, tousled the ultrafine hair on the top of Harp's head, and smiled at Naomi. "I'm thinking, on account of Tess being here for work, that she probably needs her phone to be usable. So, if it's okay, maybe I could drive her back to your place so she could get powered up again?"

"Her boss, Mr. Livingston, wants her to live

as we do," Naomi said, not unkindly. "There is a phone just down the street, next to the Esch farm."

"And she will use that for most outgoing calls, I'm sure. But if someone needs to reach her—for either professional or personal reasons, she won't get the call if her phone is not charged."

Tess felt Naomi's gaze a split second before she heard the woman's quiet yet relenting *Yah*.

"Great. I won't keep her out long. Tess? You ready to head out?"

"I . . . um . . . yeah. Sure. Thank you." As if on some sort of autopilot setting, Tess claimed her notebook and pen from the table, stuffed them into her tote bag, thanked Emma for her hospitality, and then followed Jack out of the house and across the scrap of lawn separating it from the buggy she'd arrived in and the black pickup truck in which she'd apparently be departing.

Steps from the truck, he shortened his stride enough to let her catch up. "I'm guessing, if your phone is pretty much dead, that it's probably going to need longer than the trip to Naomi's place to get back up to speed. So are you okay with driving around a little? Maybe seeing a little more of the countryside than you've likely gotten to see from Naomi's buggy?"

"You don't have to do that."

"I know I don't. But I'm offering."

159

She took in the Harper Construction logo on the passenger-side door. "Don't you have to get back to work?"

"Nah, Brad is pretty chill. An extra thirty minutes won't matter." He led the way to the passenger-side door, opened it for her, and then made his way around the front of the truck to his own spot behind the steering wheel. "So, let's get you charged, shall we?"

Nodding, she handed him her phone and then sank back against her seat as he started his truck. "Thank you for this. I really appreciate it."

"You're welcome. Can't have folks worrying because they can't reach you, now can we?"

"That's not really an issue, but, still, thank you." Aware of his questioning eyes, she turned her own attention out the window and onto the farmhouse growing ever smaller in the side-view mirror. "I liked her. She was really sweet."

"Who? Emma?" He returned her nod with his own as he took them in a westerly direction "Yeah, she's great. Straddles the two worlds like she's been doing it her whole life."

"Two worlds?"

"The Amish one she lives in and the English one Brad lives in," Jack said as he lowered their windows. "I'm not sure I could have handled it all so well if it had been me."

"What happened to them?"

"Who?"

"The people who raised her as their own."

"Wayne and Rebeccah—her parents? They're still around. I saw them at her house not that long ago."

She drew back. "She still talks to them?"

"Of course. They're her parents."

"No, your boss is."

"Right, but Wayne and Rebeccah are the ones who raised her," he said, resting his left arm atop the open window and lifting his chin to the gentle breeze flowing through the truck.

"They raised her because *they lied* to her. And to your boss. I-I don't get why they're not in jail."

"Because that's not what Emma wanted."

"But why not? They played God with her life, and with your boss's."

"I suppose . . ."

"You *suppose?*" she challenged. "*Seriously?* They created a whole world for her that shouldn't have been."

For a moment, maybe two, he said nothing, just took in the passing fields to his left and the winding road in front of them before guiding her eyes to the same with his hand. "Maybe. And I'm sure those lies were a mighty bitter pill to swallow. But what came next in terms of how she chose to handle it—was hers to choose. And so she chose."

"Based on what she knew, sure. But—"

"Brad says she chose forgiveness and love."

"And Brad? What was his choice?"

"Emma taught him to do the same."

"I-I just can't imagine that," she murmured.

"Which part? The forgiveness or the love?"

"Both."

He seemed to consider her words. "I guess, if you focus only on the lie and turn a blind eye to everything else, yeah, I can see how you'd feel that way. And, honestly, I can't say I wouldn't struggle with the same thing if I was the one in Emma's position. But that said, I can tell you I've been out at their place when everyone is there—Brad, Emma, Levi, the baby, Rebeccah and Wayne, and her siblings, and, well, I always leave feeling a whole lot happier and a whole lot lighter than when I got there. Which says to me they're onto something."

"I just . . . I can't . . ." She waved away the rest of her sentence, if not her growing agitation, and looked out the window once again, the passing fields little more than a blur in her consciousness.

"So where are you from again?"

"Connecticut, technically. But really just outside of New York City."

"Ahhh . . . So you're either climbing the walls out here or loving all the peace and quiet." The steady thrum of his fingers atop the windowsill ceased in her answering silence. "I'll take your lack of response to mean you're climbing the walls."

"It's nothing personal," she murmured. "I'm just used to a busier life."

"Things are busy here, too."

"I mean with lots of deadlines and meetings and . . ." She pulled back on words that no longer applied and, instead, pointed at a hatted man in a small cart being pulled back and forth by a horse. "What is that guy doing?"

Slowing the truck to a near crawl, Jack pulled onto the road's grassy shoulder. "He's breaking in that horse before he sells it to a family who will use it to pull their buggy. Many of the horses he gets in are retired racehorses who are used to pulling sulkies, so they transition well. But other horses can need more time and guidance."

"Have you ridden in a buggy?" she asked.

His laugh was warm, friendly. "No. I like to move a little faster myself."

"You sure?" she asked, eyeing him across the bench seat. "Because I'm not getting that."

"Ha. Ha. Ha. Might I remind you we've got a phone to charge," he said by way of explanation. "And I figured, since you're here to write about the Amish, you might want to see a bit more of the countryside than you've likely seen so far, Little Miss Uptight."

She splayed her hand between them. "Whoa. I'm not uptight."

"Then you didn't see yourself in Isaiah's barn this morning . . ."

"Wait, what? Seriously? The way I remember things, you approached me out of nowhere and started making a slew of less than friendly comments while I was trying to muck the barn."

"I was *playing* with you, Tess . . . You know, having a little fun? If you weren't so uptight you might have recognized it for what it was."

"And what was it, exactly?"

"Good-natured teasing between two adults."

"You didn't know me—*don't* know me," she protested.

"And so that means I can't try to strike up a friendship with you?"

Her answering laugh sounded bitter even to her own ears, but she didn't care. "I'm not interested in making friends with you or anyone else while I'm here, Jack. I'm here to do my job. That's it." Breaking eye contact, she swept her hand toward her phone and then toward the windshield and the road beyond. "I think I've got enough charge at this point. So, if you don't mind, I'd much rather you take me back to Naomi's now so we can both get on with our day."

"You got it."

CHAPTER 14

She wasn't entirely sure what time it was. She'd watched the sun slip toward the horizon, paint the bottom edge of the sky in a kaleidoscope of reds and oranges and mauves, and, finally, disappear from view completely as night took its rightful turn at the helm. And, still, she sat on the cane rocking chair on the front porch, staring into the darkness, her thoughts too heavy to sift through.

All her life she'd been a planner, a list maker. Lists had helped her keep track of things, to set and meet goals, and to plan her route from point A to point B. When she was old enough to write, she'd planned playdates down to the minute, and every detail of every birthday party she'd ever had. When she attended high school, she was the student everyone came to in order to know what was due and when. College had opened the door to thoughts of life beyond her childhood cocoon and, with it, came new things to plan and milestones to hit. Everything had a schedule, a time, and a place. And it was all going like clockwork until—

"You were very quiet at dinner tonight."

Toeing her aimless rocking to an end, Tess searched the darkness on the other side of the porch rail. "Naomi?" she whispered, rising to her feet. "Is everything okay?"

Footfalls on the steps gave way to her host's partially moonlit face. "Please do not get up. Everything is fine. I did not mean to frighten you. It is just that Isaiah saw you sitting out here in the dark as he was getting ready for bed."

"I'm sorry. I-I can go inside."

Naomi interrupted her move toward the door with a gentle hand. "I am not here so you will go inside, Tess. I am here to see that you are okay. You did not say very much at supper even though Reuben tried many times to make you smile."

Had he? She couldn't remember. Then again, she sort of remembered everyone laughing and Reuben's wide eyes when she hadn't . . .

"I'm sorry, Naomi. I hope I didn't hurt his feelings."

"It just means he will try again tomorrow."

She nodded. "Then I will make sure to laugh when I hear the rest of you laugh."

Even in the shadowed slivers of moonlight, she could see the woman's mouth tighten in conjunction with the grip on her arm. "Are you not enjoying your time with us?" Naomi asked.

"No, no. It's nothing like that. It's . . ." She looked into the darkness and drew in a long, steadying breath. "I don't know what to say. I guess I was thinking about something else when Reuben told his joke. I'm sorry."

"I am not here because you did not laugh at a joke. I am here because you seemed upset." Naomi released her hold on Tess and leaned back against the railing. "It did not work, did it?"

She waited for more, but when it didn't come, she lowered herself back onto the edge of the rocker. "What didn't work?"

"The charging of your phone."

"No, it worked. The phone is fine. Why?"

"You did not look happy when you returned with the Englisher."

Aware of a sudden tightness in her jaw, Tess willed herself to breathe, to relax. "The phone is fine," she repeated.

"That is good, yah?"

"It is."

She felt Naomi studying her, wanting to ask more questions, but she was grateful when none came. Instead, the woman brushed a hand down the front of her maroon dress and turned her attention toward the darkness. "Sometimes I wonder what that would be like. To be able to speak with my sisters instead of waiting for a letter to come in the mail."

"How many sisters do you have?"

"I have four."

"And they don't live here in Blue Ball?"

"No. They live far away, in different places."

"How often do you get to see them?" she asked.

"It has been many years."

"Do you miss them?"

"Yah," Naomi conceded. "But letters keep us close. And it is as Isaiah says—my friends Katie and Emma and Danielle are like sisters I see often."

"I haven't met Danielle . . ."

"You will."

She sat with Naomi's words and ensuing silence for a few moments as her own thoughts rewound to their afternoon visit. "Your friend Emma seems so happy, so cheerful."

"Yah."

"As her friend, though, surely she isn't really okay with everything, right?"

Naomi turned back to Tess, confusion pulling at her brow. "Everything?"

"With what her aunt and uncle did to her. You know, the way they played God with her life the way they did."

"I don't understand."

Gripping the armrests of her rocker, Tess toed its gentle sway to a stop once again. "Telling her they were her parents when they weren't . . . Keeping her birth father from her . . . Keeping her from him . . . All of it."

"If you are to be forgiven, you are to forgive," Naomi said, simply.

"We're not talking about someone who took her-her"—she cast about for a suitable analogy—"*kapp* and didn't give it back. Or-or someone

168

who took her picture when they weren't supposed to, Naomi! We're talking about two people who pretended to be her parents, who didn't tell her real father that she'd survived. That's nothing if not *unforgiveable*. Or would be for anyone who wasn't Amish."

Even in the limited light, she could see a cloud pass across Naomi's face. For a moment, Tess thought the woman who'd shown very little variation in emotion from the moment they'd met was about to crack, but the anger never came. Instead, Naomi's thin lips lifted in a smile. "Miss Lottie helped Emma as she helps so many. It is because of Miss Lottie, Emma says, that she did not make a decision in haste."

"Miss Lottie," Tess repeated, slowly. "Miss Lottie . . . Where have I heard that—wait! One of the twins mentioned that name. *Katie,* maybe? I think she said this Miss Lottie person helped her, too."

"Yah. Miss Lottie is a friend to many. To Katie. To Hannah. To Emma. To Danielle. To—"

"I take it she's Amish?"

"No. Miss Lottie is English. She did not take baptism."

Tess leaned forward. "So she *was* Amish?"

"She was raised in an Amish home. But she was not baptized."

"Interesting . . ."

"Perhaps Miss Lottie can help you, too."

169

"Help me?" Tess echoed, shaking her thoughts back into the moment. "With what?"

"Finding your way through all that pain you hold inside."

Pushing the door closed behind her, Tess returned the phone to her ear. "Murph? You still there?"

"Yup."

"Sorry. I was outside talking to Naomi."

"If this is a bad time, I could—"

"No! Trust me, our conversation had run its course. *More* than run its course, actually." She stepped inside the pitch-black kitchen, bumped into the edge of the table, and, after feeling around for the bench, lowered herself onto it. "I'm glad you called. I wasn't sure you would."

"You mean after you hung up on me the last time we spoke?"

"Yeah. About that. I didn't mean to do that."

His two-pack-a-day laugh tickled her ear. "Of course you did. I hit a nerve, and you were ticked off."

She held up her hand only to drop it back to the table, unseen. "Can we just call a truce and talk about something else? Please?"

"You settling in?"

"I'm surviving."

"They got you wearing one of those bonnets yet?"

"It's a prayer kapp, remember?"

170

"You said it was the same thing."

It felt good to laugh, to let go of the tension that had started in the barn that morning and built, steadily, to its near breaking point a heartbeat before Murph's call. "Seen any action yet?"

"You know I can't answer that."

"You wouldn't be much of a mentor if I didn't at least *ask*."

"Touché." He sucked in a breath, inhaling a puff of smoke she didn't need to see to imagine. "So, you find that golden egg you've been looking for yet?"

"I think I have."

"Tell me."

"Okay, so I told you about the twins, right? Katie and Hannah?"

"One left and got a pass, one thought about leaving but didn't?" Murph asked. "Yeah, you did."

Pulling the phone from her cheek, she pressed the speaker button and set it on the table. "Okay, so I met another Amish woman today. And get this . . . She was literally kidnapped at birth."

Murph's breath ceased, mid-inhale. "Kidnapped?"

"Pretty much, yeah." She filled him in with the bits and pieces she'd been able to put together and, when she was done, waited for the response she imagined.

Only it didn't come. Instead, his answering silence was broken, on occasion, by a few drags of his cigarette.

"Um, hello? Did you hear all of that?"

"I heard it."

"That's it? Seriously? C'mon, Murph. The lies? The cover-up? The acting as if all of that is normal and okay? Tell me that's not a killer story . . ."

"It could be. Sure. If this woman wanted it to be. But she doesn't. Clearly."

She stared at his name on the screen in front of her. "C'mon, Murph . . ."

"C'mon what? It's done. It's in the rearview mirror. She loved them. She forgave them."

"But they committed a crime!"

"She forgave them," he repeated.

"Who's to say that was her choice?" she argued. "That Emma wasn't strong-armed the way Katie was strong-armed to give up her talent? That these seemingly peaceful people aren't really just victims of some sort of cult or something?"

He exhaled for a beat or two. "Tell me about her."

"I just did."

"No, you told me about what *happened* to her. Tell me about *her*. Describe her the way you would in a story so that I can picture her."

"Okay . . ." She rested her elbows on the table, nestled her chin against her hands, and revisited the sunny farmhouse kitchen and the young woman who seemed to fit it perfectly. "Emma is about my height, maybe a half inch or so shorter.

Her hair—or what I could see of it with her prayer kapp on—is the color of warm honey. She has what my grandfather used to describe as smiling eyes. And she had this little spray of freckles across the bridge of her nose that reminded me a little of fairy dust."

"Okay, good. Next layer?"

"She has a baby. He's about six months, if I had to guess. Really cute. Chubby. She calls him Harp—short for Harper, her birth father's last name."

"Keep going . . ."

"Emma is married to Levi."

"Amish?"

"Yes. Though I'm pretty sure he works with Emma's father."

"Doing what kind of work?"

"Building stuff." She thought back to the panel on the side of Jack's truck. "Her father owns Harper Construction."

"Did you meet the two who raised her?"

"No. I imagine they are at their own house. But from what Jack said, Emma sees them all. *Together* even—the two of them, her birth father, the kids she thought were her siblings, et cetera. For family gatherings and stuff."

"Interesting . . ."

"I know, right?" Dropping her hands back to the table, she braced herself up and onto her feet, crossed to the refrigerator she could now make out with her adjusted sight, and helped herself to a glass of fresh milk. "As for Emma, specifically, she was very welcoming and very warm to me, Naomi, and even Jack. Really, she just seems like a genuinely happy person."

"Worth noting."

She paused her hand on the way to her second sip. "How so?"

"Not so fast. Who's Jack?"

"Jack?" she echoed. "How do you know about . . . ?" Her words petered off as her verbal recap of the day looped its way through her thoughts. "He's just some guy who works for Emma's father. He's arrogant, totally full of himself, and not worth infringing on my limited time with you. Trust me, you've met the type many times. Condescending one minute, tries for charming the next. The total former-high-school-jock type."

"Amish?"

"No."

She heard his growing smile. "Good. I'm glad to hear someone's around to keep you humble while I'm here and you're there, kid."

"Please. Don't flatter this guy. Jack Cloverton is no Max Murphy. Not. Even. Close."

The smile she didn't need to see to know was alive and well on the other side of the world erupted into a soft yet no less irritating laugh. "I'm intrigued . . ."

174

"Don't be. He's a nonissue in this Emma stuff."

"What about elsewhere?"

She set the glass on the table so hard she could hear droplets of milk spilling over the rim. "Can we just get back to our layering exercise? About Emma?"

He took another drag of his cigarette. "Yeah. Sure. So, from what you just told me about this young woman, it seems like she's made a very real choice."

"To?"

"To forgive. To move on. To live in the moment. All of it. And it's smart."

Tess lowered herself back onto the bench. "Smart? Smart how? These people—these Amish people who raised her as their own—literally played God with her life. They chose what was best for her and who was best to raise her."

"True. But let's flip her reaction for a moment. Let's say she pressed charges, or went positively nuts, or spent all her time and energy looking back at something that was already done? Would it change anything? Would she suddenly be able to go back to her childhood and experience it as an Englisher?"

Tess rolled her eyes. "Of course not. But—"

"So this Emma had two options from what I can see. She could be angry and bitter and rightfully so, or she could take control of her life and decide how she wants it to go from here on out.

Sounds to me like she chose the latter and is living a pretty good life because of it."

"But *could* she really choose? Maybe it was like it was with Katie, where she was emotionally blackmailed."

"To do what? Stay connected to people who lied to her? I don't think that applies here. The Amish are not a cult. They aren't locked in a room and told they can't leave, right? They can choose to leave if they want. There are just repercussions depending on when they choose to leave."

"My point exactly."

"So what would leaving have meant for her?"

"If she'd been baptized when she found out, a lot."

"If she cared about the Amish, sure. But if her birth father was English and she'd chosen to sever ties with the Amish folks who raised her, would being banned from them have mattered?"

It was a valid point. But—"Maybe there was something else. Maybe this Levi was already in her life and she didn't want to lose him."

"Maybe. I can't know that. But regardless of all of that, you can't discount what you told me about her. Unless you think it was all fake?"

"You mean the way Emma is?"

"Yes."

She shook her head in the darkness. "No. Her happiness and her warmth is genuine. She's exactly the kind of person you'd want as a . . ."

Pushing the glass into the center of the table, she let loose a labored sigh. "I need to keep looking, don't I?"

Another inhale. Another exhale. Another beat or two of silence. "Do you?" he finally asked.

"Well, yeah . . . You're telling me I've got nothing here in terms of Emma. That because she's chosen to forgive and move on, there's no story to be told here. And, last time, when I told you about Katie and Hannah and *their* story, you essentially shamed me away from that one, too."

"I wasn't trying to shame you, kid. I was just weighing in on the direction you were going. Like we do with each other back at the office. You played out a possible avenue for your story, and I weighed in."

"Yeah. I remember." She took one last sip of milk and then rested her cheek atop the table. "Whatever. It's all saying the same thing, isn't it? I don't have my story yet."

"Now, *that* I didn't say . . ."

She jerked upright in tandem with a series of voices in the background of the call. "Wait— what? You said—"

"Sorry, kid, I gotta go. Duty calls. I'll be in touch again when I can."

CHAPTER 15

Resting her chin on the rake handle, Tess drank in the freshly mucked stall and the odd feeling of accomplishment powering the smile she wore. "Not too shabby, if I do say so myself," she murmured into the empty space. "Not too shabby at—"

"Who are you talking to?"

Tess glanced down at the large hazel eyes peeking up at her from the stall's entry point and laughed. "I was talking to myself, Reuben."

"Yourself?"

The confused scrunch of the little boy's face turned her smile into a laugh, and her grip on the rake handle into a veritable *Ta-da!* sweep of her fingers. "Do you see this, little one? I did this. By myself. Thanks to you."

"Me?"

"You taught me how, didn't you?"

"Dat's friend taught you."

She felt her smile falter and tried her best to shake it back into place. "By the time I go back home, I'll be an egg-retrieving, stall-mucking pro. And since I've mastered those things, I think it's time for you to teach me something new."

"Mamm said you are to come to the house when you are done."

Again she looked at the stall, allowed herself one last nod of satisfaction, and then handed the rake to the little boy. "So I'm done here then?"

"Yah."

"All righty then. I guess we're going into the house." She pulled off her ball cap, looped her finger around the Velcro strap, and waved it toward the front of the barn. "Shall we?"

The four-year-old stood tall. "I am to help Dat today."

"Oh? With what?"

"The fence!"

"Ooooh, that sounds like fun . . ."

"Yah!"

They walked side by side into the late-morning sun and parted ways at the porch steps. For a moment, she simply watched as he ran toward the sheep enclosure, his excitement over helping Isaiah palpable.

"This place really has a way of getting under your skin, doesn't it?"

Tess turned toward the steps, her gaze traveling to the unfamiliar woman sitting on one of Naomi's rocking chairs. On the woman's lap was a rosy-cheeked baby bouncing up and down with pure joy. "I'm sorry, I didn't see you sitting there just now."

"It's okay. I've gotten lost a time or two—or a million—like that myself since I've been here." Wrapping one arm around her child, the woman motioned Tess onto the porch and held out her free hand. "Hi. I'm Danielle. Danielle Parker. And this busy little baby is my daughter, Grace."

"Danielle . . . Danielle . . . I think I've heard your name."

"Probably. I'm Naomi's friend. You must be Tess."

"Oh. Right. Sorry. Yes, I'm Tess." Retrieving her hand, she took a moment to note the woman's shoulder-length brown hair and the way it fell in soft waves atop shoulders left bare by a pretty pink halter top. "You're English."

Danielle grinned. "I am."

"How do you know Naomi?"

"Our mutual friend Lydia Schlabach introduced us." Danielle placed a momentary kiss atop her little girl's head before pointing her chin toward the part of the road they could just make out beyond the edge of the barn. "I live about a half mile away. Lydia and Naomi have been a godsend to the two of us"—she lifted and turned the baby so their foreheads touched—"haven't they, pumpkin?"

Tess scanned the fields dotted by the occasional windmill before bringing her focus back to the woman. "Have you always lived here, in Amish country?"

"No. I visited, once, as a child. And then came back twenty-one months ago. I've been here ever since."

"Where were you before that?"

"New York."

"City?"

"No. A suburb about thirty minutes north."

"So the Westchester area then?" she asked.

Danielle smiled. "I take it you know the area?"

"I live and work in Stamford."

"I didn't realize."

Tess made her way over to the rocking chair next to the woman and sat down. "Coming here from New York had to be quite a shock to your system, right?"

Instead of an answer, Danielle returned her lips to the top of Grace's head.

"Did you come for your husband's job or something?"

"My husband was killed in a car accident. This place"—Danielle leaned back against her rocking chair—"was where I came to *escape,* I guess. Though, really, that's not something I can ever truly escape."

"Danielle, I-I'm so sorry."

Rapid blinking chased the misty sheen from Danielle's eyes in conjunction with a deep inhale, and an even deeper exhale. "I didn't know it at the time, but this place and its people were the arms I needed while I grieved, and the strong, steady hand I needed to help me stand back up again."

At a loss for what to say, Tess said nothing,

the ensuing silence peppered only by Grace's occasional babbles. She took a moment to study the dimpled hands, the hair that curled around tiny ears, the teeth she could spy . . . "How old is she?"

"Fourteen months."

She did the mental math and swallowed. Hard. "So you were pregnant when you came here?"

"I was. Although I didn't know it at the time."

"Wow. I can't imagine what . . ." She let the rest of her needless sentence fade into nothing as she searched the woman's face for the pain she knew had to be there. But for the moment, at least, the baby's innocent joy was clearly Danielle's. "You're very strong."

"I became that here, maybe. But it took a while." Danielle closed her eyes briefly. "I actually thought about giving her to my friend Lydia. To be raised Amish."

"Who?"

"Grace."

She stared at the woman, too stunned to speak.

"I blamed myself for the accident—for not knowing, for staying behind, and for being the mother I'd convinced myself I'd been."

"The mother you'd convinced yourself you'd been? I don't understand . . ."

"My three children were in the car with my husband. My mom was, too."

The words were like a sucker punch to her

gut. "Oh, Danielle, I . . ." She reached across the space between their chairs and closed her hand around the woman's shoulder. "I'm so very, very sorry."

"I came here to escape everything—my old house, my old neighborhood, the kids' friends, reminders, you name it. But I couldn't escape the pain. The regret and the anger were all-consuming." Danielle's eyes fluttered closed again as Grace nestled against her shoulder, thumb in mouth. "Eventually, though, I found what I needed. Forgiveness, friendship, love, affirmation, and even hope. All the things I needed for this next chapter of my life. With Grace."

Again Tess was left speechless, her mouth gaped wide.

"So Naomi tells me you're here for your job?" Danielle asked, smiling. "To write some sort of article on the Amish?"

"Uh . . . yeah—I mean, yes."

"Good. Maybe you can help people understand."

She looked from Danielle, to the baby drifting off to sleep against the woman's chest, and then, finally, back to Danielle. "You mean about the way the Amish live? With no electricity? The plain clothes? The work ethic?"

Danielle's head bobbed ever so gently against her daughter's face. "You could go that route, sure, and I'm sure it would be an interesting read.

But I'm thinking about the deeper stuff, the stuff you can't see in a single visit or when you stop to buy something they've made."

"Tell me what you see here," Tess prodded.

"Well, first and foremost, community. The lessons the rest of the world could learn from them . . ."

"You mean like the fire the other day? The way they all showed up to rebuild?"

"There's that, sure. They do what needs to be done, no questions asked. But it's more than that."

"I know they follow up their church service with a meal together . . ."

"It's quite a sight, yes, but that's not it, either. It's . . ." Danielle's gaze traveled across her daughter to some distant place Tess suspected was not tangible, yet every bit as real, leaving Tess to regret not having her notebook and pen at the ready. "It's the way they *are* . . . the way they've been taught . . . the way they teach. It's not by words spoken or cutesy memes plastered and shared across social media. It's . . ." She stopped, drew in a breath, and returned her focus to Grace and to Tess. "I'm not sure how to say it so you can understand. It's more about immersing yourself in their actions, even the ones that might seem trivial."

The *creak* of rusty hinges sent their collective attention to the open screen door and the woman it deposited onto the porch with a plate of muffins in one hand and a trio of milk glasses held together by the fingers of the other. "Oh, Tess, I see you've met Danielle."

Rising, Tess liberated two of the glasses from Naomi and handed one to Danielle. "I have, yes. Though now that you're standing here, I'm realizing Reuben said you wanted me inside."

"No worries. Tomorrow we will bake a lot of bread together." Naomi held the muffin plate out to Danielle first, then Tess, and then claimed the remaining rocker and muffin for herself while Danielle carefully lowered Grace into a reclining position. "Miss Lottie said your hat is coming along nicely."

Grace startled but did not wake at the sound of her mother's soft laugh. "Perhaps it is time for Miss Lottie to get new glasses."

"You don't think it's good?" Naomi asked between bites of her muffin.

"I think it bears no resemblance to something anyone would wear on their head in winter or any other season."

Naomi's lips twitched. "It's your first try, Danielle. You will get better. Miss Lottie will see to it that you do."

"I have no doubt she'll try. I have much doubt she'll succeed."

"Don't give up. There are many things Miss Lottie helps us learn."

"Don't I know it," Danielle mused around her muffin. "Even for those of us who resist her wisdom for longer than we should."

Tess paused her own muffin halfway between her lap and her mouth. "Who is this Miss Lottie woman, exactly? I know you said she's a friend to many, Naomi. And I know Katie, Hannah, Emma, and now Danielle have spoken so highly of her."

"Yah. That is Miss Lottie."

"You said she was English, right? That she was raised Amish but was not baptized . . ."

"Yah."

"So what is it about her—*her friendship*—that resonates with all of you the way it so clearly does?"

Naomi and Danielle exchanged glances, with Danielle taking the job of answering. "It's her wisdom. She has an uncanny ability to help people find their way through the darkest of times. Myself included. Although, truth be told, I didn't embrace her words all that quickly or willingly."

"Since she left the Amish and the area, did she get a counseling degree or something?"

"I don't think so," Danielle said over a sip of milk. "Though, now that you bring it up, I'm actually ashamed to realize I've never asked. I just know she traveled extensively and that, eventually, she found her way back here. To the

186

people and the place she always equated with home."

She let Danielle's words roll around in her thoughts for a few minutes while she took another bite of muffin and a few sips of milk. "So this woman, with no formal counseling experience that you know of, took it upon herself to tell Hannah to go to New York, and Katie to stay Amish?"

Naomi shook her head emphatically. "No. Miss Lottie does not tell us what we should do. She listens and then she speaks, sharing lessons she has learned in the hope they might help others. It is up to the person speaking with her to decide if those lessons fit."

"Interesting . . ." Tess took another sip. "Can I ask how she helped *you,* Danielle?"

"Miss Lottie felt that shutting out my memories in the interest of minimizing my pain was actually having the opposite effect," Danielle said, glancing down at her sleeping child. "In my case, it took yet another wise soul to help me see the truth behind Miss Lottie's words. But I got to where I needed to be for Grace and for myself because of Miss Lottie."

"So she's a voice of reason, essentially."

Danielle's shoulders lifted in a half-hearted shrug. "I guess she's that, sure. But really she's *a friend.* To everyone. In the truest sense of the word."

"Anyone can appear that way for a while," Tess managed around the sudden lump in her throat. "Until it no longer works for them."

The gentle, measured rocking Danielle had been maintaining since Grace drifted off to sleep came to a stop. "Miss Lottie is as genuine and good as they come, Tess."

"I'm sure you think so. I'm sure—"

Grace's eyes fluttered open ever so briefly at Naomi's answering gasp. "It is not just *Danielle* who thinks so, Tess. Miss Lottie has an ear and a shoulder for all. Even you."

"I don't need her ear or her shoulder," Tess said.

"Maybe not today, but perhaps another day you will."

She shook off Naomi's words as the woman stood and gathered the trio of empty glasses. "No. Not then, either."

"Who is *your* Miss Lottie in life?" Danielle asked as she resumed her rocking. "You know, the person you go to when you *do* need an ear and a shoulder?"

"Myself."

"Not one of your close friends?"

She tightened her grip on the armrests of her rocker. "No."

Danielle's gaze sharpened on Tess as Naomi paused en route to the door. "Perhaps the person who called while we were speaking on the porch last night?" Naomi suggested.

"That was Murph."

"He is your friend?"

"He is my coworker. He's away on assignment, too, and so we check in on each other via text or phone call to see how it's going."

Naomi opened her mouth as if to speak, but closed it again in favor of carrying the glasses inside. When the screen door banged closed behind her, Tess stood and made her way over to the railing and the view it afforded of Reuben and Isaiah working on a distant fence. "Does the absolute quiet of this place ever make you go stir crazy?"

"I've actually found that I prefer it," Danielle said. "Sometimes at night, after I've put Grace down, I sit out on my own tiny front porch and just *feel* it all. The fatigue from a busy day . . . The stillness of the night air . . . Whatever memory chooses to visit me that particular evening . . . And the joy or sadness that memory brings me in the moment."

"Wouldn't you rather be in a place where you don't have to do that?"

"I *want* to do that. It's in those memories and the senses they invoke that I can still be with my family. Short of having them back in the flesh, there's nothing I'd rather do."

Tess abandoned her view of father and son in favor of the gray buggy slowly making its way along the road in front of the farm. "Me? I'd go stir crazy in this quiet if I had to be here for too long."

"Hustle and bustle can only distract you away from the pain for so long, Tess. You've got to deal with it in order to get to the other side. A good friend can help you do that. Trust me. I know this."

Closing her lashes to the buggy, Tess felt her breath grow shallow. "That is not my experience."

"Which part? The good friend part or the trust part?"

She didn't need to open her eyes to know her knuckles were blanched white by the force of her grip on the railing. "Actually, I think it's best if we change the subject. I don't relish being the pin to someone else's balloon of naivete."

The quiet thump of Danielle's rocker grew silent once again. "Which part, Tess?" Danielle repeated. "The good friend part or the trust part?"

"Why? Do you think they're mutually exclusive, as well?"

"Of course not. Why would I?"

"Because, in my experience, they are."

The quiet squeak let her know Danielle had stood. The footfalls that followed gave her time to brace for the inevitable hand-on-the-shoulder move. Danielle of course, didn't disappoint. "I don't know what this person did to you to hurt you the way they so clearly have, but I can tell you she wasn't a friend."

190

"I know that. *Now,*" Tess whispered fiercely. "But I had every reason in the world to believe she was until she . . . wasn't."

"And so now you're hesitant about getting close to anyone else?"

"There's nothing hesitant about it. I simply *won't* allow myself to get that close to anyone ever again."

"I see. And I get it. I really do. But in my case, had I continued down that same path, I'd have let the situation win—to destroy what was left of my life. If I had, I wouldn't have my daughter in my arms right now, and I wouldn't have the support system I have here in Blue Ball."

Tess ducked her way out from under Danielle's hand and crossed to the side railing. There, she looked out at the mules Reuben had told her were used in the fields. "I really don't want to talk about—"

"Don't let this person rob you of the beauty that comes with trust and true friendship, Tess. You're too young for that."

"You don't understand."

Danielle and a sleeping Grace closed the gap between them with slower, slightly more hesitant steps this time. "I'd like to. If you'll give me a chance."

"I don't *want* a friend, Danielle. I really don't. I'm good on my own." She breathed away the wobble in her voice and, when it was gone, turned to meet the pity she knew was waiting. "I'm better, actually."

"Why? Because no one can hurt you that way?"

"Exactly."

A joyless smile flitted across Danielle's face. "It may seem that way to you now. And I get that. I really do. But in the end, if you stay this course, *you* will be the one who hurts you most of all."

CHAPTER 16

Tess stopped at the end of the rutted dirt driveway and took a moment to get her bearings in relation to Naomi's front porch. She knew she was putting a lot on the single point of a finger, but it was preferable to spending the empty hours between dinner and bedtime alone in the Grossdawdy Haus, replaying all those moments and conversations in her life she wished had gone differently. And maybe, just maybe, a brisk walk would tucker her out so thoroughly her pillow would be free of tears come morning.

They were sound reasons, both of them. They just fell a little shy of the truth that had her actually venturing into the path of a sun that would soon begin its colorful descent toward the horizon.

There were no two ways about it. Danielle Parker had remained in her thoughts long after their time together on the porch had come to an end. At first she'd chalked it up to the woman's tragic story and the empathy Tess couldn't help but feel for another human being. But when the questions about Danielle's decision to raise her child in Amish country began firing away in her thoughts, she knew it went deeper—to that part of her brain that had made journalism her perfect career choice.

Quickening her step, Tess made her way along the sun-faded macadam, the questions she'd jotted in her notebook during the few precious moments between helping to set the table and the actual start of dinner itching to be asked. The key, though, was how best to ask them. Come on too strong, and she risked Danielle shutting down completely . . . Come on too weak, and she might not get the powder keg she was all but certain was there waiting to be lit . . . Find just the right sweet spot and she might actually have the story she—

A staccato *clip-clop* hijacked her attention toward an approaching buggy on the opposite side of the road. The mare, tasked with pulling the buggy, was a deep chocolate brown with a mane of black hair down its long, sleek neck. She watched it prance by, and then, when continuing to watch it would mean turning her face away from the occupants in the buggy, she fixed her gaze on them in time to catch the bearded driver's nod of acknowledgment and his passenger's shy smile.

Standing there, surrounded by the Amish countryside, it was hard for Tess not to be taken by the sheer peace that was Blue Ball—a place that was so vastly different from everything she knew. At home, at this time, the sounds making their way through her screened window would be a mixture of the occasional motorcycle, doors opening and closing on delivery vans finishing up their routes, laughter and voices from the coffee shop's outdoor tables, and more than a few dogs barking. Here, outside the now-fading *clip-clop,* the only sound came from the blades of a far-off windmill, the faint bleat of a sheep, and the creak of a barn door somewhere off to her right.

The two worlds were as different as night and day. Leaving one to put down permanent roots in another had to be daunting. Still, for Hannah it made sense. The girl was clearly far too much of a free spirit to be content in a place where the biggest excitement to be had was trying to track down the owner of a runaway horse.

But for Danielle? A woman whose days had been packed solid with places to go and things to do? The decision to move to Blue Ball made zero sense for a woman of sound mind.

Step by step Tess continued down the road, the evening sun beginning to streak the sky in varying shades of yellows, oranges, and reds. A brown-and-white dog with a red collar and big pink tongue fell in step beside her as she rounded a bend, only to disappear with a wagging tail when the name matching the one on his collar was called out in the distance. She, along with a half-dozen grazing sheep, watched until he disappeared from view.

She continued on, passing a one-room school-house with a lone tree in its front yard, colorful construction-paper flowers on its front door, and an empty swing set to its side. Next came a fenced enclosure with rows of simple white tombstones and a lone tree standing sentry nearby. Still, she kept walking, the fresh air and mild temperatures making it easy to pass another farm, another field, and another house while she soaked up every sight, every sound, and every smell she came upon.

And then, just as she was beginning to entertain the notion of turning around, a familiar laugh in the not-too-distant vicinity had her veering off the edge of the road and visually following a narrow driveway to a pale yellow cottage straight out of the pages of a child's favorite bedtime story. A second laugh pulled her attention toward a small side yard in time to see Danielle blow a round of bubbles into the air much to the obvious delight of the baby sitting beside her on a red-and-white-checked blanket. Grace's chubby little hand grabbed for each bubble she saw, then waved wildly for her mother to make more and more and more.

Stepping forward, Tess made her way over to a tree for the vantage point it provided and took a few moments to study Danielle. But try as Tess did to find something to the contrary, the joy the woman exhibited seemed completely authentic.

Movement out of the corner of her eye had Tess temporarily abandoning her view of Danielle in favor of a dirt-covered pickup truck slowly making its way to a stop beside the cottage. Seconds later, a tall man wearing a cowboy hat hopped down from the driver's side and headed toward the cottage with what looked like a takeout bag clutched in his hand. Midway to the door, though, Danielle called out, and he rerouted himself to the blanket.

From where she stood, Tess couldn't make out any words that might tell her who the man was, but the smile on Danielle's face, coupled with Grace's happy squeal over his presence, let her know the Englisher was someone special to the pair. With growing curiosity, Tess stepped farther into the protective arms of the tree and watched as the man lowered himself to the blanket, handed the bag to Danielle, and pointed Grace's attention toward the baby-size ice cream cup her mother pulled out. When the baby lunged forward, bubbles forgotten, the man's laugh mingled with Danielle's.

Were they a couple? She couldn't tell for sure. But what she could tell was that Danielle's joy was real. Whatever had prompted the woman to make Blue Ball her permanent home, coercion didn't appear to be part of the mix.

With one last look at the threesome, Tess headed back in the direction she'd come from. It was hard not to feel frustrated when every possible story idea she chased invariably rolled over and showed her its tummy. She needed something big. Something she could sink her teeth into. Something that would make Sam forget all about some silly celebrity engagement most suspected was a publicity grab to begin with.

Yet she kept falling short. Katie seemed genuinely at peace with her decision to set aside her artistic talent in order to remain Amish . . . Emma chose not only to forgive the unforgiveable but to seemingly embrace it, as well . . . And Danielle? That woman was no more the victim of some imaginary cult than Tess, herself, was.

Still, there had to be something—something story-worthy she could write about. Amish or not, the vast majority of people were out for themselves the way Brian and—

She drew in a breath and released it slowly. The story she needed was there in Blue Ball. Somewhere. She felt it just as surely as the *pop* of gravel under her shoes as she passed the cemetery, the schoolhouse, the—

Stopping in front of a grove of trees, Tess took in the footpath through its center that she'd missed the first time. Granted, it was easy to miss, its entrance point tucked between two rambling forsythia bushes, but it was there, likely worn into being over many years and by many feet.

She glanced at the sky, calculated her remaining window before nightfall, and slipped between the bushes, the quiet thud of the earth beneath her feet the lone counterpoint to the sound of her own measured breath. Step by step she made her way deeper into the woods, the canopy of trees above her prematurely rushing night's advance. But just as she contemplated turning back, the trees suddenly parted company to reveal a large pond that sparkled and shimmered with the sun's final hurrah. She felt the answering hitch of her breath and then let it go in one long, day-cleansing sigh.

Spying a large rock off to her right, she picked her way around a few fallen limbs and settled herself onto its smooth, wide surface, her gaze returning to the pond and the reflection of the setting sun that would soon bid its final farewell. And while she knew she should head back to the road before it got too dark to find her way out, there was something so utterly calming about her present surroundings she couldn't make herself move.

Instead, she found her thoughts wandering back to Danielle and Grace, their joy at being with one another as real as the bubbles that had dotted the air. They'd been so lost in each other and in the moment that they'd had no idea Tess was watching. Nor did the man in the cowboy hat, who clearly had eyes for no one but mother and baby.

That was what she'd wanted. What she'd envisioned for her and Brian. Only instead of blowing bubbles on a blanket in Amish country, she'd fantasized bringing the child they'd always talked about having to the same park they walked every Saturday morning. Brian had been certain they'd have a girl and that she'd sport the same wide forehead and high cheekbones Tess saw in the mirror every day . . . She'd been certain they'd have a boy and that he'd have the same mischievous left-cheek dimple as his father . . .

Slipping her phone from her back pocket, Tess pressed her way into her album, her thumb practically moving of its own volition—a sequence of scrolls and swipes it, too, had memorized.

There was the picture of Brian's face as Tess's father had given him her hand on their wedding day . . .

There was the picture her cousin had taken at the exact moment the minister had declared them husband and wife—Brian's smile a perfect match of her own . . .

There was the picture of them, arm in arm on their honeymoon, their total focus on each other the reason why, in the next picture, they'd been knocked to the ground by the wave neither of them saw coming . . .

There was the picture she'd taken of him while he was sleeping, the arm she'd wiggled out from under still draped across her spot . . .

There was the picture Brian had taken of her

and Mandy on the couch, with Mandy in the center of the frame . . .

The picture of Mandy and her dancing in the living room, with Mandy in the center of the frame . . .

The picture of—

"No, no, no!" Tess forced herself to look away, to see her surroundings, to remember where she was and why.

This was her fresh start. Her chance to start over again. Her chance to realize a dream that had nothing to do with anyone but herself. Her future . . . Her life . . . Her happiness . . . Her—

Gathering her breath, she took one last look at the faces of the two people responsible for the biggest wake-up call of her life and blackened the screen. "You can have each other, for all I care. Because, in the end, I *will* come out on top. Just you watch and see."

CHAPTER 17

Tess set out again just after breakfast with a plate of blueberry muffins in her hand and Naomi's directions guiding her feet. The sun, even at a little past nine o'clock, brought a welcome warmth to her face as she headed in the opposite direction of the one she'd taken the previous night.

Farm by farm she went, her eyes, if not always her full attention, skirting fields and fences, cows and sheep, windmills and barns, laundry lines and farm equipment. Somewhere along the way she exchanged waves with a young girl in a passing buggy, but other than that, it was just Tess and the empty country road with its graveled shoulder and very occasional bend that made it so she had to be semipresent lest she run into a fence post or lose her footing while traversing horse droppings.

Twice, she stopped and shifted the muffins from her right hand to her left in order to take a picture with her phone—both the Amish man atop a mule-pulled tractor, and the Amish woman and her daughter hanging laundry together, requiring the zoom feature to truly capture her subjects' expressions. She was getting some good shots—a few that could even hold their own in a photo competition with actual photo journalists, but if she was going to get herself back in Sam's good graces, she needed more. Much more . . .

Rounding the last of the three subtle bends Naomi had referenced, Tess slowed to a stop. At first glance, the house didn't stand out from the one before it or, looking ahead, the one after it, either. In fact, if she hadn't followed her host's directions to a tee, she'd think she was in the wrong place—the occupant surely Amish.

Simple at its core, the house was little more than a freshly painted white square with a few windows in front, a few windows on the side, a sunshine-yellow door, and a chimney rising from the roof. Not far from the side windows was a small garden boasting flowers in a veritable rainbow of colors. Nestled among them was a small eastward-facing wooden bench and a birdbath in full use by what appeared to be a robin or maybe a female cardinal.

Returning her attention to the house itself, Tess noted the screen door, the wide front porch, the pair of cushion-topped rocking chairs arranged to invite conversation, and the small side table perfect for holding the pitcher of lemonade and plate of cookies both Naomi and Danielle had referenced when relaying stories about the woman who lived inside.

She shifted her gaze to the other side of the house, noting the clothesline that, for now, held no clothes, and the single scooter-style bike she'd seen multiples of propped alongside Naomi's house. There were no two ways about it: to the casual observer, the home in front of her appeared to be like any other on the road, save for the small white sedan parked where a barn might otherwise be.

"Interesting." Tightening her grip on the muffin plate, Tess made her way up the dirt driveway, her thoughts accelerating past her surroundings to the woman she had every reason to hope was inside.

"You must be the writer."

Startled, Tess shifted her attention from the house to the elderly woman straightening to a stand inside the garden.

"Oh. Hello . . . I didn't see you there." Tess hurried across the lawn. "I'm Tess. Tess Baker. And yes, I'm the writer. How did you know?"

"Writers are observers, and you spent a lot of time observing just now."

She felt her face flush warm with the woman's truth. "I'm sorry, I just—"

"I'm not looking for an apology, dear. Just answering your question." Emerging from between the plants with the help of a cane, the woman offered a welcoming smile. "Besides, I was doing a little observing of my own, and I see you've brought what looks to be Naomi King's blueberry muffins."

"You're right. I did." She met the woman outside the garden's perimeter and extended her hand. "And I have to tell you, it took some mighty strong willpower not to eat one on the way here."

"Oh, I know it did." Tess's hand disappeared inside the woman's soft, wrinkly one. "I'm Lottie—Lottie Jenkins, but my friends call me Miss Lottie. So that means you can call me that, too."

"I'm honored. Thank you."

Miss Lottie pointed at the house with her cane. "While I suspect we could both eat one of those muffins standing right here, I think we'd be more comfortable up there on the porch, with a glass of milk for each of us. Unless, being a reporter, black coffee is more to your liking."

"Milk sounds good, thank you."

"Then come along. It seems all that cleaning I was compelled to do for some unknown-to-me reason last night was because the Lord knew you and I would be visiting together today." Miss Lottie led the way onto the porch and over to her front door. "And those muffins are clearly why I didn't think to make cookies. Though I can, if you like chocolate chip?"

"No, no, please. I've already invited myself into your morning. Muffins and milk are more than enough."

Inside, the woman pointed Tess toward a tiny

sitting room just beyond the kitchen. "Why don't you get yourself settled, dear, and I'll join you in a few minutes with our drinks."

"Actually, how about I help with the drinks?"

"A few years ago, I'd have had the luxury of protesting, but now"—Miss Lottie glanced down at her cane—"I will simply say thank you, that would be lovely."

She trailed the woman into the small but well-appointed kitchen, her mind's eye registering the various trappings of a baker while simultaneously soaking up the woman's instructions on where to find glasses. When both were full and on a tray alongside Naomi's muffins, they headed down the hall.

Like the kitchen, the sitting room was small yet amply sized for a woman who lived alone. A quilt-draped sofa and matching armchair were arranged around an oval-shaped hook rug in a way that encouraged conversations with guests, and winter evenings spent reading alone in front of the hearth. To the right of the sofa was an oak end table that held a lamp and a paperback mystery novel. Atop the rug was a matching coffee table.

"This is lovely," Tess mused as she set the tray down and looked around. "It makes me want to curl up under a blanket and—oh! Pictures. May I?"

"Of course."

She crossed to the mantel for a closer look at the framed black-and-white photographs that covered it from one end to the other. The pictures, themselves, were of places—some she recognized, and others she didn't. The first shot was of the Chrysler Building from the vantage point of the sidewalk below, its spire appearing to touch the clouds. The second shot was a simple bridge one might find on a hike, its mountainous back-drop breathtaking.

"Where was this?" she asked, lifting the picture for Miss Lottie to see.

"The Grand Tetons."

"I've always wanted to go there. It was on my list."

"Was?" Miss Lottie echoed.

"Yes." Setting the frame back in its spot, Tess moved onto the next picture—this one from the top of a mountain overlooking a valley. "And this?"

"British Columbia."

"Very nice." The last picture was of a vast ocean with the same common denominator she'd spied in all the rest—a solitary woman, wearing a floppy straw hat, her back to the camera. "Are all these you?"

"A much younger and more agile version, but yes. Those are all of me."

"You've done a lot of traveling," Tess mused as she took one last look and then turned back toward the empty couch Miss Lottie patted with her hand. "Do you still?"

"No. I'm where I want to be—where I feel most content and most at peace in my heart."

She considered the woman's words against bits and pieces she remembered from her visit to Katie's and Emma's, and on Naomi's front porch with Danielle. "Did I hear correctly that you were Amish at one time?" she prodded.

Miss Lottie leaned forward, deposited one muffin onto each of their plates, and handed one to Tess. "I was raised Amish, but I did not join the church."

"Meaning you weren't baptized?"

"That is correct."

"So then what?" Tess asked, across the top of her milk glass. "You left?"

"Yes."

"How old were you?"

"I was seventeen." Biting into her muffin, Miss Lottie's eyes fluttered closed behind her glasses. "I don't know how Naomi makes these so light, but she does it every time."

"I imagine your friends up to that point were all Amish, right?" she asked.

Miss Lottie paused, mid-bite. "For the most part, yes."

"Did any of them opt not to be baptized, either?"

"No. Just me," Miss Lottie said on the heels of a big gulp of milk.

"That had to make your decision a lot harder and a whole lot—

"Good heavens, dear, I can barely remember where I set my cane or whether I remembered to fill the birdbath most days, let alone how I felt about something that happened more than sixty years ago." Miss Lottie flopped back against her chair. "So tell me, what do you think of Blue Ball so far?"

"It's different than what I'm used to. But it's fine." She matched the woman's flop backward with a lean forward. "Why did you leave?"

The smile that had accompanied the woman's question about Blue Ball faded away. "My older brother had left the previous year and was banned. That first year was hard. I missed seeing him and being able to talk to him. If I'd stayed, that wouldn't have been able to change."

"So you left in order to have a relationship with your brother?"

Tightening her hands on her chair's armrests, Miss Lottie's gaze dropped to her lap, lifted to the hearth, and, finally, settled on a spot somewhere just north of Tess's eyes. "It is something my leaving allowed to happen, yes."

She pondered the elderly woman's answer in relation to her question and wondered at the change in wording. Before she could explore it, though, Miss Lottie clapped her age-spotted hands together with glee. "I imagine you're looking forward to digging into all that dough this afternoon."

"Dough?"

"Today is Saturday. There is much bread to be made."

"I'm sure Naomi can manage without me."

"Trust me, dear, you don't *want* her to manage without you. You would miss all the fun and fellowship."

Tess pulled a face. "Fellowship?"

"It started about a year ago when one of the women in Naomi's district fell and broke her arm the morning before church was to be at their farm. Naomi gathered together a few of the women from the district, and they spent the afternoon baking bread and desserts for the post-church meal as a way to help. They apparently had such fun baking together that it's become a weekly time of fellowship for all involved, and it's lessened the burden on whoever is hosting church that week. And on non-church weekends? They have treats to take with them if they go visiting."

"I didn't know."

"Many of the women will be there. Katie and Emma, and maybe Lydia, and even Danielle if Caleb can look after Grace while she naps."

"But Danielle isn't Amish," Tess protested. "She doesn't go to church with them."

"She is still Naomi's friend."

"I know. I met her. Yesterday. And I think I may have seen this Caleb person with her while I was out walking last evening."

"Cowboy hat?"

Tess nodded.

"Then that was Caleb."

She thought back to the easy way in which Danielle and her daughter interacted with the man and took another sip of her drink. "Are they dating?"

"I don't believe so, no. Danielle is not ready for that. But Caleb has been by her side this past year with a steady hand and a listening ear the way a good friend is."

Tess didn't mean to laugh. She really didn't. But neither could she hold it back.

"Did I say something funny?" Miss Lottie asked.

"No. That wasn't a ha-ha laugh. It was more of a . . ." She waved the moment away. "I take it this Caleb person lives here in Amish country, as well?"

"He does. Just a little way up Danielle's driveway, in fact. She rents her cottage from him."

Tess placed herself back at the tree and the view it had afforded of Danielle and Grace. "Oh. Wow. Okay. I didn't notice another place . . . So that's why he's here? He owns rental property?"

"No, he just has the one cottage he rents to Danielle now. Better that than have it sit empty."

"Does he have another job?"

"He's a paramedic." She sat with that for a moment while Miss Lottie took another bite of her muffin and another sip of her milk. "And when he's not at that job, he's either helping around Lydia's farm or doing jobs over at his mamm and dat's."

Tess shifted her wandering gaze back onto the elderly woman. "His parents are Amish?"

"His parents and his siblings. Caleb is the only one who didn't take the vow."

Another one . . .

"Why?" she asked.

Miss Lottie shrugged. "It wasn't right for him."

"How often does that happen?"

"You mean how often does a young person who's been raised Amish leave to lead an English life?" At Tess's nod, Miss Lottie slipped her glasses off her face, wiped them with the gardening apron she still wore, and then returned them to start. "Ten percent of the time. Maybe a little more."

She commanded the startling number to memory as a slew of new questions assembled, one behind the other, in her thoughts. "Wow. That's lower than I'd—Wait . . . I have to ask. Don't you think that number would be higher if there weren't so many repercussions?"

"There are no repercussions. If one doesn't want to be baptized, they don't get baptized."

"Yeah . . . yeah . . . I know. If they leave *before*

212

baptism, they can still interact with their family like this Caleb person and Hannah. But we're talking about kids who are only educated through the eighth grade. They've lived a sheltered life. I would imagine those factors would make the thought of leaving absolutely terrifying."

"It's scary. Certainly. But if living an Amish life is not for you, it's not for you."

"Do the parents pressure them to stay?" Tess asked, setting her plate with her half-eaten muffin back onto the tray. "I mean, I would imagine they wouldn't be thrilled at one of their kids up and walking out."

"They would prefer they stay, of course, but they'd rather them go then take a vow they later break. At least then they can still see them, be a part of their lives."

"Did you visit often after you left?"

It was fast, and it was fleeting, but there was no denying the tightening of the woman's mouth in the lead-up to her answer. "No."

"Why not?"

"I got swept up in the English world."

"But yet you're here now . . ."

"You're right, Tess. I am."

"When?"

Miss Lottie eyed her from beneath heavy lids. "When what?"

"When did you come back?"

"Almost twenty-five years ago."

"Making you what at the time? Age-wise."

"Fifty-five."

"Fifty-five," Tess repeated as her attention returned to the hearth and the pictures displayed across it. "So what made you come back? Especially when you seemed to enjoy traveling the way you did."

Miss Lottie's eyes disappeared behind closed lashes. "I was wandering in an outdoor market in San Francisco one day and I came across a sign. It said, 'Home is not a place, it's a feeling.'"

"Okay . . ."

"Once I read that, I couldn't get it out of my head. I thought about it when I woke up, I thought about it when I was drifting off to sleep at night, and I thought about it in between. And when I finally applied those words to myself, I realized the only place I ever truly felt at home was here."

"And so you came back."

Miss Lottie's nod was slow, deliberate. "This place and its people bring me peace. Even if it's from the outside looking in, now."

"But you're not really on the outside, right? You were raised here, you grew up here, you're friends with all of the Amish I've met, and they all absolutely worship you."

"The Amish worship no one but the Lord!" Miss Lottie countered, sharply.

Tess held up her hands in surrender. "Right.

My bad . . . It's just that they all speak of you as a blessing. All of them."

"It is *I* who am blessed by *them*."

Tess stood and wandered back to the mantel for a second look at the much younger Miss Lottie. "I imagine, after all that time, they were mighty happy to see you again, yes?"

"Who?"

"Your family . . . the community . . . the people who'd known you when you were a young girl just setting out on your new—" A muted *thump* stole the rest of her words and pulled her gaze back to the chair and the woman now struggling to her feet with the help of her cane. Tess hurried to help. "Miss Lottie? Are you okay?"

"I'm terribly sorry, dear, but I'm going to have to cut our visit short. There's a-a"—panicked eyes led Tess's around the room only to land, a moment later, on a corner table and its small portable phone. "I have a call I promised I'd return, and it's something I really must do. *Now*."

CHAPTER 18

Tess didn't need to turn around to know Miss Lottie's eyes were following her down the driveway and onto the road. She could feel them just as surely as she could the excitement coursing through her body at the veritable certainty she'd hit on something big.

Whether that something big was what she was looking for remained to be seen, but if she were a gambler, she'd bet big money it was.

Sure, Miss Lottie was sweet, welcoming. The woman hadn't even blinked at inviting Tess—a complete stranger—into her home for a visit. But there was no denying the way she rushed to change the subject when Tess tickled at her past, or the chill that had enveloped the otherwise cozy room when Tess refused to be deterred.

And the sudden remembrance of a phone call that had to be made on the heels of Tess's final question? Yeah, no . . . Miss Lottie clearly wanted the questions to stop and Tess out of her home.

Which left one last question . . .

Why?

Quickening her pace, Tess hurried around the first gentle bend to discover the woman and her daughter who'd been hanging laundry on the line were no longer in sight, yet the clothes they'd been painstakingly hanging were still there—soaking up the sun's drying rays. The mules in the next field were still hard at work as was the man atop the tractor-like implement they pulled.

The second bend deposited her onto yet another straightaway with more farms, more crops, and more families working together. Twice, she was the recipient of a slow, deliberate nod, and once, a small wave and a smile.

The third and final bend had her walking still faster at the notion of jumping on her laptop and doing a search on Lottie Jenkins and—

She stopped dead in her tracks, her groan so loud it earned her the attention of more than a few grazing sheep.

No internet, no search on her laptop . . .

No car, no internet café . . .

Sure, she could use her phone, but her battery could only hold out so long, and she was already looking forward to her next exchange with Murph. Especially now, when she might finally have something story-worthy to share.

She checked the time, tried to calculate how long it might take her to walk however many miles it was to something even remotely resembling modern-day civilization, and gave into the sigh the impossible task demanded. "Why couldn't I be in Belize right now?" she muttered.

"I see you're still talking to yourself. And that

you're still in the same foul mood you were when I dropped you off in this exact spot the other day."

Startled, Tess lifted her phone-holding hand to her forehead as a sun shield, then dropped it back to her side with a second and even more frustrated groan. "Is this your shtick? To sneak up on people and eavesdrop on conversations that have nothing to do with you?"

"I'm not sure how driving a pickup truck with a diesel engine can be construed as sneaking up on someone." Jack draped his arm over his open driver's side window and thumped his hand against the door's shiny black panel. "And, last I checked, the word *conversation* comes from the word *converse,* which, by its very definition, means other people are involved. Which was not the case in this"—he flicked his hand in her direction—"situation. Still, if I offended you, I'm sorry."

Oh, how she wanted to argue, how she wanted to just unleash all of the frustration involved with being there instead of Belize, with having to reprove herself to Sam and everyone else at the magazine, and with trying to fix it all while stuck in a place that still operated as if the 1900s—let alone the 2000s—had never come. Instead, she just pushed it all off with a shrug of indifference as she took the final few steps toward Naomi's driveway.

"So what's got you in such a foul mood again? Or is it *still?*"

She stopped, fisted her hands, and willed herself to breathe rather than scream. "For your information, I couldn't be having a better day. Unless, of course, you hadn't inserted yourself into it the way you have."

"Oh. So that little display just now when I drove up is you having a *good* day? The groan? The talking to yourself? The staring at the sky? Huh . . ."

"Nooo. That was me realizing my ability to fully *play out* my good day is in jeopardy because I'm stuck in a place that doesn't believe in electricity. That said, why on earth am I standing here talking to you, let alone answering anything you have to ask?"

"Because it's the courteous thing to do?"

"Ha!"

"You disagree?" he chided, propping his elbow atop the open windowsill.

"I was actually reacting to *you* using the courtesy card with *me.*" Her growing anger propelled her closer to the truck. "You do realize the first sentence out of your mouth when you crossed my path the other day was nothing short of mocking, right? And just now—when you pulled up next to me—you started all over again. What in all of that makes you think you deserve *courtesy* in return?"

"Maybe the fact I helped you out with your phone situation?"

She narrowed her eyes on his. "You mean while calling me uptight and trying to justify your behavior under the guise of establishing a *friendship?* Yeah, no . . . sorry. You, like everyone else, have a long way to go between your definition of that word and mine. And even if you somehow bridged that distance, I'm not interested."

Before he could say anything to prolong an unexpected and unwanted encounter that had already gone on far too long, Tess turned and covered the remaining distance to Isaiah and Naomi's driveway.

"Look, Tess, I think we got off on the wrong foot. Maybe we could try again—after whatever party Naomi is having is over."

"Party—what party?" She followed the path of his finger across the driveway to the four empty and horseless buggies parked alongside the barn and the small four-door sedan—

Sucking in a breath, Tess took off in a run toward her one and only ticket to civilization.

"Tess!" Naomi said, looking up from the ball of dough she was forming in her hands on top of the kitchen counter. "You're here!"

Before she could answer or even fully process who was in the room, Katie Beiler grabbed a rolling pin from the table and handed it to

Tess. "You can roll while I find the cutters."

"Yah. That is a good idea." Naomi held up the dough ball for Tess to see and then abandoned it on the counter beside a small bowl of flour.

Danielle stepped around the other side of the table, hurried over to Naomi's sewing table, and plucked a folded apron from beneath her purse. "I figured you probably wouldn't have one of these in your suitcase, so I brought an extra for you. That way you won't mess up your clothes— which I love by the way."

Glancing down at herself, Tess took in her brushed denim jeans and powder-blue top with its tiny sunflower pattern only to watch it all disappear beneath the apron Danielle slipped over her head with an encouraging smile. "Welcome to our unofficial Saturday-morning baking club, where we laugh and visit every bit as much as we actually bake."

Emma's sweet laugh joined that of Naomi's, Katie's, and Danielle's. "Yah. That is true. But we *do* bake." The young mother guided Tess's attention toward the table and the loaves of bread cooling on racks across its center. "See? And that is before the cookies."

"You made all of this already?" Tess asked, smoothing her hand down her borrowed apron and stepping farther into the room. "While I was at Miss Lottie's?"

Danielle's hands came together with a happy

221

squeal. "So you met her? You met Miss Lottie?"

"Yah. She took muffins to her this morning," Naomi said.

"So?" Danielle prodded. "Isn't she wonderful?"

Katie returned to the table with a basket of cookie cutters and then thought better of it and headed toward the counter and Naomi's dough ball instead. "Hannah and I thought about stopping to say hello to Miss Lottie on the way here, but Hannah was critiquing my driving the way she always does, and I could not think straight."

"*Your* driving?" Tess echoed. "I thought you could only ride in a car, not drive it."

"We did not take Hannah's rental car. We took Abram's buggy."

She felt the answering sag in her shoulders a split second before Danielle's gentle push toward the counter and the dough. "You must talk *and* roll, Tess. It is the only way we get anything done."

"Yah. That is true." Stepping to her left, Naomi dug her hands into a large mixing bowl with even more dough. "Did you enjoy your visit with Miss Lottie?"

"I did, she—"

"Talk *and* roll, Tess. Talk *and* roll."

Trading smiles with Danielle, she scooped some flour into her hand, ran her palm up and down the rolling pin, and brought it down atop the dough. Then, slowly, she began to roll, the back-and-forth motion somehow calming even as her thoughts worked to deliver an answer that might help her learn more. "I think it's neat that Miss Lottie chose to come back here after so much time. Even when she no longer had familial ties in the area."

"She had family here," Katie said. "My mamm and us."

Tess stopped rolling to stare at the Amish twin. "You're related to Miss Lottie?"

"Yah."

"How?"

"She is my mother's aunt and my great aunt."

"I didn't know that, Katie!" Danielle said, placing two cookie trays on the counter beside Tess. "How wonderful."

Katie nodded, pleased. "It is something I don't think to say because she was just Miss Lottie to me and Hannah for so long."

She knew Danielle was waiting for her to select a cookie cutter and begin cutting the dough, but her eyes, her every brain cell was locked in on Katie. "Are you saying you didn't *know* she was your aunt?"

"My *great* aunt," Katie corrected, not unkindly. "Yah. I found out after Mamm had gone to be with the Lord."

"Why would your mother keep something like that a secret?"

"Mamm did not know."

"I don't understand. How could she not have known?" Tess asked.

"My grossmudder was only six when her sister left. It would be many years before she would meet my grossdawdy and have my mamm."

"Wow," Danielle said, temporarily abandoning her job as cookie-cutting sergeant. "How old were you when Miss Lottie came back to the area?"

"Hannah and I were babies."

"Babies?" Tess echoed. "So we're talking twenty-plus years ago?"

"Closer to twenty-five."

"And none of you knew until a few years ago?"

"Miss Lottie put it together when Mamm began talking to her about Hannah's choice not to be baptized."

Tess glanced inside the basket Danielle scooted closer to her elbow but couldn't make herself focus on anything other than the unfolding story. "And she didn't tell your mamm then? Why on earth not?"

Katie shrugged. "She was afraid it would change Mamm's feelings about her."

"But why? Miss Lottie left *before* baptism, right?"

Again, Katie shrugged. "I don't know. I just know she felt that Mamm needed a friend when Hannah started speaking of leaving, and again when"—Katie glanced down at the ground and swallowed—"when Mamm got sick. Miss Lottie thought it was more important she continue being Mamm's ear. And so she was."

"Like she is for all of us," Naomi added.

It was a lot to take in, a lot to process. But still—

"I still don't understand how Miss Lottie wouldn't have known all along. How others in the community wouldn't have known . . ."

"Miss Lottie was raised a Miller, like my gross-mudder. When my grossmudder married, she became a Fisher and moved into another district. When Mamm married Dat, Mamm became a Beiler and moved here."

"And Miss Lottie is now English and a Jenkins," Tess said, playing it out.

"Yah."

"Okay, so where did Jenkins come from? Was Miss Lottie married?"

Katie paused her fingers around the stray piece of cookie dough she'd quietly liberated from the side of Naomi's bowl. "I don't know. I've never thought to ask, and—mmmm, Naomi, this is very good dough. You should try some."

"Try some? I have been sampling it since Tess got here."

Katie squirreled away another scrap of dough. "At least *you* have an excuse, Naomi. You are with child."

"Yah, I am with child. But that is not why I've been eating tiny bits of dough. I've been eating it because it's too good not to, *and* because Tess has not cut cookies from the first batch. Since she hasn't, I have nowhere to put it but in my mouth."

"Tess," Emma teased. "You better cut those cookies, fast, or you will become a scapegoat for all of us."

Nods, powered by laughter, made their way around the room, claiming Tess in the process. Looking down at the dough in front of her, she, too, helped herself to a scrap, rolling it into a bite-size ball she promptly popped into her mouth. "Oh. Wow. You're right. This is good."

"It's *all* good." Danielle selected a simple flower-shaped cookie cutter and handed it to Tess. "The dough and this time together. In fact, being here—laughing with everyone—is actually making me want to try my hand at quilting again just so I can spend more time with all of you."

"I thought you switched to crocheting, Danielle," Katie said, sticking her finger in the bowl once again.

"I did. I thought I could get the hang of that better. But I'm as inept at that as I am quilting. But, maybe, if we sat together, I would get the hang of it better. And if not, at least it would be fun."

"I have been teaching Tess how to quilt,"

Naomi said, pointing a flour-spattered finger at Tess.

"What Naomi *means* is she *tried* to teach me, but"—Tess cringed—"I was helpless. Truly, truly helpless."

Danielle giggled. "I know the feeling. It took me so long to catch on to what I was supposed to be doing that Naomi actually fell asleep."

"I was resting!" Naomi countered. "That's all!"

"Do you always snore when you're resting?"

The laughter borne on Danielle's retort echoed around the room. "Ooh, she got you there, Naomi!" Emma said, lifting the completed tray of cut dough off the counter and carrying it over to the oven.

"Maybe it's an English thing. Maybe we're born without the quilting gene." Danielle set the second ball of dough in front of Tess and then wandered over to the kitchen bench and sat down.

"You just need more practice," Naomi said. "The two of you. Together."

"I'm game if she's game."

Tess paused her dough rolling. "I'm only here for another three weeks . . ."

"That's plenty of time, especially if we are all there to help," Emma interjected, returning to stand by the counter. "Katie? Are you in?"

"Will there be cookies?"

There was no denying it felt good to laugh, and laugh Tess did. There was something so easy about being there. Something so real about Danielle, about Naomi, about Emma, about Katie, about—

She paused her hand on top of the circle cookie cutter she'd selected for the second batch and looked at Katie. "Didn't you say you and Hannah came here together?"

"Yah."

"Then where is she?"

"Reuben took her out to see the new kittens he found in the barn this morning," Naomi explained. "And knowing Reuben, he has expanded the introductions to include every animal in the barn."

Katie's nose scrunched along with the emphatic shake of her head. "I don't think it's Reuben that has Hannah staying away from the kitchen. It's the baking. She thinks we're working hard in here, and Hannah doesn't like work."

"That's okay." A mischievous smile accompanied Naomi's hand to her aproned abdomen. "That just means more for the baby."

Danielle's gaze dropped to her delicate silver wristwatch a moment before she stood. "Oops, I've got to go. Grace should be waking from her nap any minute, and I don't want to take too much advantage of Caleb's offer to watch her. But this has been so much fun, as always. And Tess? It's been great having you here this time."

"It's been great being here." And it was true. Then again, anything could be great for a while . . .

"Which pans are yours again, Danielle?" Emma asked. "I could help carry them to your car."

Tess's glance shot back to Danielle. "That's *your* car out front? The white one?"

"Yes."

Wiping her flour-drenched hands off on her apron, she took a fast step back from the counter straight into Katie. "Oh. Sorry. I just need to—"

"I think this last tray should be the watering-can shape," Katie said. "Hannah bought it for me, and she'll be pleased if we use it. Plus it's a fun one, don't you think?"

Tess took the shape from Katie's hand, gave it the expected once-over, and then set it on the counter next to the partially rolled-out dough. "It'll be a cute one, for sure. But maybe one of you could cut this batch instead? Because I'd really like to catch a ride into town with"—she glanced up and around the room—"wait. Where's Danielle?"

"She left."

"Left the house or *left* left?"

Emma crossed to the mouth of the hallway, craned her neck to the right, and then ventured back to the table with a shrug. "She just pulled out."

"Seriously?"

"Don't worry, Tess. We will do this again," Naomi said, rounding the counter and handing the rolling pin back to Tess.

"And maybe we really can quilt together some time soon, too. I think Danielle looked really happy at that idea," Katie added. "It's good to see her smiling so much."

Emma wandered over closer to the group. "She really seems to be doing okay, doesn't she?"

"Yah." Naomi carried the dirty bowl to the sink and returned with a wet cloth to wipe up its floured imprint. "I spoke with Lydia the other day. She said Danielle's birthday is coming up next month. Perhaps we should do some special things on that day."

"I can make a cake!" Emma said, beaming.

Naomi slowed her cleaning efforts. "Perhaps Isaiah can make a clock for Danielle's mantel . . ."

"Ooh, I like both of those ideas." Katie drew her hands together. "And I can draw a picture for her! Something she can hang in her house! Perhaps Caleb will have some ideas for me."

Shaking off her lingering disappointment over missing out on a ride into town, Tess forced herself to finish rolling the dough and to cut it into Katie's requested watering-can shape. When the cookie sheet was full, she slid it into the oven and turned back to the women. "Maybe it could have something to do with Grace. Like the other night, they were out on a blanket and Danielle was blowing bubbles for Grace. There was something so beautiful in the way Danielle was looking at her. Maybe you could capture something like that."

"I can't draw their faces, but I can figure out something," Katie mused.

Emma leaned against the counter, her smile contagious. "And what about you, Tess? What could you do for Danielle for her birthday?"

"I don't know," she admitted. "I really don't know her all that well."

"You could make her a quilt, if you would not give up so easily," Naomi countered.

Tess's laugh drew matching ones from Emma, Katie, and Naomi. "Uh, yeah . . . no. Nice try, Naomi."

"I am nothing if not persistent."

"A quality I admire. Truly." Slipping the apron over her head, Tess gave into the yawn she was powerless to stop. "Hey, Naomi? If it's okay, would you mind if I took a pass on dinner tonight and just headed over to my place now, instead?"

"Yah. That is fine. If you would like, I could send Reuben over with a dinner plate for you when it's time."

"No, it's okay. I'm not really hungry right now."

"We are having chicken and *brown-buttered noodles* . . ."

As if on cue, her stomach rumbled, inciting even more laughter.

"I see you have had Naomi's noodles," Katie teased.

"Boy, have I . . ." Tess sighed at the memory. "They're incredible."

"Then it's settled. Reuben will bring a plate when it's time, and I will be sure to include extra noodles."

"Thanks, Naomi. I'm sorry my stomach gave me up just now."

"Are you really?" Emma asked, winking.

"You're right. I'm not." Tess folded the apron and tucked it under her arm. "I'll walk this over to Danielle's sometime tomorrow. In the meantime, this was a lot of fun. Thank you!"

"It was good to see you again, Tess," Emma said, following her to the hallway.

Katie stopped behind Emma and added a wave. "It was so much fun!"

"Remember, you'll get the hang of quilting if you keep trying," Naomi added across the top of her friends' heads.

Grinning, Tess stepped onto the porch, inhaled the late-afternoon air, and then headed down the steps to the dirt—

"Someone looks mighty happy right now."

She glanced to her right to find Jack emerging from the barn with what appeared to be an end table in his hands. "Great. You're back."

"I never left."

"You robbing the place?" she asked, changing direction in favor of his truck.

"Nope. Just picking up stuff for one of the display homes Brad has opening up next week. He likes including furniture made by Amish folks like Isaiah." Jack set the table inside the truck's bed and closed the tailgate with a firm hand. "You win the lottery or something?"

"The lottery? No. Why?"

"You were actually smiling just now."

"You mean before I saw you?"

Crossing his arms in front of his chest, he leaned back against his truck and grinned. "Touché."

"Sorry, couldn't resist."

"You could pretend to try, though," he said on the heels of a rich, deep laugh. "But seriously, you seem . . . *happy.*"

There was no argument to be had. He was right. "I guess I just had a good time inside with Naomi and the other women. They seem so . . ." She cast about for the right word and finally settled on the only one that fit. "They seem so *normal.*"

"I remember when I came to that conclusion, too. Especially after growing up in the area and always seeing the Amish as so different. Yeah, they travel around by horse and buggy instead of a car. Yeah, they're not into the latest fashion trend or, really, anything resembling fashion in the last century. And, yeah, they have an issue with things that don't seem like a big deal to the rest of us—like electricity. But at the end of the day, when you remove all that stuff, they laugh, and they cry, and they feel things just like we do."

She, too, leaned against the truck, her thoughts traveling back to Naomi's kitchen and the ease she'd felt as she'd interacted with Naomi and Katie, Emma and Danielle—four women who'd treated her as if they'd known her every bit as long as they'd known one another.

"There it is again."

"What?" she asked, shaking her focus back to the driveway and the man standing not more than three feet away.

"That smile. It makes your eyes sparkle."

Just like that, she could feel the lightness beginning to slip away, taking with it any semblance of a smile. "And you're trying too hard to create something that isn't there."

"Create something? With what?"

She gestured toward herself and then swept her hand outward toward the house, the barn, and, finally, Jack himself. "All of it. This town . . . the people . . . you . . . And you couldn't be any more off base if you tried. I'm just here to—"

"Do your job," he finished. "Yeah, I know."

"Okay. Then we're good." Walking backward, she hooked her thumb toward her final destination. "Now, if you don't mind, I have to head inside and do a search on places within a taxi drive of here where I can get on the internet at some point tomorrow."

"New Holland Sip and Click."

She stopped, mid-turn. "Excuse me?"

"That's the closest place that fits what you're looking for." He left his spot beside the truck bed in favor of opening the driver's side door and sliding into place behind the steering wheel. "Coffee is pretty good. Brownies, even better."

"They have Wi-Fi?"

He nodded.

"Wow. Okay. Good. Thanks."

"I can swing by in the morning about ten, if that works?"

Again, she stopped. "For what?"

"To save you a cab fare."

CHAPTER 19

Resting her cheek against the window's edge, Tess looked out over the dusky countryside and tried to pick out the barns and houses that went with the people she'd met so far. She knew, from the direction Naomi had gone in each case, that Katie's house was somewhere ahead and to the left, and Emma's more to the right. She wondered if Katie was sitting outside on her front porch with Abram and Hannah, or if Hannah was entertaining them inside with stories of city life, across a cup of coffee and a piece of shoofly pie. She wondered, too, if maybe Emma was getting Harp ready for bed while Levi checked on the barn animals one more time.

There was no way to know for sure, but when you lived a life with little to no variation as the Amish did, her guess was likely pretty close if not on the mark completely. Yet, despite knowing neither scenario was worthy of a picture, let alone a feature story in a national magazine, she couldn't help but wish she were there, with Katie and Hannah and Abram as they sipped their coffee, chased every last bite of pie around their plates, and laughed together over moments shared from their day . . . Or maybe watching from Harp's bedroom doorway as Emma rocked her son to sleep amid the same symphony of crickets making its way through her own screened window at that exact moment . . .

A persistent vibration from the kitchen table broke through her odd reverie and sent her scrambling for the phone. The sight of Murph's name had her lowering herself onto the bench, with a smile she felt clear down to her bare toes. "Murph! Hi! How are you?"

"Besides wishing I was you right now? Fine."

Her answering laugh was more snort-like than she intended, but it fit, too. "Right . . . The legendary Max Murphy wishes he was in Amish country instead of embedded in enemy territory with the elite of the elite."

"I woke up exhausted and out of sorts. You sound"—he paused, took a drag on the cigarette she knew he had between his fingers—"different, somehow."

"Different, how?"

"Can't put my finger on it yet, but I will. For now, though, catch me up."

"You first."

"I already did. Remember the exhausted-and-out-of-sorts part? Your turn."

Rolling her eyes, she stood, helped herself to a glass of milk and the cookie Naomi had sent over with Reuben at dinnertime, and returned to the table. "Fine, but I'm going on record and saying that Secret Mission Murph is zero fun."

"My apologies, kid. Rules are rules. Besides, I'd rather hear about you."

"I'm about to take a bite of a cookie, which I'll then follow with a gulp of milk."

"Ahhh, I see how this is going to go. Which means I should probably just head off and—"

She bolted upright. "No! I was just playing. I'll talk!" Turning the cookie over in her free hand, she noted the watering can's distinctive shape and the answering smile it brought to her lips. "I actually helped make the cookie I'm about to eat."

"Oh?"

"Naomi started this baking day with a few of the other women. They do it every other Saturday afternoon as a way to lighten the baking load for whoever is hosting church that week. They bake bread and cookies together. Or, at least, that's what they did today. Katie and Hannah— the twins—were there, though I never saw Hannah. Apparently she was in Naomi's barn the whole time. Emma was there, too. And so was Danielle."

"That's not a name I remember you mentioning," Murph said.

"Who? Danielle?" At his audible affirmation, she took a bite of her cookie and chased it down with some milk. "She's English. She came here to stay with a friend from childhood after her family was killed in a car accident. The friend is Amish. Name is Lydia. But I haven't met her yet. Anyway, from what I've been able to piece together, Danielle found out she was pregnant after the accident. She even considered giving her baby to Lydia to raise, but she didn't go through with it. She and her now-toddler-aged daughter are living here full-time now. In a cottage on Lydia's brother's property."

"Wow."

"I know." She took another bite of cookie, another sip of milk. "And even more so when I thought her staying here—rather than going back to New York like anyone else would've—was my story."

"Your story? How so?"

"I thought maybe she'd been pressured into staying. Like a cult might do."

A beat or two of silence was followed by another drag of his cigarette and, then, more silence. "Did I say something wrong?" she asked.

"No. Just trying to wrap my head around that thought process when it sounds to me like this Danielle woman probably just wanted a fresh start for her and her child."

"Okay, so I reached a little. But if I'd been right? Can you imagine *that* story?" She waited through another round of silence, another inhale, another exhale. "But don't worry. I think I might have found something better."

"And what's that?"

She finished her cookie and the last of her milk and then carried the empty glass over to the sink. "You know that feeling you get when something just feels too good to be true? Well, I'm getting that about this woman who lives here. She's English now, but she was raised Amish. Left for like forty years before she decided to come back to the area."

"Okay . . ."

"These women around here? They all seem to worship her." Tess crossed back into the sitting room, bypassing the window this time in favor of a simple upholstered chair. Sinking onto it, she drew her knees to her chest as a resting place for her chin.

"I'm pretty sure you're barking up the wrong tree with that statement. The Amish worship no one but God."

She released her feet back to the ground. "Okay, so maybe *worship* isn't the appropriate word choice in this case, but seriously, Murph? It's not too far off. Naomi? Katie? Hannah? Emma? And Danielle? They've all sought this woman's counsel for something, and they refer back to the things they learn from her all the time."

"Maybe she's a therapist."

"She's not."

"Maybe—"

"Murph, I went to her house this morning. To meet her. She welcomed me inside and was exactly the way everyone described her. *Until* I started asking her questions about herself, that is." Tess could feel the excitement bubbling up inside her all over again and let it propel her back off the chair and over to the window. But this time, the view in front of her bowed to the one currently replaying in her thoughts. "She gave a few vague answers to some things I asked, but changed the subject often. Of course, I changed it back the first chance I could because, well, it's what we do, right?"

She took the grunt in her ear as a sign she had his full attention and continued. "You could literally feel the temperature in the room dropping with each question I asked. Next thing I knew, she was making up some bogus story about having to make a phone call. But *Murph?* She wanted me out of there. Big time."

"I take it you think she's hiding something?"

"I sure do. And I'm going to move heaven and earth to find out what it is."

She counted her way through his three inhales and answering exhales before he spoke again. "How old is this woman?"

"I'm putting her at about eighty. Give or take a year or so on either side."

"And you say these women you were baking with today care about this woman?"

"Absolutely. They insert her into conversations all the time."

"So she's their friend . . ."

"Naomi calls her a *friend to all*." Tess drew in a breath, held it, and let it out against the window. "But I don't want to say any more about this until I know where it leads. Once I do, I'll share, okay?"

"Roger that, kid."

"I'm glad you called. I was thinking about you while I was eating dinner."

"Was it something good? Because the food here is pretty awful."

"It was chicken, which was good all on its own. But, Murph? Naomi makes these brown-buttered noodles that are incredible. I had them for the first time earlier in the week, and I guess I must have commented about them enough that she made them again tonight. For me."

He cut his inhale short. "You sound happy, kid."

"Well, yeah . . . I might finally be onto something."

"And you baked?"

"I did."

"And someone took the time to notice something you liked?"

"They did, but what's your point, Murph?"

"No point. Just playing through everything you told me about your day. It's what I do—what we *both* do. Or should, anyway."

She grinned. "Ahhh, yes. The life of a reporter."

"Indeed."

"I'm glad you called, Murph. It was a real lift."

"I'm not sure I deserve that credit. Not this time, anyway. But, yeah, it was good to talk to you, too. I'll be in touch again soon."

CHAPTER 20

It was three minutes to ten when she spied Jack's black pickup truck making its way past the barn en route to the Grossdawdy Haus. Grabbing the tote bag with her laptop, notebook, and phone inside, she stepped onto the small front porch and shut the door.

"Good morning, Tess. Ready to get some coffee and the world's best brownie?"

She hiked the tote strap higher on her shoulder and fast-stepped her way over to the passenger door. "If you mean am I ready to get on the internet without worry about using all my battery—yes. And then some."

"Got everything you need?" he asked as she slipped into place on the bench seat beside him. "Paper? Pen? Computer?"

"I've got it all. Though it still feels weird not to lock the door behind me. Especially when"—she glanced over at the main house and then at the barn—"they don't seem to be back from church yet."

"And won't be until early evening." He pointed to her seat belt, and when it was fastened in place with her tote bag at her feet, he piloted them toward the barn. "As for locking doors? It's just the way the Amish are. They live by the honor code."

"Just because they do doesn't mean everyone else does," she mused.

At the end of the driveway, he turned right, the truck's wide tires sending up dry dirt and pieces of tiny gravel in the side-view mirror. "You can charge your phone on the way to the coffeehouse if you need to."

"I-I actually do, thanks." She dug her hand into her tote, located her phone and its power cord, and plugged it into the charging port. "I used up a lot of its life last night on a call, but it was worth it."

"Long conversation?"

She couldn't help but smile as she revisited her time with her mentor. "I always wish it could be longer, but it worked."

He took them past many of the same places she remembered from her walk on Friday evening— the spot where the creek traveled beneath the road, the spot where the dog had shown up and walked with her for a few steps, the one-room schoolhouse with the swing set, the spot where she'd slipped off the road and found the pond, and, up ahead, the cemetery with its simple white headstones.

Bathed in midmorning sunlight, everything looked brighter than she remembered but still just as quiet. "It was quiet out here like this the other evening when I was out walking. I assumed it was like that because it was the post-dinner hour and the sun was getting ready to set. But everything looks as quiet now as it did then."

"That's because it's Sunday. If it was a weekday, there'd be kids at that school, and farmers out in their fields, and women hanging wash and tending gardens. Same thing on a Saturday, with the exception of the kids-at-school part."

She looked down each of the next three driveways they passed, Jack's words proving to be true in every case. "There's not a single buggy anywhere. Not next to a barn, not in front of a house, not even on the road with us."

"You want to see where they all are?" he asked, his blue eyes sparkling. "At least the ones from this area?"

"Sure."

Letting off on the accelerator, he took the next turn and headed north on another deserted and far narrower road that took them alongside the outermost edge of the last farm they'd passed. Here, like as had been the case in all the driveways, there was no sign of human life.

"Where are we going?"

"Look right there," he said, pointing her attention toward a field on the driver's side of the truck. "There's all the buggies you've been looking for."

She sat up tall in her seat, craned her head to

the left, and gasped so loudly it echoed around the truck's cabin. "Was there another fire?"

"No. No fire."

"Then what's with all those buggies? I mean there's not as many as the other day, after the fire, but there's still"—she lifted her own finger and began to count as he stopped the truck in the middle of the road—"fifteen of them!"

"Actually that last one to the side of the barn is a bench wagon, not a buggy. But it's here, like the buggies, for church."

"So this is where Isaiah and Naomi and the kids are right now?"

"Yes. They'll be inside that house, with everyone else who came in those buggies, for about another forty minutes or so."

"But they left just after seven thirty this morning!"

"It's a three-and-a-half-hour church service from what I've been told."

"Wow."

"And when they're done? Some of the benches they're sitting on will be configured into tables so they can share a meal and visit with one another. It's quite a sight."

"I saw one of their group meals earlier in the week when a bunch of them came together to rebuild a barn in a neighboring district. There were tables and people everywhere, and they never seemed to run out of food. It was crazy."

"You thought *that* was a lot of people? You should've seen this same field back in February. The owner's oldest daughter was getting married, and there had to be upwards of four to five hundred people here—no exaggeration." He shook his head at the memory. "Can you imagine hosting something like that, and then, a few years later, your kid comes to you and tells you they're getting a divorce? You'd kill them."

She felt her smile drain away, replaced instead by something more befitting of the anger stirred by his callous words. "And if the divorce wasn't her fault?"

"It takes two, as my grandmother always says."

Clenching her hands into fists, Tess willed herself to breathe, to remain calm, to dismiss his response as the ignorance it clearly was. But it was hard. More than anything, she wanted to open her door, grab her tote bag, and walk back to the Grossdawdy Haus. But to do that meant walking away from the one thing that might actually make her time in Amish country worthwhile.

"Think you could cook for that many people?" he asked, abandoning his view of the home's buggy-filled front yard in favor of Tess. "Or would you be looking at your guest list thinking, *I'm calling the caterer?*"

"I wouldn't be getting married, period." She retrieved her phone from its resting spot atop the center console and pushed the screen to life, her gaze finding her email even as her words remained directed at Jack. "So . . . About this internet café place . . ."

For a moment, the silence in the truck was so thick she almost looked up. But, instead, she scrolled through the same messages she'd already read through over breakfast. When she reached the end, she exited and moved on to her news app, the weight of his gaze on the side of her face heavy.

"Isn't that why you want to go to an internet café—so you can do whatever you're doing right now?" At her shrug, he sighed and reapplied his foot to the gas pedal. "I'm glad I've never seen the appeal."

"To?" she asked, moving on to her pictures.

"Spending my time watching other people live their lives instead of living my own. Then again, that's sort of what you do as a reporter, right? Report on what other people are doing and thinking instead of doing your own thinking and your own doing?"

Clenching her teeth, she lowered her phone to her lap and lifted her gaze to his. "Actually, I'm doing and thinking all the time in my job. I hunt down the stories, I make the necessary contacts to tell them correctly, and I write them."

"But it's not something *you've* done that you're writing about. It's what someone else has done or learned or invented or whatever." He stopped at a stop sign, scanned the road to their left and right, and then crossed onto a busier, less rural road. "Again, one step removed. You're the observer, not the participant. Like you're doing with your phone right now instead of being a part of"— he pulled his right hand off the steering wheel and gestured at the landscape beside them and the road in front of them—"this, and what I was showing you and telling you about back there."

"*You* weren't part of that. You, too, were observing, as you call it."

"But I was seeing it in real time. And you were seeing it in real time. What you're doing on that phone isn't the same thing because you're looking at whatever you're looking at as seen through someone else's eyes and in someone else's time."

"But if someone says something completely ignorant *here*"—she shook her phone at him— "I can stop reading and move on. Unlike was the case *back there,* as you keep referencing."

He lifted his hand as if to wave her off but stopped, instead, his brow furrowed. "Wait. What did I say?"

"It doesn't matter. Really."

"Clearly it does. I just don't remember saying anything . . ." His sentence trailed off as, judging by the expression on his face, his mental rewind of the past ten minutes finally delivered him to the moment in question. "Oh no . . . You were married, weren't you?" he asked, his voice raspy.

"Seventy-five guests in the backyard of my parents' home. Party tents, floral archway, caterer, and even a pair of rented doves—the whole nine yards. And . . . yeah . . . What your grandmother says? About it taking two? She's right, it does. Only I suspect she means it in a very different way than—" She exhaled away the rest of her explanation. "Look, it doesn't matter. It's done. Over. Nothing to discuss, nothing to share."

He raked his hand through his hair, then returned it back to the wheel with tangible discomfort. "I'm sorry, Tess. I wasn't really thinking—*obviously*. I just . . . I mean, I—"

"Please stop," she said. "All I want is for you to drop me off at this internet place you told me about. That's all."

CHAPTER 21

Although she'd had her doubts, Sip and Click was, in fact, the epitome of a modern-day coffeehouse. From the chalkboard menu listing the various drink options, to the glass-fronted cabinet with an array of food items ranging from breakfast breads and muffins, to sandwiches and salads, Jack's suggestion checked all the boxes. Even the state-of-the-art milk steamers and frothing machines were as they should be, with the prerequisite smiling but efficient barista moving from one to the other with the ease of a seasoned employee.

When the drink order before hers had been filled, the employee tasked with manning the register smiled at Tess. "Welcome to Sip and Click. What can I get for you?"

She scanned the colorful columns on the wall above the woman's head. "I'm looking for hot chocolate, but I'm not seeing it . . ."

"White or regular?"

"You can do a white chocolate hot chocolate?" Tess asked.

"We sure can."

"Then, yes. Please. I'd love that."

"What size?"

She took in the trio of cups beside the register

and dipped her hand into her tote bag for her wallet. "Let's go with a medium."

"Anything else?"

"No."

The cashier eyed Tess's bag. "And that's for here, right?"

"Yes. Please." She paid the amount due, took the numbered tabletop placard she was given, and made her way down a long tiled hallway, past book-filled shelves and cozy reading nooks. At its end, she was deposited into a sunny atrium with couches, overstuffed chairs, tables of all shapes and sizes, and a dozen or so people in various configurations.

Then a burst of laughter to her right revealed a large community-style table and eight chairs occupied by senior citizens. The couches and chairs on the opposite side of the room housed a few lone readers, as well as a young teenage couple sharing a pair of headphones, a giant-size chocolate chip cookie, and some not-so-subtle flirting.

Bobbing her head to the left, Tess caught sight of an empty table tucked into a back corner and made a beeline in that direction. Once there, she pulled her laptop out of her tote, powered it up, and got straight to work.

Her first search was on Lottie Jenkins herself— a search that revealed a number of people with that name. She searched her way through a writer from Texas, an accountant in Wisconsin, and a small business owner in Oregon—three very different women with the same name, and none of them right.

Next, she tried narrowing her search by including a few of the places the elderly woman had mentioned or the pictures on her mantel had revealed. A search specific to San Francisco—the place Miss Lottie had mentioned visiting when she'd been hit with the idea of moving back to Lancaster County—turned up a real estate transaction from thirty years ago, but it went nowhere.

She remembered mention of an older brother and his part in Miss Lottie deciding not to be baptized, but without a name or any further details, it was another dead end.

"Think, Tess, think," she murmured. "There's got to be something."

"Ma'am?"

Looking up from her computer screen, Tess found a smile for the same woman who'd taken her order. "Oh, right . . . my hot chocolate . . . I'd forgotten that was coming. Here, I'll clear a spot for it."

She shoved her notebook to the side of the table and leaned back to afford the woman an easy reach for setting down the drink and—

"Oh. No. That brownie isn't mine," Tess said, waving off the plate being set next to her hot chocolate. "I mean it looks amazing, don't get me wrong, but I didn't order that."

"I know, but *he* did." The woman nudged her chin and Tess's attention toward an all-too-familiar face seated on the far side of the room. "He said it's his way of apologizing for putting his foot in his mouth earlier."

She looked from the shrugging and sheepishly smiling Jack to the white chocolate drizzle dripping off the top of the brownie and found that her urge to decline the treat was quickly bowing to her stomach's gurgle of anticipation.

"I say enjoy every last bite while you let him squirm." The cashier-turned-server dug a napkin out of her pocket, set it beside the brownie plate, and then headed back down the hallway to her original post while Jack made his way over to Tess.

"You're still here," she said by way of greeting.

"Because you are."

"I told you I would call a cab when I was done."

"I know you did."

"But you stayed anyway."

He pointed at the brownie. "I didn't want you to leave without trying one. They're pretty amazing."

"You didn't have to get me one."

"Yes, yes I did. I was a total jerk earlier."

"Let it go. *I* have." She took a sip of her hot

chocolate and immediately went back for another. "Oh. Wow. That's good."

He pointed at her plate again. "Trust me. It gets better."

"I really wish you hadn't."

"Okay, but I did. So try it."

"One bite," she conceded.

"Ha! Good luck with that . . ."

She grabbed hold of the fork the cashier had set atop the plate and took a bite, the moan it elicited earning her more than a few knowing smiles from nearby tables. "Oh. My. That's-that's—" She took another bite, and another. "Wow. Just wow."

"Told you so."

She smiled around yet another bite of brownie and pointed to the vacant chair across from her own. "You want to sit while I finish this?"

"I don't want to interrupt your work."

"You're not. Unfortunately."

He cocked an eyebrow. "Meaning?"

"Meaning my whole reason for having you bring me here has turned up absolutely nothing." She took one last bite and then closed her computer. "Ugh. Ugh. Ugh. I was so sure I had something."

"For a story?"

"I thought so. But it appears my potential subject's time away was skeleton-free, and so I'm back to square one. *Again*."

Jack took a sip from his own lidded cup and leaned back in his chair. "So, tell me about your job—what you like about it, what you don't, if it's your end goal, that sort of thing."

"I thought you already knew everything there was to know about what I do for a living," she countered between sips of her own drink.

"Why do you say that?"

"Because you said you did."

"When did I say that?"

"Less than"—she glanced down at her phone screen—"thirty minutes ago. You told me that writers are observers, not doers."

He winced. "Yeah, about that . . . I'm not usually such a jerk, even if it seems otherwise."

"Whatever. Anyway, getting back to your question, I wanted to be a writer from the time I was a little kid," she said, bringing them back on track. "When other kids in the neighborhood were setting up lemonade stands and puppet shows, I was running around interviewing people about what they thought of the lemonade, and writing behind-the-scene profile pieces about the puppets and the puppeteers."

His answering laugh was warm and kind and it encouraged her to keep going, to keep sharing. "So when it was time for us to go to college, we found a school that had journalism for me, and business for Mandy."

"Is Mandy your sister?"

Stilling her hand on her to-go cup, Tess stared at Jack. "How do you know about Mandy?"

"I know you just said her name. And that the college you went to had journalism for you, and business for her."

"Oh. Right. I . . ." She shook off the explanation she didn't want to give, let alone speak. Instead, she used another sip of her drink to collect her thoughts and to get a handle on the emotions she didn't want to share with anyone, most especially the man looking back at her, waiting. "Anyway," she said, clearing her throat. "I found my way to the magazine where I work now and, after a shaky start, unearthed my groove again thanks to Murph."

The intrigue in his eyes dulled ever so briefly. "Who's Murph?"

"The one I use all my phone's battery power with," she said, smiling. "Murph is a legend in my business—or, at least, where I work."

"Tell me."

She laughed. "That's what he says to me all the time—*tell me*." She pushed her now-empty cup to the side in favor of her notebook and ran her finger along its spiral edge. "For whatever reason, he saw something in me when I started. How, I'm not sure, but he did, and he took me under his wing as his mentee—something my boss said Murph has never done. And I am a better writer because of it. No doubt."

"How?"

"I think it was my third day on the job, when I was lost in my own head. He sat on the edge of my desk and asked me why I was there. I told him I wanted to write stories that stayed with people long after they stopped reading. He nodded and then started reading something I was writing on my computer. I don't think he got to the end of the first paragraph when he stopped, motioned for me to grab my notes, and then led me into his office. I'd barely shut the door behind me when he told me he'd already forgotten what he'd read, and that my stories were never going to be unforgettable if I didn't take the time to see beyond the obvious."

"That had to hurt," Jack said across the lid of his cup.

"It did. That's why I burst into tears."

"I bet he felt like a heel."

Her answering laugh turned a head or two in their direction. "Uh, no. Max Murphy tells it like it is. No holds barred. But he'll also follow it up with a reason and suggestions for those who want to learn."

"And you wanted to learn . . ."

"I did. Once I stopped crying, anyway." Abandoning her notebook in lieu of the drink she'd finished and the computer she'd already closed, Tess leaned forward on her elbows. "He started asking me questions about the people I'd spoken to for my story—questions that, at first, seemed unimportant. Like . . ."

She stopped, took in the faces at their neighboring tables, and then refocused on Jack. "Let's say I was doing a story on your boss and his business. The obvious would be that he builds houses, that he employs folks like yourself, et cetera. But the not so obvious would have me sitting down with some of the people he's built homes for."

"To talk about their take on the job he did?"

"Sure, I could do that. But, again, that's the obvious. The not so obvious would be what happens inside their new home—the memories that have been created there, the milestones that have been reached. Like the Thanksgiving meal in the dining room that included their military child . . . Or that moment they walked through the front door with their new baby, or the picture in front of the fireplace from Great-Grandma's hundredth birthday celebration . . . It's in getting down to those moments and making them come alive on the page that you can truly help forge a real and lasting connection between the reader and the subject."

"So what you're saying is you have to always be thinking, right?"

"Sure. But it's also about stepping back and seeing below the surface so that readers can, too."

"That's really interesting." He drained the rest of his drink and set his empty cup beside Tess's. "I'm not sure how good I'd be at that."

She considered his words and found that they delivered a memory to her mental doorstep. "Actually, you made a rather Murph-like observation just yesterday."

"I did?" he asked. "When?"

"It was when I'd come out of Naomi's yesterday and saw you in the driveway. I was surprised about how normal she and her friends all seemed despite being Amish. You said—and I'm paraphrasing here—that, at the end of the day, when you remove all of the Amish stuff, they're people just like the rest of us."

He was silent for a moment despite the smile making its way from one end of his mouth to the other. "Hmmm . . . So maybe I'm not a total buffoon?"

"I didn't say *that*," she said, splaying her palms.

Their respective laughter mingled and then faded into something uncomfortably comfortable.

"So, now what?" he finally asked.

"In terms of my story?"

"For starters."

"That's a good question. I'm not sure yet. But I'll figure something out. I have to. My job is kind of riding on it."

"Maybe you need a little time away, a little time to clear your head. That's something that always works for me when I've hit a wall at work or in my personal life or whatever." He slipped the handle of her tote bag off the back of his chair and handed it to her across the table. "There's a pond not far from Naomi and Isaiah's place that I like to hit up when I need to clear my head. Maybe it'll work for you, too."

She glanced up from her task of putting her belongings into the bag. "I think I may have found that pond on Friday night when I was out walking. It's not too far from that schoolhouse we passed on the way here, right? And the trail to get to the pond is easy to miss if you're coming from the direction of Naomi's?"

"Yep, that's the place. So you've been there?" he asked, his question tinged with . . . *disappointment?*

"Briefly, but yes. I was kind of lost in my own head when I noticed the footpath through the trees. But by the time I found it, it was getting close to dark, and I didn't want to spend so much time that I couldn't find the path back out." She slid her notebook alongside her laptop, tossed in her pen and her phone, and followed him to the trash bin in the corner while he deposited their cups inside. "I can see why you'd like to go there, though. There was something very peaceful about it, like you could easily daydream a whole day away there."

"Been there, done that," he said, laughing.

"Many times. Miller's Pond just does that to people and has for a—"

She knew he was still talking. She could see his mouth moving as they fell in step beside each other on the way toward the exit. But she'd stopped hearing anything the moment he mentioned the name of the pond.

Miller's Pond . . .

Miller's—

"That's it!"

He stopped, mid-step. "What? What's it?"

"I was looking at who she became, not who she was!" Hooking her thumb toward the table they'd just vacated, Tess shrugged an apology. "It looks like I'm going to need to call that cab, after all."

"Why?"

"It's something you just said. It means I need to get back on my computer."

He pulled a face. "Something *I* said?"

"It was hearing the name of the pond that made me realize I didn't look at enough to be able to call it quits." She pointed toward the table again. "I'm sorry. I really need to see if there's something there."

"Then I'll wait."

She looked from the table to the window, and back to Jack. "I can't ask you to do that. It's your weekend and it's a beautiful day and you don't need to be wasting it waiting on me."

"I can read." He pointed toward the bookshelves

in the hallway. "It's been far too long since I've read anything other than a blueprint. So go do what you need to do and, when you're done, come find me at one of the outdoor tables. That way I'm enjoying the beautiful weather and a book at the same time."

She watched him make his way over to the bookshelf and then hightailed herself back to the same spot in which she'd given up prematurely.

Lottie Jenkins had been Lottie Miller in her youth. And while there was no doubt the elderly woman had grown increasingly uncomfortable with Tess's questions, the first sign of squirming had come while talking about her original departure from the Amish.

This time, when her computer booted up, she put the woman's maiden name into the search bar and hit Enter. When nothing relevant came up, she narrowed her efforts specifically to Lancaster County and, again, got nothing.

Her frustration mounting, she deleted Lottie's name completely and, after staring at the blinking cursor, cast a wider search to include nothing more than the approximate time frame in which the woman chose to leave everything she'd ever known. And to do so for more than four decades without a single glance back . . .

Slowly, Tess scrolled her way down the first page, clicking in and back out of several items. Nothing.

Slowly, and with waning hope, she scrolled her way down the second page, clicking in and back out of different hits. Nothing.

Slowly, and with thoughts that were starting to wander outside into the sunshine, she clicked on the first item on the third page and began to read. Halfway down the page, all thoughts of sun and books and the blue of Jack's eyes disappeared along with her breath.

CHAPTER 22

"Care to share?"

Tess abandoned her view of the farms she wasn't really seeing anyway to find Jack splitting his own attention between the road in front of them and her. "I take it I missed a question?"

"Nope. You've just got me all curious about your answer back at Sip and Click."

"My answer? My answer to what?"

He slowed to a stop at a four-way intersection and then continued straight, the truck taking them down the very same roads they'd traveled two hours earlier. "When I asked you if that grin you were wearing when you came out to find me meant you'd found something, you said *maybe.*"

She remembered the exchange. "Okay . . ."

"Well, your smile *then,* and"—he glanced over at her—"your smile *now* has no *maybe* about it."

"I'm"—she tried to rein in her smile, but it didn't take—*"hopeful."*

"I see that. Which brings me back to my question. Care to share?"

"Ahhhh." Leaning into the headrest, she thought back to the article that had changed everything. Maybe. "It *could* all be nothing."

"Or it could be everything," he countered.

"Let's hope."

"And it has to do with this person you needed to research?"

"I'm not sure." And it was true. She wasn't. But the timing was right . . . "I so wish I could call Murph right now and play this off him."

"So why don't you? We charged your phone on the way."

Her sigh stole his attention from the road once again. "Murph is away on assignment just like I am."

"They sent him to an Amish community, too?" he asked.

"Ha! No. Murph got a real assignment, like I was supposed to."

"You weren't supposed to come here?"

"Hardly. But I missed a big story, and so I was sent here instead."

"I see. And Murph? Where'd he go?"

"He's imbedded with a Special Forces unit somewhere in the Middle East."

Jack's whistle filled the cabin before the breeze coming through their open windows carried it off with what was left of her smile. "Seriously? I'd love an assignment like that."

"You and me both."

"Where were you supposed to go?"

"Belize. To get an up-close look at efforts to relocate coral." She rested her arm along the passenger side window sill and sighed again. "Instead, I'm here."

"I'm not complaining."

"Because you're not the one who was supposed to go to Belize."

"Touché." They drove another mile, maybe two before he spoke again. "But you talked to this Murph guy just last night, right? So he's reachable."

"He calls or texts me when he has a window."

At the end of the road, Jack turned left, the barns and farmhouses they passed beginning to look familiar.

"You could bounce stuff off me," he said after a while. "I know I'm not a reporter, but I've got ears. And maybe, since I've lived here my whole life, I might actually make a good sounding board."

"You're too young. You wouldn't have been around during the time frame in question. Chances are your parents wouldn't have been around, either."

He slowed as they approached and then passed the cemetery. "My granddad is still alive."

"Is he from this area, too?"

"Born and raised." Pulling to a stop on the road's grassy shoulder, Jack shifted the truck into park and guided her curious eyes onto the other side of the road with his chin. "I could show you Miller's Pond in the daylight, and you could tell me what you found that had you looking like the cat who swallowed the canary right up until the whole Belize thing came up."

"Oh, I don't know. I probably should head back to the farm and see if I can help Naomi with something."

"Naomi won't be back from church yet. Not for another few hours, at least."

She reached into her tote bag for her phone and checked the time. "It's coming up on one thirty. She left for church before eight."

"The service wrapped up around eleven thirty, but everyone sticks around to eat and to visit for hours afterward."

"How do you know all this stuff?" she asked.

"The Amish have been my neighbors more or less my whole life. You figure stuff out." He nudged his chin and her gaze across the street a second time. "So? What do you say?"

She started to decline but, at the last minute, settled on a half-hearted shrug.

"Fantastic. Let's go." He shut off the engine, stepped out of the truck, and waited for her before he crossed the road. At the break in the trees, he held back a branch and motioned her to take the lead along the narrow path. "This is one of my favorite times of the day to come here. This and first thing in the morning."

"Why is that?" she asked, picking her way around the same rocks and downed limbs she'd traversed two days earlier.

"I like first thing in the morning because of the

songbirds. There is something mighty peaceful about sitting here, before the workday starts, just listening to them sing the way they do. Makes me wish I could stop out here every morning instead of just on Mondays."

"Why Mondays?"

"Good way to start the week off," he said, stepping beside her as the path widened.

She stole a seconds-long peek at his profile, then willed herself to look away. "I wouldn't have guessed that about you."

"What? That I like listening to songbirds?"

"That you'd intentionally seek them out."

Shrugging, he drew to a stop as they reached the clearing, then swept his hand and her attention toward what seemed like a million pinpoints of sunlight dancing along the surface of what she now knew was Miller's Pond.

"Wow! It's . . ." She cast about for just the right words but came up short. "Wow."

"Beautiful, right?"

"Oh yes. It's *magical*." She stepped closer to the water's edge. "Is this normal for this time of day?"

"On a sunny day like this? Absolutely."

"Wow."

"Some days when I stop out here, I just stand and take it all in for a little while and then head back to my truck. On other days, when maybe I have a little more leeway in my schedule, I'll chill out on that rock"—he pointed to the same flat-topped boulder that had caught her eye Friday evening—"right there for a while. It's a great place to think, to veg, and even to sneak in a little nap."

"A nap, eh?" she echoed, laughing.

He grinned. "Only once or twice." At her raised eyebrow he tried again. "Okay, okay, maybe three or four times. Six, at most."

"Well, regardless of how many times you've actually drifted off out here, I can see why you would. It's really peaceful. A real hidden gem, so to speak."

"Hidden from the road, yes. But known by many. Especially the Amish." Bending over, he sifted his fingers through a smattering of rocks and retrieved two—one he handed her and one he kept for himself. "Ever skip rocks?"

"Once. When I was little." She held it flat inside her fingers, cocked her wrist back, and launched it across the top of the water.

"Wow. Three skips. Nice!"

"My grandfather could skip it four and sometimes five times, and I thought that was the coolest thing." She watched her rock disappear beneath the water's surface and then brushed away any residual dirt. "But I only got to try once or twice during that visit. He died shortly after."

"I'm sorry to hear that. How old were you?"

"Six." Tess squinted against the sun's rays and

nudged her chin at Jack's hand. "Let's see what you can do."

Jack cocked his wrist back and forth and then sent his own rock skipping across the water while she counted aloud. "One, two, three, four, five! Very impressive."

"Granddad taught me, too. Only I'm fortunate to be able to say that he's still around to give me a refresher course every now and again." He stepped back from the pond's edge and pointed toward the rock. "Let's sit for a little while before I take you back to Naomi's."

She started to reach for her back pocket to check the time, but let it go. With Naomi and Isaiah and the kids tied up for the foreseeable future, there was nothing to rush back to. And if she did, she'd just be alone with her thoughts and questions. Nodding, Tess followed Jack over to the rock, claimed her spot, and looked out over the water as he, too, sat. "How old is your grandfather if you don't mind me asking?"

"Well, my mom was twenty-five when she had me, so that makes her fifty-eight. And I'm pretty sure my grandfather was twenty-three when my mom was born. So I'm going to say—wait. Yes. He's eighty-one. I know this because we had a big birthday bash for him last year when he turned eighty."

"They're about the same age, that's for sure," she murmured.

"Who is?"

Tess shook off his question in favor of her own. "And he grew up around here?" she prodded.

"He sure did. In the next town over, actually."

"New Holland?"

"That's right. Do you know it?"

"I hadn't heard of it until about an hour ago." She hiked her feet up and onto the rock and rested her chin on her knees. "But it's on my radar now."

Reclining back, he draped his arm across his forehead and grinned up at the clouds. "Will you tell me what you're after if I promise to channel this Murph guy?"

"Do you remember your grandfather ever mentioning something about money going missing from the home of an Amish bishop when he would have been in his late teens?"

"Not that I recall," he said, moving his arm a smidge to afford eye contact with Tess. "What kind of money are we talking about?"

"Twenty thousand dollars."

Whistling, he sat up. "From the bishop's house?"

She nodded.

"I've always heard the Amish are good about coming together for a crisis and stuff, but—wow. And it went *missing?* How?"

"Wait." She turned so as to face him more than the pond. "Why did you say that about coming together for a crisis? How did you know the money was for that?"

"I didn't," he said, pushing his fingers through his hair. "I just know the Amish are self-supporting of themselves and their own, and so if the bishop had that kind of money gathered in one place, it's a safe bet it was being collected for something.

"Like, for instance, if a kid is hospitalized for some reason, whatever cost the family can't pick up is absorbed by the rest of the families in the district. Same holds true for paying a teacher and purchasing supplies for a school—the money to do those things comes from the families inside the district. If they need more because a hospital stay goes on for longer than expected, they might hold a mud sale to raise more, but it's all coming from their own pockets." At her answering nod, he dropped his hand back to his side. "So I'm guessing, from what you just said a minute ago, the missing money was for something like that?"

She looked back at the water, only this time, instead of seeing the sparkle from the sun's light, she saw the words of the article that had reignited her excitement. "Apparently, the money that went missing had been donated by various Amish families. It was earmarked for some structural improvements to a school, and to help pay the medical expenses of a young Amish boy who'd been burned in a barn fire."

"Okay . . ."

"The money disappeared from the bishop's

home after something called a hymn sing."

This time Jack's whistle not only claimed her full attention but that of a bird perched on a nearby branch, as well. "Wow."

"You know what that means?"

"A hymn sing? Sure. It's a chance for the teens in a district to come together and, essentially, hang out. They're held later on a Sunday, after church and the shared meal, and usually at a different house than where the church service was held that day."

"So why the whistle just now?" she asked, picking a leaf up off the rock and twirling it between her fingers.

"Hymn sings are for *Amish* teens," he said. "I wouldn't expect one of them to steal anything, let alone that kind of money. It doesn't fit with what I know, I guess."

She dropped the leaf back onto the rock and returned her feet to the ground. "And you might be right. Because, from what I was able to piece together, there were rumors it wasn't an *Amish* teen."

"Someone saw something?"

"Maybe, maybe not. The police tried to investigate when it first happened, but they met with little cooperation from the families of the teens present that night."

Jack nodded. "That makes sense on account of the fact the Amish tend to shy away from police."

"The person writing the cold case article I found said there had been rumors of two English boys hanging around on the road the night of the hymn sing."

"So one—*or both*—took it and ran?" Jack asked.

"There was no proof, nor a name the police could follow up on to find out. The Amish weren't talking, and those who were willing to talk off the record didn't know the English boys by name. All they *did* know was that the boys were there because one of them was apparently smitten with someone who was on Rumspringa at the time."

"Ah . . . okay." Jack slid off the rock and followed her back to the water's edge. "Yeah, that happens, sometimes. I went to high school with a guy who fell for one of the Amish girls on Rumspringa. Fell hard, in fact. But then he started applying to college, and she wanted to live an Amish life, and so they broke it off and went their separate ways. End of story."

"The Amish are okay with their daughters dating English guys?" she asked.

"Not particularly, I imagine. But Rumspringa is the time when Amish kids experiment with our life—our clothes, our music, our good and bad choices, et cetera. After they do, though, close to ninety percent decide to go ahead and get baptized."

"And the others?"

"They leave." He bent down, grabbed up two more skipping stones, and turned them over and over between his fingers. "So what happened? This Amish girl's parents wouldn't let the cops talk to their daughter about the English kid who was lurking around the hymn sing the night the money disappeared?"

"Nope."

Stilling the rocks inside his hand, he arched his brow at her. "Nope, they wouldn't? Or nope, that's not what happened?"

"Nope, that's not what happened."

He waited for her to say more, and when she didn't, he let the rocks drop from his hand back to the ground. "C'mon, Tess! You can't go all cliff-hanger on me like this. It's cruel."

Oh, how she wanted to tell him there was so much more to the story than he could possibly imagine. But she couldn't. Not yet, anyway. Not until she knew for certain her hunch was right. And once she did, he could read about it like everyone else—in the story she'd already titled in her head: *Deception in Plain Sight.*

"Hello? Earth to Tess . . . What happened?"

"She left."

"Left what?" he echoed.

"The Amish, and the area."

He stared at Tess for a beat, maybe two, and then looked out over the water. "When was this again?"

"Almost sixty-four years ago."

"Sixty-four years ago," he repeated. "And this is what you were looking for on the computer today?"

"If my hunch is right, yes." She retrieved one of the rocks he'd dropped and ran her thumb across the flattest side. "But as Murph likes to say, a hunch *can* be a fact, but a fact is *always* a fact. Which is why I'm wishing I had a time machine right about now."

His eyes returned to hers. "What if I have one I can let you borrow?"

"You have a *time machine?*" she echoed, dryly.

"I do." He guided her away from the pond and toward the path. "C'mon. I'll show you."

CHAPTER 23

Even without the official introduction, she'd have known she was meeting Jack's relation. Their eyes boasted the same deep blue hue, their nose the same firm angle, their thick hair the same hint of a cowlick, and their smiles the same mischievous twitch.

"Tess . . . Pretty name for a pretty girl." Releasing her hand in favor of his grandson's shoulder, Tom Richter nodded his approval. "If she's as sweet as she is pretty, Jack, you've found yourself quite a keeper."

Shaking off the answering gape of her mouth, Jack motioned Tess toward the patio chair closest to the one the elderly man had been sitting in when they arrived. "Tess isn't my girlfriend, Granddad."

"You sure?"

"Yes, Granddad, I'm sure." Rolling his eyes for only Tess to see, Jack helped the man back onto his seat with gentle and steady hands and then pulled close a third chair for himself. "So how goes it? All good?"

"It's better now." Tom looked again at Tess, his smile growing ever wider. "So how do you two know each other?"

"We just do, Granddad."

Tom swatted at his grandson's answer as if it were an unwelcome gnat. "I was asking *Tess,* which means I want *Tess* to answer."

Shrugging off Jack's mouthed *Sorry,* she scooted her chair closer to the elderly man. "We met while I was mucking a horse stall out at the Amish farm where I'm staying and—"

"I'm sorry, Granddad, I have to interrupt here for a minute," Jack said. "When we met, Tess was just staring into the stall like it was going to muck itself. So I gave her a few words of encouragement."

"Words of encouragement?" she echoed.

"That's right."

"I don't remember any words of—"

"You didn't muck it for her?" Tom asked, eyeing his grandson.

Jack's cheeks flamed pink.

"It's okay, I didn't need his help."

Jack's left eyebrow lifted at her. "Scoop and roll? You don't remember that?"

"Oh, I remember. I just know I would've figured it out all on my own without your—"

"Scoop and roll?" Tom straightened proudly in his chair. "I taught Jack how to do that when he was no bigger than my knee. Works well, don't it?"

"Don't it?" Jack repeated, grinning.

She met and held Jack's eye for a silent count

280

of three before turning back to his grandfather. "It sure does."

Pleased, Tom leaned back in his chair, plucked a pair of glasses from the front pocket of his shirt, and slipped them into place. "So what farm are you staying at?" he asked.

"She's staying out at Isaiah and Naomi King's place, Granddad. In the Grossdawdy Haus. Tess writes for a magazine, and she's here on assignment for work."

Tom's gaze narrowed on hers. "You're staying? For how long?"

"A month in all."

"What kind of reporter spends a month on a single story?"

"Granddad!"

She stopped Jack's protest with a hand. "No, it's okay. It's a fair question. Newspaper reporters don't. They can spare a few hours on a story— tops. But I work for a national magazine that comes out twice a month. Meaning we have more time to devote to a story or a series of stories if our boss feels it's warranted. Most of the time that might mean a few days here, a few days there. But once a year, a few of us get sent out on a bigger assignment. Amish country is mine this time."

"What are you writing about?"

"I'm not sure yet," she said. "Right now it's really just about seeing what it means to be

Amish—how they work, how they live, how their world fits alongside ours, that sort of stuff. It could be a setting piece, a travel piece, a lifestyle piece, or something entirely different. I'll know it when I see it."

He sat with her answer, giving Tess time to fit a few easy-to-find pieces into the puzzle that was Jack's grandfather. There was the raised flower bed off the backside of the patio with its uniform rows of vegetable plants . . . There was the local newspaper, folded to make the nearly completed crossword easier to fill in . . . There was the mystery novel, turned spine up, balanced atop the armrest of his chair . . . And there was the—

"Just be fair and truthful."

Her gaze traveled back to his. "Did you say something?"

"I said, *Be fair and truthful.*"

"With what?"

"Whatever you write about them."

"Of course. I wouldn't write anything that was untrue."

Seemingly satisfied, he nodded at his grandson. "You could start by asking her on a date, you know."

"Granddad!" Jack dropped his head into his hands and groaned. "You've got to give this whole dating thing a rest. Please!"

"I taught him right, you know." Tom added.

Jack's groan grew louder. "Granddad, please . . ."

"I'm here for work and that's it," Tess said.

Tom's slight shoulders dipped in defeat. "You gotta fella at home?"

"All righty then, moving on," Jack said, snapping his head up off his hands. "Granddad, do you remember hearing something about money disappearing from one of the farms? Money the Amish raised to help pay medical expenses for a child who'd been burned in a barn fire?"

The elderly man drew back, stared at Jack for a moment, and then grabbed the newspaper off the table and began to unfold it. "It happened *again?* When? What page?"

"No, no. It's not in the paper. Not now, anyway." Jack set a gentle hand atop his grandfather's. "It's an old story. One that happened back when you were in your late teens."

Tom's slump of relief was followed by a refolding of the paper and a slow nod. "I remember. It was a lot of money at that time—*a lot* of money."

Tess and Jack leaned forward in unison. "Can you tell us about it?" she asked.

"The Amish in that particular district had been raising money for that boy for weeks. What they couldn't raise just by donating themselves inside their district, they raised by way of a big mud sale.

She looked from grandfather to grandson and

283

back again. "Jack mentioned that word earlier, but I don't know what that means."

"A mud sale?" Tom set the edge of his elbows against his armrests and propped his chin atop tented fingers. "It's something you really should see if you're wanting to learn about the Amish and the way they do things. It's basically an auction they have to raise money for the local fire department in most cases. But sometimes they have them to raise money needed for other things."

"Like medical bills," she prodded.

"Like medical bills. They'll auction off everything from handmade furniture and quilts to farming equipment and baked goods. It's quite a sight."

"They auction these things off to other Amish?"

Tom nodded, but it was Jack who answered. "Some, sure. But these mud sales are open to the English, as well."

"And so they had one of these mud sales when they were raising the money for this Amish boy back then?" she asked in an attempt to keep from steering too far off topic.

"They had two, actually. One in the early spring, one in late spring. Between what they raised at those and the money the Amish had donated on their own, they had just about twenty thousand dollars to help pay this young boy's bills. But then it all went missing—stolen right out of the bishop's house during a hymn sing."

Jack's chair creaked with his sudden shift. "But how? I've driven by hymn sings before. There are kids everywhere. How could someone do that without anyone else noticing?"

"That kind of busyness can be a distraction just as much as a distractor."

"Meaning?" she prodded.

Tom took off his glasses, rubbed his eyes, and then, slowly, settled them across the bridge of his nose, once again. "When you get young people together—Amish or otherwise—they're so busy talking and visiting and focusing on each other it's not out of the realm of possibility someone could slip by them and into a house, aided or unaided."

"Aided or unaided?" She scooted forward onto the edge of her chair. "Does that mean you think more than one person was involved?"

Tom's gaze mingled with hers for a brief moment before lifting to a spot far beyond the man's backyard. "I've always suspected there was, although I can't say all parties actually *knew*."

"*How,* Granddad? Someone had to know what was happening . . ."

"Of course. But that doesn't mean all three knew."

She heard Jack's quiet gasp and knew it was an echo of her own. "You think there were *three?*" Jack asked.

"I know there were three. I just don't know how

many of them were party to what happened."

"What *do* you know about that night?" Tess asked.

It was fast, and it was fleeting, but something that looked a lot like pain made its way across the elderly man's face a second before his labored shrug. "That I should've went with JJ out to the bishop's farm the way he asked."

She and Jack exchanged glances, while Tom closed his eyes and continued. "But I told him I had homework I didn't have."

"Who was JJ and why did you lie to him, Granddad?"

"JJ was my best friend. And I lied to him because it was just supposed to be *us* that night— with *me* being JJ's wingman, not Carl. And so I lied about my homework."

"Who was Carl?" Tess asked.

"A bad egg, through and through."

She considered asking for a pause in the conversation so she could run out to the truck and get her notebook and pen, but they were too close to the part of the story she was dying to hear. Instead, she did her best to commit the names she'd heard thus far to her memory and dove back in. "What happened?"

"They went out there just like JJ wanted. And I imagine they walked back and forth on the road in front of the bishop's place until she saw them and came over."

It took everything Tess had not to yell *yes* at the top of her lungs. Instead, she tucked her hands under her thighs and worked to keep her voice even. "Who?"

"The bishop's daughter. Dorothy."

Defeat made her back sag against the chair as Jack picked up the baton she no longer cared about. "The *bishop's* daughter?"

"That's right," Tom said, his nod labored. "We met her at the ice cream parlor in town. She was on Rumspringa, and JJ fell hard. So hard, in fact, he was convinced he was going to marry her one day."

"Did she like him, too?"

"She did. Very much."

"Did the bishop know about JJ?" Jack asked.

"No. Dorothy knew her dat wouldn't be happy that she'd fallen for an Englisher." Tom palmed his mouth only to let his hand slip back to his lap. "Like JJ, I thought Dorothy was shy and real sweet. But we were both wrong."

She felt Jack's eyes, knew he was trying to gauge whether her intrigue matched his, but she was too tired, too defeated to give him what he wanted. After a moment, maybe two, he moved on without her. "You think she was part of stealing the money?"

"I know she *knew* about the money. I was there when JJ told us how much money her father would be giving to the little boy's family that next week. But JJ was *proud* about it . . . *proud* that his girl was part of something so good. But then the money went missing, and the two of them just up and disappeared."

"JJ and Dorothy?" Jack asked.

Tom shook his head. "*Carl* and Dorothy."

It was Tess's turn to close her eyes. To feel the pain of a tale she knew intimately. "She ran off with JJ's *friend?*"

"That fella was no friend of JJ's! If he was, he wouldn't have stolen his girl!"

A long, low whistle had her opening her eyes to discover Jack had stood. "Where'd they go?"

"Don't know, don't care," said Tom.

She tried to clear her throat of the lump that had lodged itself midway up her throat, but when it wouldn't budge, she gave up and hoped Jack would ask the only remaining question she cared about.

"And JJ?" he asked, as if on script. "What happened to JJ?"

"He pulled away from everyone, including me. Spent all his time working so he could donate everything he made to that family. Still, he took the boy's death real hard."

"The boy *died?*" Tess and Jack echoed in unison.

Tom cleared the lump from his own throat and sighed. "About three months later. Of course the money had nothing to do with that, but JJ couldn't seem to separate one from the other. All he saw was that Carl had been there that night because *he* brought him, that Carl didn't come back to school the next day or any day thereafter, that Dorothy made the out-of-left-field decision not to be baptized and to move away not more than twenty-four hours later, and that on the heels of both of those things, the money the Amish had raised to pay the boy's medical bills was missing."

"Any chance JJ's despondency was because he'd helped steal the money?"

Tom was already shaking his head before the last word was out of her mouth. "No, I don't. JJ was—and is—a standup guy. I think he was as surprised by everything that happened as anyone else."

"Yet he didn't tell the cops?" Jack asked.

"He didn't, but that was only because he didn't know for sure and didn't want to level accusations that might not have been accurate. What he did know was that he'd gone in search of somewhere private where he could go to the bathroom. When he got back, Carl wasn't standing where he'd left him. So JJ wandered around looking for him and finally found him back by the tree some ten minutes later. He asked Carl where he went, but Carl wouldn't give JJ a straight answer. All he did say was that they had to leave because he had to hurry and get home."

"And Dorothy?" Tess asked out of sheer curiosity. "Where was she when Carl wanted to leave?"

Tom was silent for a minute as he looked toward the garden Tess knew he wasn't really seeing. "I don't know. You'd have to ask JJ."

"He's still alive?" Jack asked.

"He is, and you know him."

Jack looked from his grandfather to Tess, and back again. "I do?"

"Sure. Lives behind the filling station."

"Wait. You mean Old Joe Wilder is the JJ you've been talking about this whole time?"

"He is indeed."

"Why am I just now hearing this story?" Jack asked.

"Because it was a long time ago, and he's been hurt enough at the hands of other people." Tom said. "Didn't feel the need to add to it."

Jack sat in silence for a little while, his thoughts impossible for Tess to read. And, really, what difference did it make. The story that had brought them to where they were wasn't the story she'd hoped it would be.

"Is this why Old Joe has never married, Granddad?"

Tom's nod was slow, pained.

"But that was so long ago," Jack argued. "Surely Old Joe isn't still blaming himself."

"It's more like he never got over what he thought Dorothy was."

"But she *wasn't* what he thought. Not even close. Surely he can see that now, right?"

"It doesn't matter if he can or can't." Tess stood, the excitement she'd felt upon their arrival long gone. In its place was a pain so raw and so familiar it took every ounce of restraint she could muster to be the voice of a man she'd never met yet understood completely. "If he could be that wrong about something he believed with his whole heart *before,* why would he put himself in that position ever again?"

"Because that was sixty-some-odd years ago and it wasn't his fault!" Jack laced his fingers behind his head in frustration. "What's that thing you're always saying to me, Granddad? Something about a bad apple and"—he snapped—"I know! One bad apple does not a bushel make."

Tom grabbed hold of a cane tucked discreetly against the far side of his chair and worked himself forward, stopping just shy of actually standing. "Well, now I know you've at least *heard* me, which is a step in the right direction . . . But even so, as true as I know that expression to be, I also know that if one apple was bad enough to make you sicker than you've ever been in your life, you're not going to try another unless you're absolutely sure it's a good one."

"Which you can't be," Tess said, stepping forward to assist Jack's grandfather. "Ever."

Bypassing his cane in favor of Tess's hand, the elderly man stood, steadied himself, and held fast to her gaze. "*I* can be. And I am."

"You can be and you are *what,* Granddad?"

"Sure of one apple, at least. Two if you count Old Joe."

CHAPTER 24

"So?" Jack asked as he backed the truck down the driveway and onto the empty, two-lane rural county road that fronted his grandfather's yard. "On to Old Joe's place now?"

Shaking her head, Tess lassoed her thoughts away from the feel of his arm across the seatback behind her, skirted them around the unsettling way in which his grandfather had seemed to read her in a way she didn't want to be read, and laser-focused them onto safer, if not disappointing, territory. "No, there's no need. My hunch proved to be completely off base."

"You sure?"

She didn't mean to sigh, but she couldn't stop it, either. "I'm sure."

"Sorry." His fingers brushed the back of her hair ever so gently as he retrieved his hand for a farewell wave to his grandfather and to shift the truck out of reverse and into drive. "Still, it was a really cool story, don't you think? It sure had me hanging on my granddad's every word."

"It was quite a story, no doubt," she murmured.

"So do something with it, anyway, no?" He lowered their respective windows and then headed west, his gaze moving back and forth between the road and Tess. "Surely we're not the only ones who would find that story intriguing. And who knows? Maybe it would lead to a viable tip even after all these years."

"My boss sent me here to learn and write about the Amish of today, not sixty-four years ago."

"But you knew that time frame when you were all excited at first, right?"

She took in the English houses and driveways for a few moments and then rested her head against the seatback. "Because I thought it was going to lead me back to the present day and it didn't."

"I see."

"And now I'm back to square one in terms of trying to *knock it out of the ballpark* for my boss."

"No pressure, though, right?" he said, laughing. "My boss says that kind of stuff to me, too."

She opened her mouth to tell him it was Murph who said it, not Sam, but, really, what difference did it make? Murph said it, Sam expected it, and it was looking more and more like she'd be hard-pressed to make it happen. Instead, she turned her attention back outside and to the tracts of land that became larger as they crossed back into the more Amish-heavy areas.

They drove in silence for a while, each lost in their own thoughts. For her, it was about revisiting, again and again, the way Jack's grandfather had seemed to be able to see right through to everything she didn't want him or anyone else to see. In the moment, she'd been stunned. But now, there was a growing restlessness that had her feeling off-kilter somehow and—

"Hey, would you mind if we stopped by to see Joe real quick, anyway?" he asked. "I think hearing all that stuff got me feeling a little bad, and I'd just like to check in on him. We won't stay long, and it's not all that far out of the way if I make this turn up here at the stop sign."

Oh how she wanted to say no—to ask him to just bring her back to the farm. But she couldn't. He'd spent a huge chunk of his day chauffeuring her from useless whim to useless whim, and the least she could do in return was humor him this one time.

"Sure. That's fine," she said, shrugging. "For a little while, I guess."

"Fantastic. Thank you!" At the stop sign, he turned left. "Like Granddad said, Old Joe lives behind the filling station you'll see as we come around the next bend. He's got a little shop where he fixes just about anything that's broken. In fact, I've lost many an hour watching him put things back together."

She made herself nod and act like she was all in on the small talk, but she wasn't. Not really, anyway. Instead, her thoughts kept conjuring up apples, and bushels, and—

"Man, it just kills me to think that Old Joe has been by himself all these years because of some girl he fell for when he was a *teenager*." Jack eased up on the gas pedal as they rounded the bend. "I mean isn't time supposed to heal all wounds eventually?"

"Betrayal is just . . . It's just *different*. It destroys your trust in the one"—closing her eyes momentarily, she steadied her breath, her voice—"*or ones* who betrayed you, sure. But it also destroys your trust in yourself."

Slowing the truck to a crawl, they inched their way past the filling station and then onto a narrow dirt lane framed by overgrown trees and brush. "But it was Dorothy and this Carl guy who were in the wrong, not Old Joe," Jack protested. "They were the bad ones, not Joe."

"But *he picked them*."

The second she closed her mouth, she regretted having opened it in the first place. It wasn't that the words themselves weren't true, because they were. But it was the emotion with which she'd said them that had earned her the full weight of Jack's questioning eyes.

"Is that it?" she asked, rushing to point his attention away from her and onto the simple yet neat-as-a-pin cottage that was now no more than three car lengths away.

"Yeah, that's it but—"

"Oh, and that must be his workshop, yes?" She shifted her finger toward the equally neat shed with the wooden sign bearing the name

Joe's Fix-It Place. At Jack's muted assent, she unclicked her seat belt and waited for the truck to come to a complete stop. "This isn't what I envisioned. At all."

He cut the engine. "How so?"

"I don't know, I guess I was expecting something old and maybe a little dilapidated. More like the filling station—which *is* exactly as I envisioned."

"I'm not sure how much faith I'd put in someone's ability to fix things if, well, they couldn't fix things," he said, sweeping his hand toward both the house and the shed.

Her answering laugh sounded a tad forced even to her own ears, but in lieu of the conversation she'd successfully avoided, it worked. "So? Should we see if he's home?" she asked.

"He's here. He's always here. Listen . . ."

Sure enough, the silence she'd rushed to fill just moments earlier was just as quickly broken by a steady tapping from the vicinity of the workshop. "He's hammering something," she said.

"Sounds like it. Let's go."

Stepping around the front of the truck, they headed in the direction of the shed, the continued *tap-tap* all the guidance they needed. "Hello? Joe? It's Jack—Jack Cloverton."

The tapping ceased in favor of footsteps across wood and, seconds later, the soft creak of the door and its reveal of a man clearly the same age as Jack's grandfather. Like Tom, the man sported a thick crop of hair and relied on the assistance of glasses to see what needed to be seen. Unlike Tom, though, the man moved with an ease that defied their shared age.

"Jack!" Stepping down onto the flagstone walkway that served both the house and the workshop, Joe Wilder bypassed Jack's hand in favor of a strong hug. "How have you been, son?"

"Good. Busy at work."

"Great . . . great." Joe released his hold on Jack to turn his welcoming smile on Tess. "And I see you brought a friend. Hello, and welcome. I'm Joe."

"And I'm Tess—Tess Baker."

"Tess," he repeated as if commanding it to memory. "I take it one or both of you needs something fixed?"

Jack shook his head. "Actually, we were out at Granddad's a little while ago, and I realized it's been far too long since I stopped by to say hi."

"Well, isn't this a treat then." Reaching behind his back, Joe removed his tool belt and set it just inside the shed door. "I guess this explains why I felt called to make a pitcher of lemonade this morning."

Jack was waving his hands before Joe was done speaking. "We don't want to keep you from your work. I just wanted to check in and make sure you're doing okay, that's all."

"I'm fine, son. But Tess and I could use us a nice glass of lemonade, isn't that right, Tess?"

There was something infinitely appealing about Joe Wilder that went far beyond his warm welcome. What it was, exactly, she wasn't sure. But it was there, and it was strong, and it had her nodding along with the man even though she wasn't the slightest bit thirsty at that moment.

"I guess we're staying for some lemonade then," Jack said, grinning. "Lead the way, Joe."

The walk to the house, while short, took them past well-tended flower beds and a doghouse crafted and painted to resemble a miniature beachside cottage in everything from the color scheme and nautical detailing to the faux seagull that sat on its roof. She slowed down to take in the canine owner's name spelled out across the top of the doorway in pieces of a captain's wheel.

"Did you make this, Joe?" she asked as she crouched down for a closer took. "It's incredible."

"I did. I'd been seeing that place in my head for decades and figured if it wasn't in the cards for me, why not make a version of it for Bailey."

Jack cocked his head toward the backyard as if listening for something, and then shifted his gaze in the direction they'd just come. "Where *is* Bailey? Shouldn't he have been waiting by my truck when I got out?"

"I lost Bailey four months ago, son. Died in his sleep."

"Aw, Joe, I'm sorry," Jack said. "I didn't know."

There was something about Joe's answering shrug that tore at her heart. The movement, while simple enough, spoke of a grief that went far beyond the loss of a treasured companion to an emptiness he'd become gifted at hiding behind a ready smile, a welcoming demeanor, and a well-kept home.

"So how's the home-building business going, Jack?"

"Great. My boss just picked up a tract of land we're going to start building homes on in the next few months." Jack took control of door-holding duty so Joe could lead Tess into the small yet tidy kitchen.

A peek in the sink as she passed by revealed a single glass and plate to go with the single counter stool and place mat. Nearby, a hardcover thriller novel sat waiting to resume its role as faithful dining companion.

At the doorway to a darkened sitting room, Joe motioned Tess and Jack toward a plaid couch while he hurried to open window blinds she suspected were rarely opened. In fact, if she were to guess, Joe Wilder spent little time sitting on the couch. Instead, he likely went from bed to his workshop and back again each day with only an occasional stop in the kitchen for sustenance as needed.

Maybe, when Bailey was alive, he hadn't

shunned inactivity as much, but without the dog, the need to keep self-reflection time to a minimum meant staying busy, busy, busy . . .

"There we go. Can't have you thinking I live in a cave." Joe waited for them to take a seat and then excused himself just long enough to retrieve three glasses and the pitcher of lemonade from his refrigerator. When everyone had a glass, he took a seat across from them and smiled at Tess. "I'm going to go out on a limb and say you're not from around here, Tess. Am I right?"

"You are. I live in Connecticut, actually."

He leaned back, took a sip of his drink, and deposited the glass on a table near his left elbow. "See, now I was expecting you to say you were from the Midwest somewhere."

"I spent the first half of my childhood in Missouri," she said across the rim of her own glass.

"Okay, yes. I thought so."

Jack looked from Joe to Tess, and back again, his eyebrow inching upward. "Okay, so what am I missing? How did you know that?"

"I can't put a finger on it, exactly. It was just a sense." Joe leaned back, tented his fingers beneath his chin, and took a slow, measured breath. "So what brings you here, to New Holland, Tess?"

"To *New Holland* specifically? That would be Jack's time machine for all things local." She took a quick sip of lemonade, liked it enough to go back for a second, and then rested the glass back on her leg. "To *Blue Ball* where I'm staying? That would be my job. I'm a writer for *In Depth* magazine."

He shifted his full attention to Jack. "Time machine?"

"A-k-a Granddad."

"Ahhh," Joe said, grinning. "I thought for a moment you'd kept that old refrigerator box of your grandmother's we painted together when you were barely taller than my hip."

Dropping his elbows onto his knees, Jack leaned forward with a laugh. "Wow. I forgot all about that box." He glanced over at Tess. "I had this supercool teacher when I was in fourth grade who was all about making history fun. He assigned everyone a time period to bring to life for our classmates. I got the mid eighteen hundreds."

"Laura Ingalls's time!" she said.

"Pretty much," Jack conceded. "So my grandmother made a period-appropriate outfit for me to wear, Granddad made an old slate tablet for me to show what kids wrote on in school back then, my mom taught me how to make butter in a baby food jar, and Old Joe here helped me make a time machine everyone could use to transport themselves back to my time period. Needless to say, I got an A plus."

"I imagine you would've," she said, winking across at a still-smiling Joe. "While I never thought to make a time machine, I had fun with a refrigerator box when I was little, too. Only I turned mine into a magic box equipped with a secret door in the back. I managed to convince a neighborhood kid I'd actually made myself disappear until his older brother came looking for him for dinner and blew my hiding place wide open."

She liked the sound of Joe's laugh. It was warm and comfortable and genuine. Like . . . *Jack's?*

Pushing the thought aside, she took advantage of the good-natured banter between the two to really take in the room. To her left was a bookcase brimming with thriller novels and the occasional history-based tome. To her right, beyond Jack's head, she could see the framed sketch of a windmill standing proudly in the middle of a field. And along a shelf on the far wall, she spied a clock and a few seashells on either side of it.

"So, did it work, Tess?"

At the sound of her name, she returned her focus to their host. "I'm sorry, I was admiring your collection of seashells, and I think I may have lost the conversation for a moment."

Joe waved away her words and, instead, looked over his shoulder at the same shelf before turning back to Tess. "You like seashells, too?"

"I like anything that makes me think of the

ocean," she said. "Even doghouses, apparently."

"As do I." He seemed to disappear from the room for a moment, but when he finally reengaged eye contact, he was fully present once again. "Did Jack's grandfather make a good 'time machine'?"

"He did. But it didn't take me where I thought it would."

"I'm sorry to hear that," Joe said, widening his gaze to include Jack, as well. "Is there something *I* might be able to help with seeing as how I've lived here my whole life, too?"

She traded glances with Jack. "No, no. It's okay. It's just—"

"Tess is right, Joe. There's no sense in making you revisit all of that again. She thought it was going to lead somewhere very different than it did."

"It?" Joe asked.

Squirming under the weight of his curiosity, Tess forced her eyes back to the shelf and prayed Joe's would follow. "So, did those seashells all come from the same beach, or different beaches entirely?"

"The same beach." Joe slid his own attention onto Jack. "How far back did you have to go?"

She met Jack's eye and led it down to his wrist-watch.

"How far, son?" Joe repeated.

"Sixty . . . *ish* years."

"Sixty*ish* or sixty-*four?*" At Jack's barely perceptible nod, Joe palmed his mouth, held it there a beat, and then dropped his hand down onto his armrest. "Why is *In Depth* magazine interested in missing money from sixty-four years ago?"

"They're *not. I'm* not," she said, between swallows. "I-I just came across it while looking for something else during that same time frame."

"I see . . ."

"Joe, tell me you don't still blame yourself for going that night," Jack said.

Tilting his chin upward, Joe stared up at the ceiling, his very aura an answer in and of itself. "I knew Tom wasn't going with me that night because of Carl. He didn't like him. Didn't trust him. And I didn't, either. I'd seen plenty of examples at school to know this kid's moral compass was lacking. But Carl got wind of where we were going, and he was determined to go along. I guess I knew on some level I didn't want him there, either, but I was so focused on just being there, and seeing her—even from a distance—that I didn't pay it the due it deserved. And when your granddad backed out, I saw only that Carl was still going, not the why behind Tom's decision not to."

Jack held up his hands in an attempt to stop his grandfather's friend from going down what was clearly a road littered with painful memories. "You were what? Sixteen? Seventeen?"

"I was just shy of eighteen."

"Okay, and you wanted to see a girl you had a crush on. I'm pretty sure that's—"

Pushing off his chair, Joe wandered over to the window. "It was more than just a crush, son. I loved that girl. Loved her the moment I stepped up to the counter at that ice cream parlor and she asked me what she could get for me. I knew, in that moment, she was my person."

"At seventeen you did, sure," Jack countered.

"It had nothing to do with my age." Slowly, and with obvious effort, the man turned around, his steps back to his chair heavy. "But I don't expect people to get it. Most don't. And I pity them for that."

Tess stared at their host. "You *pity* them? Really?"

"Of course. To know someone is your person? And to have them know you are theirs? It's—"

"A complete farce." She pulled back at the truth she hadn't meant to share aloud in that moment but found that she couldn't stop there, either. "You can only know your own thoughts and feelings, and your own level of commitment. But someone else's? No, you can't ever fully know that. So why bother?"

Jack turned to her, his brow furrowed, his mouth partially gaped. "Wow. So I take it you won't be quitting your job to write romance novels anytime soon, eh?"

"What?" she asked, feigning surprise. "*Once*

upon a—run! Run! Trust me, don't go there. The end . . . You don't think that would sell?"

"Yeah, probably not."

Shrugging, Tess turned back to Joe and pulled a face. "*I* would buy that book, wouldn't you?"

"No, because *I* would rather have known a love like that for even just a little while than to never feel it at all," Joe mused, eyeing her closely.

"If it was real, maybe . . ."

"If you felt it, it was real."

"No!" She rocketed up and off the couch, earning her a healthy dose of surprise from Jack in the process. But she didn't care. "Love is a two-way street, Joe! Commitment is a two-way street! Respect is a two-way street!"

"Okay, and what about *the hurt?* Is that only real if it impacts *both* parties, too?" He followed her around the room with eyes that saw more than she wanted them to see. "Maybe you're right. Maybe I was deluding myself about her feelings for me all those years ago. But I know *my* love was real, and I know I haven't felt like that for anyone else since."

"Have you *let* yourself?" Jack asked.

"It's not about letting myself, son. It's about not finding anyone that touches my heart the way my Lottie Dottie did."

The punch of Joe's words stopped her dead in her tracks. "What did you just say?"

"It's not about letting myself? It's—"

"I thought her name was *Dorothy,*" she rasped.

The smile that started in one small corner of the elderly man's mouth soon grew to claim his eyes, as well. "It was. But to me she was—and always will be—my Lottie Dottie."

CHAPTER 25

"Tess?"

Looking up from the business card she wasn't seeing, Tess made herself focus enough to take in Jack's worried brow. "Yes?"

"Are you okay? You really seemed to check out there at the end."

"I'm . . ." Her answer trailed off as she looked beyond Jack to the steering wheel, the windshield, and, finally, the country road in front of them, her memory of actually getting in the truck sketchy at best.

"You two seemed to have a real connection," he said, commanding her attention once again. "That's why I didn't have the heart to tell him you wouldn't be sticking around long enough to need *that*."

She followed the nudge of his gaze back to the simple white square in her hands.

Joe's Fix-It Place
"Fixing What Needs Fixing"
New Holland, PA

"Sadly ironic, isn't it?"

"What is?" she asked, running her fingers across the raised lettering.

309

"His slogan."

She read the card again. "Why? Is he not good at fixing stuff?"

"No, he's amazing at fixing stuff. For *other* people."

"Meaning?"

"He's a great guy, Tess. He's kind, he's smart, he's motivated, and he's creative. Yet he can't fix the part of him that someone broke sixty-four years ago."

She looked from the card to Jack, and, finally, to the string of farms passing by her window in a never-ending sea of green. "Part of me wants nothing more than his precious"—she pulled a face at her window—"*Lottie Dottie* to see the profound effect she's had on his life. But people who can do what she did so cavalierly don't care about anyone's feelings but their own."

"I guess." Something about his shift in tone called her back into the truck's cabin in time to watch him drape his wrist over the wheel and sigh. "Me? I try to see someone like that as one person out of many. But, yeah, even so, I . . ." Shaking his head, he looked out his window and sighed again. "It doesn't matter. Life is about rolling with the punches, right? You get knocked down, you get back up, you move on. It should be so easy, but it's not."

"It is, if you're ready for them when they come."

"What? The *punches?*" he asked, glancing between her and the road.

"Yes."

"How, pray tell, do you think you can do that?"

"You gather information."

"Information?"

"Sure. If you know what triggers the punches, you can avoid them." She tilted her head against the seatback and blew out a labored breath of her own. "And if you don't, you end up mucking stalls instead of scuba diving along the Great Barrier Reef. Consequence for an action, as they say."

"Fair enough. But I'm pretty sure Joe couldn't have prepared for his punch."

"He wasn't quite eighteen. He didn't know yet. But he hasn't gotten punched like that again . . ."

"Because he hasn't gotten back in the ring."

Parting company with the headrest, she shrugged. "Exactly."

"Whoa. Hold on a minute," he said, continuing his back-and-forth between the road and Tess. "You're saying the way he's lived the past sixty-four years is *okay?*"

"No, of course not. I hated hearing the way he still talks about her. She's not worth the energy. But he has a job he's good at, and a fascination with the beach that makes him happy, and—if he could just let that be enough—he'd be fine."

"I like my job, and I like taking trips, but even

311

I know I'd rather share those things with . . ." Jack's words bowed first to a laugh and then to the faintest shake of his head. "Wow. If only my granddad could hear me now. He'd be patting himself on the back in pride."

"Your grandfather?" she echoed. "Why?"

"He's been after me to get back in the saddle, so to speak, and I've been resisting—saying I'm fine, and that I don't need anyone, and all the usual deflection stuff one says after they've been burned. But honestly? Watching Brad's kid and how happy she is *not* holding on to anger, and, now, knowing the full story behind why Joe is the way Joe is, it's making me . . ." He raked his hand through his hair. "I don't know. It's just making me think, I guess. I mean, Emma isn't bitter. At all."

Tess, again, looked out at the passing landscape, the scattered livestock and occasional farmhouse little more than a blip in her conscious thought. "She should be. Very much so. People she had every reason to believe she could trust betrayed her horribly."

"True. But if she had gotten mad and lashed out the way you or I think she should've, would she be the happy person she is today? And what about the people around her—her husband, her baby? Would they be as happy as they are if she had chosen the bitter route? And what about Brad? The only way he might have benefitted from

312

Emma being bitter is that he'd have had her all to himself. But then what? If she was bitter, she wouldn't be fully open to what he has to offer, and that would end up hurting him—and her—in the long run."

"So the people who essentially kidnapped her get a free pass?" Tess argued, turning back to Jack. "They get to go on never being punished for what they did?"

"I don't know. I just know that *Emma* chose happiness over bitterness, and it looks really good on her."

He slowed to accommodate, and then safely pass, three separate buggies, each filled to capacity. A little girl in the back of the third buggy smiled shyly at Jack's wave. "Looks like folks are starting to wrap it up and head home. Which means by the time I get you back to Isaiah and Naomi's, they should be—"

"What about Joe?"

"What about Joe?" he countered.

"Do you think he should just forgive her?"

"I think he *has,* don't you?"

"He shouldn't. Her actions and her cruelty have put a cloud over his entire life. And because of that, all of the truly good things in his life are forever muted for him."

Another burst of buggy traffic mandated another slowdown, another need to pass. When they were safely on their way again, he loosened

313

his grip on the wheel. "Look, I don't like the muting thing, either. Trust me. But if he'd gone the route of bitterness, I'm doubting that doghouse would look the way it does, and I'm doubting he'd be inviting people in for lemonade, and I'm doubting he'd be the kind of guy who'd help a kid make a time machine for his fourth grade social studies project."

"Maybe. Maybe not." She turned back to the window and the breeze. "Would you want to get even if you could?"

"With?"

"The person who burned you."

His answering laugh held none of its usual richness. "Heh. I'd be lying if I said that thought never entered my mind. Because it did—many times. Still does, every now and again, especially when"—his momentary silence propelled her gaze back to his—"I see what I'm missing out on because I'm holding myself back."

"No, because she burned you," she corrected.

He palmed his mouth, held it there for a moment, and then returned his hand to the steering wheel with a grunt. "It's funny how clearly I'm hearing myself in you right now," he mused.

"Hearing yourself in *me?*"

"In you. In your words. Everything you're saying is all the same things I've been saying to Granddad for months. Yet now that I'm not sitting across from him on the patio . . . or at a table in the pub . . . or a chessboard in his living room, I'm finally *hearing* him. Hearing *myself*. And you know what? He's right. I may be holding myself back because she burned me, but I'm missing out because *I'm* holding myself back."

"Semantics."

"I don't think so." He slowed to a stop at another four-way intersection, waited for a truck to cross in front of them, and then continued, his eyes fixed on the road even though it was clear his thoughts were taking him somewhere very different. "I got hurt. There's no denying that. But sitting around, spending my time and my energy waiting for her to get hers? I'm better than that. I've seen who she is now, so why would I want that back, you know? And as for the whole eye-for-an-eye thing, doesn't that just end up blinding us both?"

"Don't you want her to hurt the way she hurt you?" Tess asked.

He moved his head as if weighing her words. "No. I want to be happy."

"See, now I think this whoever-she-is finally getting a dose of her own medicine *would* make you happy."

"For a moment, maybe . . . But then the person my folks raised me to be would rear his head, and I'd feel bad because that's not who I am. So it's time to move forward and find my happy."

She studied him for a moment. *"Find* your happy? Why? Don't you like your job?"

"I love my job. I love building houses that are going to become someone's home. Like Emma and Levi's place . . . I helped Brad and Levi build that, and now it's this place where Emma and Levi are raising their son, and where they gather their family together for special meals, and where her friends come to see her—like that day I saw you there. What's not to love about that?"

"Okay, so you have your happy."

"C'mon, Tess, a job doesn't make a life."

"You haven't met Murph. His job at the magazine is his life."

"And when he goes home?"

"He sleeps."

"And on the weekends?" Jack asked.

"He's at the office."

"And you think that's normal?"

She sighed. "I think it's smart. Everything about his life is in his hands. No one can come along and mess it up. And he's a veritable legend in the business. The reception area and most of the hallways in the building have his awards hanging on the wall."

"And if he ever gets sick? You think that job is going to hold his hand? Or those awards are going to be any real comfort?"

"No. But at least he knows what is and what isn't right up front, instead of blindly believing something *is* only to be blindsided into knowing it *never was*."

She felt the truck slow once again and was surprised to realize they'd reached Naomi's farm. A glance down the driveway as Jack turned in yielded no sign of Isaiah's buggy, but that was okay. She needed time to think, to plan, to—

"Tess?"

Glancing at the dashboard, she tried to gauge the likelihood Murph would still be awake. She had so much to tell him, to—

"Tess?"

She slipped Joe's card inside her tote bag and then readied her hand on the door as Jack pulled to a stop in front of the Grossdawdy Haus. "Thanks for taking me to the coffee shop, and everywhere else we went today. It was exactly what I needed."

"I'm glad. I had fun, too. But, Tess?"

"Yes?"

"Maybe, for as long as you're here, anyway, you could try to be a little more open to stuff outside the job. Just to see . . ."

She drew back. "Excuse me?"

"Look, I can't know what happened with your ex-husband unless you choose to tell me. But what I *do* know is that he's just *one* guy and—"

"You're right. You don't know." She pushed open her door and stepped down onto the driveway, all thoughts of Murph and her story

317

and more Belize-like assignments in the future temporarily sidelined by near-blinding anger. "And that *one* guy, as you say? Yeah, no . . . My job is so much more than enough."

"Tess, I don't think—"

"Goodbye, Jack."

CHAPTER 26

It had taken six, maybe seven laps around the interior of the Grossdawdy Haus before her fist-clenching anger downgraded to a more general irritation, but it was a step in the right direction. Yes, Jack had been way out of line in his recommendations for her life, but, really, what did it matter? Soon, she'd be out the door and on her way back to her life—a life that was quite fine, thankyouverymuch.

First, though, she had a story to write. And, oh, what a story it was shaping up to be . . . Betrayal, deceit, heartache—it had it all.

Finally giving into the squeal she'd had to stifle in Joe's living room, Tess reached inside her tote bag and pulled out her phone. A check of the time and the realization that Murph was likely sleeping had her hesitating on sending him a text for all of about a second.

> You awake?
> I've found something!
> Something really, really good!

She pressed Send and waited.
One minute . . .
Two minutes . . .

Three—

"Murph, you're awake!" she said, pressing the phone to her ear.

"I am now."

She knew that was her cue to feel bad, but it missed its mark. Instead, she began pacing the house again, powered this time by pure excitement. "I found it! I found my story! And, Murph? It's a doozy!"

The sleepy fog that was his voice just seconds earlier parted. "Do I need to move my outfielders out into the road?"

"Actually, even if they're standing in the next town over there will be no catching *this* ball."

"Nice!" A series of grunts in her ear let her know he was on the move, likely leaving whatever he'd been sleeping on in favor of the open air and, thus, a place to smoke. The sound of a door opening and shutting, followed soon after by an audible inhale, let her know her assumptions were more likely right than wrong. "So, what do you got?"

"You're sure you're ready?" she teased. "Because if you want to go back to bed, I can wait."

"Oh. Cool. Okay, yeah, let's do that. Talk to you—"

"Don't you dare hang up!"

"Then start talking. Pronto."

"So do you remember that woman I told you

about?" she asked, tightening her grip on the phone. "The English one that all these Amish women seem to think is so wise?"

"Miss Lottie, right?"

"Yes, good memory!"

"Former Amish?" he added. "Left when she was a teen? Came back to the area after being gone for a while?"

"Now you're just showing off. But yes, that's the one!"

Another inhale, another long exhale. "Tell me, kid."

"She's not at all what they think she is!"

"Okay . . ."

Tess toed the bench back from the table and dropped onto it only to return to her feet in favor of a little aimless pacing. "She didn't leave because her older brother was banned."

"He wasn't banned?"

"I don't know. Maybe he was, maybe he wasn't. It doesn't matter."

Another inhale. Another exhale. "I'm still listening, still waiting . . ."

"She stole money from her father's house—money that had been raised to help some Amish kid who'd been severely burned in a barn fire."

The next inhale that had begun in her ear ceased. "What kind of money are we talking about?"

"Just shy of twenty thousand dollars. Which, sixty-four years ago, was probably a lot of money."

"It was. Keep going."

"She had an accomplice. An English teenager. He didn't return to school the next day, and she up and left the Amish, never to be seen or heard from again until she showed back up almost forty years later."

"No one recognized her?"

"She was seventeen when she left. She came back in her late fifties. She's eighty, eighty-one now. She was Dorothy Miller when she left, but goes by Lottie Jenkins now and—one second . . ." Tess made a beeline back into the kitchen for her notebook and pen, made a story note to herself on a fresh page, and then returned her attention to her colleague. "Sorry about that. I thought about something I need to look into and wanted to jot it down before it gets pushed to a back burner. But that's done now, so where were we again?"

"I was asking whether anyone recognized her?"

"Oh . . . right . . . Okay, so she fessed up about her Amish ties to the twins at some point, but these people wouldn't think to dig for more details. They take everything and everyone at face value. She left before baptism so she could maintain a relationship with the older brother who left after baptism. Period. End of story for them. Besides, the missing money was simply that—missing money. The Amish didn't seem all that interested in finding out who took it. They just set their mind to raising the money again."

"You have an eyewitness?"

"Close enough." At his audible sigh, she prattled on. "It's why she left, I know it. But that's not really my main angle here. Yes, she stole—from a kid who ended up dying from his wounds, no less! But now, here she is, sixty-four years later, deceiving the Amish once again."

"By not telling them?"

"By not telling them, sure, but also by presenting herself as this kindly old woman who opens her heart and her door to all who are troubled. Naomi actually refers to this woman as a *friend to all!*"

"From what you've told me about her so far, she *is,* isn't she?"

"Uh, they think she is," Tess said, pressing the phone even harder against her cheek. "But clearly she's lying to them about everything. And why? I mean, what's she up to now? What's her game *this* time around?"

Another inhale. Another, longer exhale. "She's actually helped these women, yes?"

"I don't know. I guess—I mean, Katie seems to think so. And Emma seems to think so. And Danielle seems to think so. But what difference does that make? She's deceiving them, Murph! She's portraying herself as their friend! And all the while she's lying to them about something as basic as who she is!"

"You said they know she is former Amish."

"*Now,* maybe. But she hasn't told them she's

a thief!" Tess moved from room to room, barely registering her surroundings. "Don't you think they should know that? Because I sure do."

She waited for him to say something, but there was only silence.

Pulling the phone away for a moment, she verified they were still connected. "Murph? Can you still hear me?"

"I can hear you just fine, kid." He took another drag of his cigarette. "But have you not felt the same lightness I've been hearing from you off and on since you've been there?"

"What are you talking about?"

"Like the other day, after you baked with them . . . You were *happy,* kid."

"I've always liked to bake, you know that."

"When you first started at the magazine, sure. I gained ten pounds your first two weeks in the office. But that all stopped when—"

"So I helped make some cookies yesterday and it was fun. Why is this even part of our conversation right now? Don't you hear what I'm telling you about my story?"

"It wasn't just the act of baking that had you so happy yesterday. It was being with those women and having fun."

Tess stopped in front of the window and looked out into the gathering dusk. "I'm pretty sure if I said that, it was because you asked."

"It wasn't what you may or may not have said

in response to a question, kid. It was everything else—your tone, your lightness, your voice, your aura."

"My aura?" She spun back toward the kitchen for yet another loop of the two rooms. "Which you can sense from the other side of the world? C'mon, Murph, just stop. Can't we just get back to the whole reason I woke you up in the first place? *Please?*"

He exhaled long and hard. "I never strayed off that."

"You just—" Pausing midway back to the living room, she collapsed onto the less than comfortable sofa and groaned. "Okay. Fine . . . While I don't know why any of this matters right now, yes, I felt some lightness, as you call it, when we were making cookies. Big deal."

"And earlier? When you met those twins? It was the same way."

Was it? She couldn't really remember . . . Then again, she'd liked them, liked their banter and the way they'd made her feel at ease.

"It's easy to forget things here," she conceded. "It's probably just being in a place where he never was, you know?"

"You're talking about Brian, right?"

She rolled her eyes. "Yes, though I'd rather not be. But since you keep harping on this lightness you've picked up in me a few times, I'm addressing the likeliest *why* behind it."

"It's allowed you to really put Brian and Mandy—and what they did—behind you," he mused.

Again she returned to her feet for yet another round of pacing. "For the umpteenth time, Murph, I put those two behind me a long time ago. Which is why I don't need them seeping into all these conversations with you. I want to talk about my job. I want to talk about this story! It's really got some potential to be something."

"You really think people are going to care all that much about money that went missing sixty-four years ago? Because they might, for a minute, but it's not the kind of subject that's going to stick with them the way I think you'd like it to."

The same anger that had propelled her around the room in the wake of Jack's unsolicited life advice was back. "If you'd let me get some momentum here, you'd realize the story isn't about the money. It's about someone who has made betraying people a way of life for decades. I mean think about it, Murph! These women trust her! They believe she cares about them! They practically sing her praises—or as much as the Amish sing the praises of anything besides God! And she's not what they think she is. Not even close. She's—"

"She's *your Mandy* in this situation. And they're *you*. I get it."

His words stopped her cold. "That's not true! That's . . ." She lowered herself onto the wooden bench and ran her free hand atop her still-open notebook. "If exposing this liar for what she really is saves these women even an ounce of the heartache I felt, how can that be a bad thing? Because, as it is right now? When this paragon of virtue in their eyes eventually *dies,* they're going to mourn a person who isn't real! That's not okay! Not even close!"

The silence was back. "Murph?"

"I'm here."

Retrieving her pen, she drew a small star next to her question about Lottie's last name while she waited for something that never came. "Thoughts? Input? Anything?" she prodded.

"I'm just trying to wrap my head around the irony of all this, kid, that's all."

"What irony?"

"You. Going from betrayed to betrayer."

She stared at her pen . . . the paper . . . the front door, his words draining anything resembling warmth from her body. "I'm not betraying anyone!"

"Naomi? The twins? The one who was raised by her aunt and uncle? The widow with the baby?"

"I'm doing my job, Murph!" she said, slamming her pen down on the table. "I'm chasing the smoke like you have always told me to do! And

I'm telling the facts—facts people want *and need* to know!"

"Sixty-four years later? Does it really matter?"

She couldn't believe what she was hearing, or that she was having to explain that which needed no explanation. But she was hearing it, and, clearly, she did need to explain. "If it was just about the money, maybe you're right—maybe it wouldn't matter. But these people are genuine and kind and welcoming and . . ." She pulled the notebook closer and reclaimed her pen. "This woman being back here? Pretending to care about these people while knowing full well what she's done? It's a total slap in their face, Murph! It's a betrayal in the truest sense of the word! How is that okay? Wait, let me answer that. It's *not* okay! Not. Even. Close."

More silence. This time, though, she waited him out. She had nothing left to say. If he didn't get it, that was on him, not her.

"Well, I guess you've found what you wanted to find."

"I have."

"Then I wish you well with it, and I hope it brings you everything you're wanting it to bring."

"I want to prove to Sam that I'm good enough at what I do to go somewhere like Belize . . . I want to see my name on a plaque out in the reception area . . . I want to know that I've finally found my place, my thing in life . . ."

"And you want a little payback on the Mandys in this world," he said. "Perceived, or otherwise."

"If I can do that, too, why not?"

"Good question, kid. Good question."

CHAPTER 27

Tess wasn't entirely sure how long she'd been sitting there staring, unseeingly, at the now-blackened phone screen atop her notebook. Maybe a minute, maybe ten. It didn't really matter, though. All she really knew for certain was that the limited light still filtering in through the window was fading faster than the residual irritation she couldn't quite shake. Murph had taken their usual fact-gathering ritual into territory that had felt a lot more like a personal attack. She wasn't taking on the part of betrayer. She was looking out for the betrayed. How Murph could miss *that* was inconceivable.

Then again, from the outside looking in, maybe the story about Miss Lottie could seem like Tess was trying to make something out of nothing. Maybe. But stories like this kept people glued to their television sets through entire seasons. Surely that kind of interest, that kind of fascination could and would translate to print.

There was the chance, of course, that the betrayer being eighty years old might not sit well with some of *In Depth* magazine's readers, but it being a pattern of behavior that spanned more than six decades would likely be enough to offset the age card in the end.

And the fact Miss Lottie's deception was aimed

at the Amish? A group of people known for their quiet and peaceful ways? Slam dunk, for sure . . .

Her mind made up, Tess reached inside the tote bag she'd yet to move off the table and pulled out her laptop. If she worked efficiently, she could easily settle on the lede to her story without using too much of the battery she'd charged at the coffee shop. Then, when she was satisfied with it, she could spend time with her notebook and the questions she still needed to answer before the rest of the story could be written.

She didn't relish the hurt she knew Katie and Hannah and Danielle and Emma would feel when they came face-to-face with the truth about Lottie Jenkins, née Dorothy Miller. But their hurt would be so much worse if they continued trusting this woman while Tess sat by and said nothing.

No. She simply couldn't and wouldn't do that. Murph would understand when he read the finished story.

Placing her fingers atop the keyboard, she began to type . . .

Amid the clip-clop of the horses and the snap of laundry drying on the line in Blue Ball, Pennsylvania, the fingers of deceit have

No.
She backspaced and began again . . .

In a place known for its unwritten honor code, deceit has been

No.
Again . . .

Amid the quiet Amish countryside in Blue Ball, Pennsylvania, a deception has been growing like an unseen cancer.

"Like an unseen cancer?" she murmured. "Uh, no."
She started again . . .

They said she was a friend to all. But really, Lottie Jenkins was a friend to none. Raised in

"Ugh. Ugh. Ugh."
A soft knock stole her attention from the back-space button and sent it toward the door's upper glass panel and its curtained view of the kapp-wearing figure standing on the other side. Rising, she stepped over the bench and made haste to open the door.

"Naomi, hi," she said, motioning the woman inside.

"It's late. I don't want to intrude. Especially when you're working."

She followed the woman's gaze back to

the table and the almost-garish glow of the computer against the last of the day's natural light. "I appreciate that, but I'm not being all that successful. Unfortunately."

"It will come, I am sure."

"Thanks." She looked beyond the woman to the horse Isaiah had unhitched from the buggy and was leading into the barn. "I didn't hear you come back. Did you have a nice day?"

"Yah. Did you?"

"I had a very *enlightening* day."

"That is good, yah?"

"Yah—I mean, yes. Very, very good."

"Will you still be doing *that*"—Naomi pointed Tess back to the glow of the computer—"tomorrow?"

"Writing? Yes. But don't worry. I'll get my morning chores done. As well as anything else you need me to do first."

Naomi nodded. "Katie, Emma, Danielle, and I would like you to come to the celebration tomorrow afternoon."

"Celebration?"

"Yah. We are having a birthday party, and we have many cookies and sandwiches still to share."

She ran through the names Naomi mentioned and narrowed in on one that was missing. "Is it Hannah's birth—no. It can't be. If it was Hannah's birthday, it would be Katie's birthday, too . . ."

"It is not Katie and Hannah's birthday."

"Oh, okay. You just didn't mention Hannah so I thought maybe it was some sort of surprise for her."

"Hannah went back to the big city Saturday night, after our day of baking."

"She did?" Surprised as much by the answering slump of her shoulders as the reason for it, Tess forced a carefree smile. "That's great!"

"Hannah left a letter and a gift inside a purple bag that Katie is to bring when she comes. But you do not have to worry about a gift. I will say mine is from the both of us, and that will please Miss Lottie."

"Miss Lottie?" Tess echoed.

"Yah. Tomorrow is Miss Lottie's birthday. She will be eighty-one." Naomi glanced back at her husband as he came out of the barn. "You will come, yah?"

"To a birthday celebration for Miss Lottie?"

"Yah." Again Naomi's gaze led Tess's back to the table and the computer. "When the celebration is over, you can get back to your work right away and I will send Reuben over with a dinner plate as I did the other night."

"I really shouldn't—"

"We would very much like you to come, Tess. And I am sure Miss Lottie would want you to be there, too. Especially now that she has met you, and spent time with you in her home."

It was on the tip of her tongue to challenge her host's assumption, but, then again, Naomi wasn't yet privy to everything Tess had uncovered about the beloved Miss Lottie. And, even more important, neither was Miss Lottie herself . . .

"Actually, on second thought, I'd love to come."

Smiling, Naomi clasped her hands together. "I'm so glad. Katie, Emma, and Danielle will be, too."

"Good." Tess returned the woman's smile with one borne on something very different than joy. "But don't worry about adding my name to your present, okay? I think I have the perfect gift for Miss Lottie."

"How wonderful! She'll be so surprised!"

"You have no idea," said Tess.

Tess rolled the lamp into the kitchen and sat back down in front of the darkened computer. There would be time to craft the perfect opening paragraph later. Now, her energy and her focus needed to be on how best to bring the truth to light.

She could go to the party for Miss Lottie and casually mention the missing money and how the Amish had worked hard to raise it for a little boy who'd been badly burned. Surely the woman would squirm at first mention . . .

She could take an even more laid-back approach and ask about instances when money had been raised for sick children and see how long it took before Miss Lottie grew restless . . .

She could wait for a moment when everyone was sitting together to press Miss Lottie about her decision to leave the Amish. Those questions had made the woman uneasy when it was just the two of them together; perhaps with more eyes watching, the show would be even better . . .

She could make a point of telling all of the women about the sweet and creative fix-it man she'd met the previous day, and then, when someone asked his name, she could look straight at Miss Lottie when she answered . . .

Or, maybe better yet, when it came time for Miss Lottie to open her gifts, Tess could hand her a wrapped box with Joe's business card inside . . .

There were so many good and viable options for how to let the cat out of the bag where Miss Lottie was concerned. The problem was how best to get the reaction she needed while making sure Miss Lottie got what she deserved.

Pulling her notebook into the spot vacated by her cast-aside computer, Tess studied the brief notation regarding Lottie's last name and grabbed her pen. Beneath it she began listing questions and thoughts as they popped into her head.

What happened to Carl? Did they stay together afterward? For how long?

What did they do with the money? How long had they planned it?

Did she ever feel any guilt over leading Joe along?

How did she assimilate into the English world without the same safety net she'd had during Rumspringa?

What's the game now that she's back?

Tess stopped, looked back at the last line, and considered its place on the list. Getting straight answers to the first few questions would be difficult enough. But asking a career con woman to come clean on her current game was sure to be an exercise in futility.

Then again, if Tess was as good at what she did as she knew herself to be, she could—*and she would*—find the answers to every one of her questions, with or without Lottie Jenkins.

"Look out, Belize," she whispered. "It's not over between us."

CHAPTER 28

It was a perfect day for a small outdoor gathering. The sun was shining, a gentle breeze was blowing, and the faintest hint of something floral played a game of cat and mouse with Tess's sense of smell. Every time she thought she had its source figured out, it would recede again. But that was okay, because in between each quick whiff she was busy helping Naomi put the finishing touches on Miss Lottie's birthday gathering.

The sandwiches were made, the cookies were waiting, and the cake frosted. The table Isaiah and the boys had carried into the backyard for them had been wiped and set. And the trio of roses Naomi had taken from her garden had been clipped and placed inside the drinking glass-turned-vase that now graced its center. But the readiest of all was Naomi, who flitted from detail to detail with the grace and lightness of a ballerina.

"It's fun to see you so happy," Tess mused, eyeing Naomi across the pitcher of milk she carried out of the house.

"Have I not looked happy before?"

"No, it's not like that. It's just"—she lowered the pitcher onto the table—"a different kind of happy. I don't really know how to describe it. I just know it's like the way you were on Saturday, when we were baking. And the way you were out at Emma's, too."

Understanding shimmered in the amber flecks dotting Naomi's hazel eyes. "God has blessed us both with good friends."

"Us both?"

"Emma and Katie and Danielle are now your friends, too, Tess."

"I've only know them for what—eight days?" Tess countered, stepping back from the table.

"You became my friend in the buggy that first day."

"I became someone *you'd met,*" she corrected. "And since then we've gotten to know one another better, but—"

"You haven't started eating cake without us, have you?"

Tess's gaze traveled to the side of the house and the familiar face rounding its corner.

"Emma, you're here!" Naomi hurried around the table and took a covered bowl from the young mother's hands.

"So is Danielle and Katie. They are moving very slow."

As if on cue, first Katie and then Danielle stepped around the house with full hands and matching smiles that rivaled the sun's brightness. "We are not moving slow, Emma. You're just moving extra fast because of Naomi's cake."

"Have you not eaten one of Naomi's cakes?" Emma asked, turning back to Katie. "Because if you had, you would move fast, too."

Katie met both Naomi's and Tess's eyes before rolling her own in amusement. "I have had Naomi's cakes many times. But I know that she would not be eating it before the birthday girl is even here." Katie stopped, glanced at the back door, and then back at Naomi. "Miss Lottie isn't here yet, right? We didn't see her car."

"She isn't. But soon, I am sure." Taking a plate from Danielle, Naomi peeked beneath its tin-foil covering. "Your special eggs look delicious, Danielle."

"I'm worried I might have forgotten something on account of being distracted by my daughter, but if so, I have a good excuse."

"You did not bring her?"

Danielle shook her head. "She wasn't up from her nap yet, so Caleb said he'd sit on my couch and read a book until she woke up, and then bring her to me here if she gets fussy."

"Does Grace even know how to fuss?" Katie asked.

"When she wants me to blow more bubbles, she sure does." Danielle stepped around Katie to hug Tess. "I'm glad you decided to come, Tess. I was hoping you would."

"She met Miss Lottie, remember? That means Tess knows how special she is," Emma said, ready with a hug for Tess when Danielle was done. "Don't you, Tess—oh! Miss Lottie! You're here!"

All eyes turned toward the side of the house and the elderly woman making her way in their direction. In a flash, plates were deposited onto the table in favor of swarming the gathering's guest of honor. Tess hung back, observing, processing, and committing it all to the mental notebook in her head.

The observer in her noted the obvious details about Miss Lottie: the gray hair, the wire-rimmed glasses, the simple pale blue dress, the sensible shoes, the tight grip atop the curved wooden cane, and the seemingly genuine smile that grew wider with each woman's warm embrace.

"Happy birthday, Miss Lottie," Naomi said, sweeping her hand, and the elderly woman's gaze, first toward the flower-topped table and then toward Tess. "And look who else wanted to be here for your special day—Tess!"

Aware of everyone's eyes, Tess offered up a quick wave as her greeting. "Happy birthday, Miss Lottie."

"Thank you, Tess. I'm glad you're here."

It sounded sincere, she'd give the octogenarian that. But she knew better. The memory of Tess's questions was there in the subtle dulling of Miss Lottie's smile—a smile Tess knew would be long gone by the time the party was over.

She managed what felt enough like a nod to appease those who might be watching and then stepped back to accommodate Naomi's path to the table's lone non–bench seat. "Come, sit, Miss Lottie. There are sandwiches and eggs for lunch, and we have things we would like to say to you on your special day."

"Good heavens, child, I didn't want you to make such a fuss." Miss Lottie took in the table and the women claiming spots on the bench around it, and then slowly, carefully sat down. "All this food? The flowers? You all being here? This makes me feel very special."

Danielle rested a gentle hand across Miss Lottie's. "You should. Because you are. To all of us. For so—*so* many reasons."

A chorus of *yahs* rang out around the table, followed by Naomi's sandwiches and Danielle's deviled eggs being passed around. When everyone's plate was filled, Naomi drew in a breath laden with unmistakable emotion. "Miss Lottie, when Isaiah wanted to get married, I was afraid. I knew I liked him, and I knew he was kind, but, still, I was afraid—afraid to not live with Mamm and Dat anymore. Afraid to have children of my own. Afraid of things that I know are silly now but didn't think were silly then. But you heard me crying by the pond that one day and you let me talk it all out, listening to every word I had to say. And when I was done, you told me it wasn't silly. That it was okay to be scared about leaving the only home I knew. That my mamm probably felt the same way before she married my dat and to look at how that all turned out.

"By the time I went home that day, I felt better—excited even. And that was because of you, Miss Lottie. Because you listened, and because you knew the right thing to say. Like always."

Miss Lottie patted Naomi's hand like one might a small child's. "There's no need to go over this now. It's in the past. You have made a wonderful home with Isaiah."

"And we"—Naomi motioned to Katie, and Emma, and Danielle—"have let you hush our attempts at thanking you for too long, Miss Lottie. But not today. *Today* we're going to make sure you know how you've touched each of us with your wisdom and your kindness."

Nodding along with the others, Katie leaned forward. "You listened to me, too, Miss Lottie. At a time when I really had no one else to turn to. Mamm had passed, Hannah was in New York, and I didn't know what to do about my drawings, and Hannah wanting me to move to New York to be with her, and Levi wanting to get married, and . . . *everything*. I'd convinced myself into believing that Hannah was the one with all the choices and that, because of Mamm's death and Dat needing someone to help with the children,

I had none. But somehow you helped me to see that I had a lot of choices in life and that I'd made some pretty big ones to that point. And because of you, and the way that you listened, and the things that you said and didn't say, I was able to clear my head and my heart enough to really see *me* and what matters most to *me*."

Shaking her head, Katie made herself take a breath. "And somehow you managed to do so without me having any idea what *you* thought I should do."

"Same for me," Emma interjected. "When I found out Mamm and Dat weren't my real mamm and dat, I was angry. I didn't want to talk to them and I didn't want to hear anything they had to say. I wanted to hurt them for keeping the truth from me my whole life. But you, Miss Lottie, you told me to never make decisions in anger, and that if I did not give them a chance to answer my questions, I would never know the whole truth. And you were right. I needed to *listen* to know the truth about what they'd done and why, and to know what my heart felt about it all so I could make the right choice for my life moving forward.

"And like Katie just said, I didn't—and still don't—know what you thought I should do about all of that."

Miss Lottie set the rest of her sandwich down on her plate. "They were not my decisions to make. They were yours—both of you. You made them on your own, as you should. It was your life, Katie. It was your life, Emma. Not mine. And, Naomi? You would have realized all the same things without me."

"Maybe," Naomi said with a gentle shrug. "But your kindness helped me to set aside the fear so I could realize it—and enjoy it all—so much sooner."

A quick yet strangled sob pulled all eyes onto Danielle in time to see the woman wiping a pair of tears from her cheeks. "I-I was so angry . . . and so very . . . *bitter* when I met you, Miss Lottie." Danielle stopped, squeezed her eyes closed, and, after a few deep breaths of her own, began again. "Looking back, it pains my heart to think of the things I said on your front porch that day. You were trying to offer me sympathy over the loss of my family, and I just wanted to know if I could give my baby up to Lydia to raise. I imagine there was shock on your face when I asked—in fact, I'm sure if I let myself revisit that moment, I'd see it there plain as day, but you never made me feel like I was an awful person. Instead, you tried to help me. You told me that the only way I'd be able to pick up the pieces of my life was to focus on the good and to let my memories of Jeff and the kids fill me up until I was walking on my own again." Danielle tried to stem the flow of tears making twin paths down her cheeks, but when it became clear it was a losing battle, she gave up and grabbed hold of the birthday girl's hand once again. "Do you remember that, Miss Lottie?"

"I do."

"You told me that my not being in the car with them wasn't a reflection on me as a mother, but rather an indication that it wasn't my time. That I was meant to still be here so I could be Grace's mamma."

"And what a wonderful mamma you are to that baby girl," Miss Lottie soothed while wiping at Danielle's tears with her free hand. "Just as you were to Maggie, and to Spencer, and to Ava."

Tess was glad for the limited time she'd known these women as that gave her the perfect reason to let the others descend on Danielle with hugs and gentle words while she worked to dislodge the lump inside her throat. Naomi, Katie, Emma, and Danielle believed Miss Lottie was their friend, just as Tess had believed Mandy had been hers. They had poignant examples to back up their belief just as she'd had about Mandy—examples that might even have swayed her opinion if she hadn't known the truth.

But she did. And there was absolutely no way on God's green earth she was going to sit by and let Lottie Jenkins continue playing them for fools. Not on her watch, anyway.

Plucking her glass off the table, Tess took a quick sip of her milk. "So . . . I met a very nice gentleman yesterday afternoon. His name is Joe."

"Joe Stoltzfus?" Katie asked.

"No."

Emma finished her sandwich and looked up at Tess. "Joe Gingerich?"

"No."

"It couldn't have been Joe Hotchstetler, as church was at his place yesterday," Naomi said.

"No. This Joe is English. He owns a fix-it shop out in New Holland." She felt Miss Lottie's eyes lift to hers but kept her own bouncing between Naomi and the others. "He's actually lived in the area all of his eighty-one years or so."

"He's eighty-one?" Emma asked, placing another half sandwich on her plate.

"He is."

Emma turned her ever-present smile on the birthday girl. "That's just like you, Miss Lottie!"

"I was thinking the same thing." This time, when Miss Lottie looked at Tess, Tess was ready and waiting. "Though when this Joe was a kid, he went by a nickname."

"Like Harp," Emma mused.

Nodding, Tess continued pinning Miss Lottie, daring the elderly woman to look away, to cough, to shift in her seat, to reach for her cane, to suddenly recall an appointment she'd forgotten. When there was nothing, Tess leaned forward. "His nickname was JJ."

Miss Lottie's answering gasp was enough to

let her know she was right, but in the outside chance the woman thought Tess hadn't put two and two together, she hit it home the rest of the way. "And JJ had his life absolutely destroyed by a girl named Dorothy. Dorothy Mill—"

"Naomi?"

Startled away from the moment, Tess glanced toward the corner of the house and the tear-soaked face of an Amish girl she guessed to be in her late teens. Before she could fully process the sight, though, Naomi and Katie were on their feet and making haste around the table to reach the stranger.

"Miriam, what happened?" Naomi asked as she grabbed hold of the girl's left arm and motioned for Katie to take the right. "Are you okay? Are you hurt?"

"Is-is it your mamm?" Katie added.

Miriam shook her head and then looked to Miss Lottie as a fresh set of tears rolled down her cheeks. "I-I went to your house, Miss Lottie, but your car was *here*. When Isaiah saw me, he said I would find you back here." The young woman's tears began to flow harder, faster. "But I . . . I did not know . . . I-I would be interrupting a-a meal. I . . . am . . . so . . . sorry."

"Shh . . . Shhh . . ." With Katie's help, Naomi led the distraught girl to Danielle's hastily vacated spot next to Miss Lottie. "Miss Lottie is here, Miriam. We all are."

"I should wait. Until later. When your meal is—"

"Come now, child. Sit," Miss Lottie said, reaching for Miriam's trembling hand. "You need us now, and we will be here for you now."

Like a doe ready to dart at a moment's notice, the young girl slowly and hesitantly lowered herself onto the bench, her shoulders hitching with each sniffle, each strangled sob "It-it is not me-me that Da-David wa-wants to court. It is . . . it is Ar-Arleta."

"Arleta Graber?" Emma asked.

A tear dropped from Miriam's eye down to her lap. "Yah."

"But I thought the Yoder boy liked *you*." Naomi placed one of the sandwich halves on a napkin and set it in front of Miriam. "He is always smiling at you and asking if you have brought him cookies. Even Isaiah has noticed."

"Yah," Miriam said between sniffles. "But it is just my baking that he likes, not me. It is Arleta he smiles at without asking about cookies."

Katie and Emma exchanged a look of surprise, with Katie breaking it first. "Perhaps you are wrong, Miriam. Perhaps he was smiling at Arleta because she said something funny. She can be a very funny girl sometimes."

"Katie is right," Emma said. "Arleta is funny. She even said something that made me laugh yesterday while I was holding Harp after our meal."

349

"David's smile was not because Arleta is funny. It is because she is pretty and smart and"— Miriam pressed back a sob with her fingertips— "everything I'm not."

"Maybe you're wrong, maybe—"

Miriam stopped Naomi's words with a hard shake of her head. "No. Last night . . . at the hymn sing . . . David gave Arleta a ride home in his buggy."

"Oh," Katie whispered, as Naomi and Emma looked down at their respective laps.

Miss Lottie's wrinkled hand reached across the corner of the table and slowly pulled Miriam's hand away from her mouth. "It's okay to cry and it's okay to hurt, child. You gave a part of your heart to David and that is *never* a bad thing, even if it feels that way now. The ability to love is a gift—a gift you've been given and that you, in turn, give to others."

And just like that the young girl scooted to the end of the bench and let herself be enveloped in Miss Lottie's arms. Seconds turned to a minute, and a minute became ten as the girl's heart-wrenching cries lessened and, finally, faded into sporadic hiccups.

"One day soon, though, someone will bring you home in their buggy because while you are pretty and smart, too, you will also be right for each other." Miss Lottie released the girl from her arms but held fast to her gaze. "And when

that day happens—and *it will* happen, child—
it will be because the smile you bring him and
the smile *he* brings *you* will fill both of you right
here." Miss Lottie pointed to Miriam's heart.

"But David *did* make me smile," Miriam
whispered, so softly Tess had to strain to hear
the girl's response. "Every time I brought him
cookies."

"Of course. Because you are kind, and you
like doing things for people that you think will
make them happy. But what I am talking about
is different," Miss Lottie said, her voice a quiet
mixture of comfort and firmness. "Yes, you will
still do nice things because that is who you are.
But when you find the right man, he will smile
at you simply because you—the person you are,
Miriam—will make him want to think about
you and *your feelings,* too. Because they matter,
child. They matter, and *you matter,* very much.
Never, ever forget that."

Miriam wiped her tears with the back of her
hand. "I don't know if I want to fall for someone
again. It hurts too much."

"I know it feels that way now. And it will
probably feel that way for a while. But David
wasn't the right one for you, child. Don't cheat
yourself of the one who is right because of one
who wasn't. You're far too special for that."

Her throat tightening, Tess reached for her glass
with hands she didn't realize were trembling.

"Tess?" Danielle whispered from her new spot at Tess's elbow. "Are you okay?"

She transitioned her intended sip into more of a gulp and then lowered the glass back to the table, her eyes stinging. "I'm fine."

CHAPTER 29

Tess dropped her hand to her side as Danielle's car, and the women waving from its passenger side, finally disappeared from view, leaving her alone on Naomi's front porch with Miss Lottie.

"We can talk at your place, or we can talk at my place," Tess said nudging her chin toward the Grossdawdy Haus. "Or, if you'd rather, we can go back inside and talk in front of Naomi while she prepares dinner for Isaiah and the children. It's your choice. But either way it happens now."

With the slightest of nods, Miss Lottie tightened her grip on her cane and made her way back to the door, her call to Naomi through the screen summoning their host in short order. "Naomi, I want to thank you again for a lovely day. It was so thoughtful of you to do this for me."

"It was all of us, Miss Lottie." Naomi pushed an errant strand of hair back under the front edge of her kapp and then returned her hand to the dish towel she clutched with the other. "We wanted you to know how special you are to all of us."

"And I do. Thank you. Thank you, too, for the quilt you made for me. That was a wonderful surprise, as was the book of poetry from Danielle, the pencil sketch from Katie, the book on hairstyles from Hannah, and the homemade candy from Emma."

Naomi's answering smile quickly bowed to worry as she stole a glance at Tess. "The quilt is from me *and* Tess," she corrected.

"And it's lovely."

"Would you like to stay for supper?" Naomi asked.

"No, dear. I'm going to spend a little time with Tess and then make my way home when we're done."

"That's good." Naomi looked past Miss Lottie to Tess. "Should I have Reuben bring over a plate when it's time to eat?"

"That would be great, thanks, Naomi." Backing away from the door, Tess waited for Miss Lottie to turn and then walked side by side with her down the porch and over to the Grossdawdy Haus.

Once inside and settled at the table, she ignored her notebook and its list of questions in favor of waiting the woman out.

She didn't have to wait long.

"Is he well?" Miss Lottie asked.

"Who?"

"JJ."

Tess's answering laugh echoed around them. "And you think you have a right to that information because why?"

"I don't."

"You're right, you don't. But I'm going to answer it, anyway, because I want you to know, just as I want *them*"—she hooked her thumb toward the front door—"to know, too."

Lifting her chin, Miss Lottie met Tess's eyes. "I would never hurt them. You must know that."

"I don't know that."

Pain lowered the woman's sightline back to the table and hands that fidgeted at its edge. "Please," she rasped. "Tell me about him. About his life, his family, his—"

"Family?"

"His wife, his children, his grandchildren . . ."

"There is no wife, no children, no grand-children. Because of you."

Miss Lottie's chin quivered as she lifted it again. "Because of me?"

"That's right. You were his *one*—the one who led him to believe you cared and then ran off for the great unknown with *his friend!*" Tess rocketed up and off the bench so hard it toppled over. "Do you know how that gets inside a person and makes them doubt their worth? Their judgement? Their-their . . . *everything?*"

"I—"

She stopped Miss Lottie's attempt to speak with a splayed hand. "Don't. Just don't. Because the truth is you don't know and you don't care."

"I didn't run off with that boy."

She paused in her effort to right the bench.

"Right. And I'm supposed to believe the timing of your"—she simulated quotes with her fingers—*"choice to leave the Amish* on the heels of money being stolen from your father's house was a coincidence?"

"No."

"Well, that's a start." Tess set the bench back in its place but opted to lean against the kitchen countertop instead. "Proceed."

"I *did* leave because of the money, but it wasn't to be with Carl."

"Please . . . Don't insult my intelligence."

Miss Lottie plucked off her glasses, set them on the table, and closed her eyes. "I was talking to a friend at the hymn sing when I saw JJ and Carl standing by the big tree. At first, I thought they were just English boys wanting to make fun of us. But when I looked closer, I saw that it was JJ and I got very excited.

"I'd met JJ when I was working at the ice cream parlor. After that first day, he came back again and again. He ate so much ice cream I told him he might start to moo. And that's when he told me he didn't even *like* ice cream all that much and that he just came all the time so he could see me. I thought that was silly since he was English, but he didn't seem to care that I wore a kapp even on Rumspringa. Soon, he started to walk me home, and we would talk the whole way. He would ask about the Amish ways and things I dreamed about, and he would tell me about his high school, and his parents, and his best friend—"

"Tom Richter," Tess finished for her.

"You know Tom?" Miss Lottie asked, popping her eyes open.

"I've met him, yes."

Miss Lottie waited for more but when Tess didn't deliver, she continued. "I had never thought I would leave my community until I met JJ. But with him, I *did* think about it. All the time, in fact. He was good and kind and—"

"And so you ran off with his friend. How lovely."

"I didn't see any other choice," Miss Lottie said, her voice, her face pained.

"You mean like telling JJ you weren't interested? Like not stealing money that was meant for an injured boy? *Those* choices?"

"I didn't want him to get in trouble because of me."

Tess stared at the woman. "Excuse me?"

"Carl was waiting for me on the road the morning after the hymn sing. I was going to work and he was supposed to be in school, like JJ." Miss Lottie seemed to fade out of the room, led away, no doubt, by her memories. "But he wasn't. He said things to me that I didn't like— about my clothes and my hair and what he would like to do to me. I tried to ignore him, to tell myself he would go away at some point, but he didn't. His words got more and more frightening, but I still stayed quiet. That is when he told me he took the money from my father's jar—money my community had raised to help pay the doctor bills for little Petey Esch."

Mesmerized, Tess returned to the table-side bench and waited for more.

"At first, I didn't believe him," Miss Lottie said. "I forgot that I'd told them about the money, and that I'd snuck Carl inside for a drink of water during the hymn sing when JJ had to go off somewhere for a few minutes. But then Carl reached inside his pocket and *showed* me the money. When I saw it, I told him he had to give it back, that it was not his to take, but he said no. That is when I said I would tell the police and they would make him give it back."

"Okay . . ."

"He said if I did that, he would tell the police that it was *JJ* who stole the money."

The ludicrousness of the woman's words pulled her out of the story. "But *Carl* had the money, not JJ."

"He said he'd put it in JJ's bag at school and then tell the police where to find it."

"He was going to *frame* him?"

Miss Lottie nodded. "He said that when they found it there, they would put JJ in jail for the rest of his life."

"They barely put murderers in jail for life these days."

"This was sixty-four years ago, and I was seventeen and unfamiliar with the English police," Miss Lottie said by way of explanation. "I believed him."

"So what? You ran off with this guy?"

Her gaze returned to Tess's. "I left, but not with Carl."

"But he never came back to school, and you left your home."

"I can't speak of what Carl did or where he went. I know only what *I* did," Miss Lottie said. "I knew it was only a matter of time before my dat realized the money was missing. I was afraid that if I told him what happened, he would go to the police and Carl would put that money in JJ's bag the way he said he would. So I went back home, took some of my things, and left my parents a note saying I wanted to live an English life like my brother."

"Did you tell *him* what happened?"

"My brother?" At Tess's nod, Miss Lottie shook her head. "No. I only stayed with him for a little while. Once I had earned enough money from a waitressing job, I moved out. Spent the next almost-forty years working a slew of jobs and traveling."

"And where did your marriage fit in in all of that?"

Miss Lottie drew back. "I never married."

"Then how do you explain the name change from Miller to Jenkins?"

"I changed it. Legally."

"Why?"

Once again, Miss Lottie, while still present in the room, disappeared to somewhere far beyond its confines. "I was ashamed of what I had done—of the position I'd put my dat and the community in by bringing that boy in our house. And when I learned little Petey Esch had died, I knew I didn't deserve to carry my father's name."

"So you picked the name *Jenkins* out of a hat?" Tess asked.

"No. I took it so I would always have a piece of JJ."

"A piece of JJ? How?"

"JJ was short for Joseph Jenkins—Joseph Jenkins Wilder."

The weight of the woman's words hung so heavy Tess could barely breathe, let alone think straight. "I don't know what to say, or what to— wait!" She sat up tall. "Why didn't you tell Joe what had happened? *He* knew he hadn't taken the money."

"Carl said he would tell JJ things that were not true about me . . . Awful, horrible things. Things that didn't happen between Carl and me when I let him inside for a drink, but that he would tell as if they did."

"Wow. This kid was awful."

Miss Lottie buried her face in her hands, her words a bit more difficult to decipher from behind their temporary cover. "He will have his day with the Lord if he hasn't already."

"So you did what you did to protect JJ and because of the shame you felt over the money being stolen . . . I get that. But why did you choose to come back here twenty-five years ago?"

"I wanted to come home—to the last place where I'd ever really felt at peace."

"Yet you came back as Lottie Jenkins, and not Dorothy Miller," Tess said. "And you told no one until years later."

Miss Lottie's nod was slow, labored. "Family-wise, there was no one left to tell, or so I thought. And when I finally realized Katie's mamm was my kin, Hannah was thinking of leaving and I felt my friendship was needed more. And then when their mamm became sick and we knew she wouldn't recover, I decided to let things be."

"Yet you told *Katie* after her mamm's passing. Why her? Why then?"

"I would like to say it was all about helping her through a difficult time, but I think the true reason is that *I* needed that connection, that sense of having real ties. *I* needed to acknowledge that kinship. *For me.*"

"And Joe—I mean *JJ?* Why didn't you try to find him?"

"I was fifty-six when I came back, Tess. Why would he have cared if some Amish girl he'd met in an ice cream parlor forty years earlier was back in town? Especially when that same Amish girl had left without an explanation or a goodbye?"

Tess sat with the story for a while, processing and replaying bits and pieces in her thoughts while sneaking peeks at the elderly woman seated on the other side of the table. "You haven't found that peace you came back for, have you?"

Slowly, Miss Lottie returned fully to the room and to Tess. "No, not completely. But perhaps now, through you, I will."

"Through me?"

"And your story."

Her story . . .

She'd almost forgotten about that.

"Maybe I need people to know that money was stolen because of me . . . that my actions hurt many people . . . that I brought shame to my mother and father . . . that I ran away because I was weak, and stayed away because it was easier . . . Perhaps then, when the truth is finally out, I will truly be at peace."

CHAPTER 30

Tess pushed the last of her dinner off to the side and reached for her computer, the cursor rhythmically mocking her inability to write anything worth keeping. She'd tried, of course. Many, many times. But every time she typed so much as a sentence, she deleted it off the screen, unhappy with her wording, her direction, her everything.

Glancing at her notebook and the notes she'd made after Miss Lottie's departure, she willed herself to get her act together, to find the words that were proving elusive. What she'd attributed to hunger had been proven wrong by her near-empty plate. And what she'd attributed to needing a little space from the subject at hand hadn't panned out as a viable excuse, either, on account of the book she'd tried and failed to read during the first half of her meal.

The vibration of an incoming text message cut through her mental browbeating and sent her attention toward her phone. The name on top of the message was the answer to a prayer she hadn't prayed. And the one-word question it contained had her thumbs fairly flying across the tiny keyboard.

Yes, I can talk!

She hit Send, stuck her tongue out at her computer, and then carried her phone into the bedroom to wait for Murph's call. Falling backward onto her bed, she stared up at the ceiling, ready to pounce on the phone the second it—

"Hey, Murph." Tess pressed the phone to her ear. "What are you doing up so early?"

"Haven't gone to bed yet."

"Night mission?"

"Can't answer that, kid."

"But you're back where you can text and call me, right? So that must mean it went well?"

"Still can't answer."

She pulled a face he couldn't see and then zeroed in on the sounds she could hear in the background of the call. "Are you eating chips?"

"Pretzels, actually." Chewing was followed by a swallow and a gulp of something. "I'm guessing by your tone and the fact you responded to my text that you haven't written me off after our last conversation."

"Our last conversation?"

"About your story."

"Right." She scooted up and onto her pillow and planted her stocking feet on the colorful quilt. "Well, you ticked me off, that's for sure. But we're not always going to see eye to eye on a story, right? It happens."

"Still chasing it?"

"The story?" At his grunt of assent, she fixed her gaze on the last of the day's light as it receded from the room. "I've caught it."

All chewing stopped in her ear. "Meaning?"

"I talked to her. About all of it."

"And?"

"Technically, she didn't steal the money."

"So we're supposed to believe it was just a coincidence that she took off for the hills the very next day?" he asked.

"The one who *did* steal it threatened to frame her boyfriend if she tried to tell anyone the truth. She knew it was only a matter of time before her father discovered the money was missing and she was ashamed—for bringing this boy into her home, for hurting the family of the little boy who needed the money for medical expenses, and for knowing she'd have to lie to her father in order to keep her boyfriend from getting in trouble for something he hadn't done."

As he ate his way through what sounded like an entire bag of pretzels, she told him everything she'd learned about Dorothy Miller, and about the woman's eventual road back to Lancaster County as Lottie Jenkins. When she finished, the chewing ceased.

"And your friends?" Murph asked. "How did they take it?"

"I haven't told them. Yet."

"Oh?"

Dropping her legs flat against the bed, she elbowed her way up to a seated position. "I was starting to when Miriam showed up."

"Who's Miriam?"

"A young Amish girl who came looking for Miss Lottie." Tess swung her feet over the edge of the bed and onto the floor, a growing restlessness stirring a sudden need to move. "She'd had her heart crushed by a boy she liked, and so she did what all the women around here seem to do when they are upset or lost—they go running to Miss Lottie."

"Why do you think that is?"

Tess wandered to the bedroom window and looked out at the barn. "I think it's because Miss Lottie has this way of making you think. It's like . . ." She cast about for the right words only to shake her head in defeat. "I don't think I can describe it."

"Try."

"Well, like, today, before Miriam got there . . . Naomi and everyone took turns letting Miss Lottie know how she's helped them in their lives. And one thing they all had in common was the feeling that Miss Lottie had empowered them to get through whatever trial they were facing.

"For Naomi, it was the fear of the unknown when it was time to leave her parents' home and marry Isaiah. Miss Lottie let her share her fears and then helped her see it all from another perspective—one of looking forward to all the wonderful things to come."

Drawing in a breath, she allowed herself to revisit the table, the party, and the people as she took Murph with her. "For Emma, it was the shock of finding out her parents weren't her parents, after all. From what she said, Miss Lottie never really said what she thought of the whole thing or what she thought Emma should or shouldn't do. Rather, she encouraged Emma to seek the truth, and then, and only then, could Emma know what was best for herself."

"Sound advice," Murph mused between gulps of something.

"*Katie* sought Miss Lottie's help when she was trying to figure out whether she should leave the Amish or stay. And whether she truly had a choice considering the fact that staying meant having to give up a passion, and leaving meant giving up her family. Again, Miss Lottie didn't tell Katie what she thought she should do. She just listened, and imparted words that made Katie think and, finally, choose what was best for *Katie*."

"Okay . . ."

"Then there's Danielle. This woman lost her entire family. Bam! Gone! From what I gathered about her, she was despondent, angry, guilt-ridden, and convinced she'd been a horrible mother. So when she found out she was pregnant, she wanted to give the baby to someone she thought was more worthy. Miss Lottie never made her feel judged in that plan. Instead, she listened and, when the time was right, told her what she needed to hear—that Danielle's husband and kids would live on forever in Danielle's memories if she'd let them, and that maybe she was spared because she was meant to be the new baby's mother. And you know what, Murph? This woman still hurts—you can see it plain as day at times. But there's so much joy there, too."

She backed away from the window and wandered back to the bed. "And then there was Miriam. Until she showed up, all this talk about Miss Lottie and what she's done for all of them was just that—talk. The kind of yay-rah-rah you'd expect to be shared about someone on their birthday. But with Miriam, I got to see it myself."

"See what?"

"This woman is more than just a listening ear. She gives people hope when they need it most."

"Hope?" Murph prodded.

"Yes. Hope. Hope that they can and will make it through whatever darkness they find themselves in. Hope is how Naomi found the courage to embrace the future, how Emma was able to forgive, how Katie was able to figure out where she belongs, how Danielle learned to keep living and to embrace what comes next, and how Miriam . . ."

She lowered herself onto the edge of the bed. "Miriam left believing that the reason this boy didn't choose her is because *he* wasn't right *for Miriam*. That the one who *is* right for her is still out there, and that when she finds him he'll—and I'm paraphrasing here—truly appreciate what he has in her."

"Hmmm . . . Sounds like Miriam got some good food for thought there." The crunching in her ear ceased, followed, seconds later, by the sound of the pretzel bag being crushed into a ball. "So are you going to tell your friends about Miss Lottie's past or are you going to let them read about it?"

"That implies I've actually written something," she said, free-falling onto the bed.

"And I take it you haven't?"

Hooking her arm over her eyes, she blew out a breath. "Nope. And it's not from a lack of trying, that's for sure. I just can't find my starting place. I keep writing and deleting, and writing and deleting, and it's driving me nuts."

"You'll have that."

"Does that mean that's happened to you, Murph?"

"A few times, sure."

"And?" she asked. "What did you do?"

"I stepped back. When I did, I realized I was trying to write the wrong story."

CHAPTER 31

After a restless night of tossing and turning, and a handful of morning chores she was becoming more proficient at with each passing day, Tess closed her fist against the sunshine-yellow door and knocked.

Seconds turned to minutes while she waited, her thoughts returning to the quick phone call she'd made en route to her destination and the way her request had gone unquestioned even though she'd done nothing to earn that right. Yet.

She lifted her hand to knock a second time but dropped it to her side as the door creaked open and Miss Lottie peeked out.

"Good morning, Tess."

"Good morning, Miss Lottie."

"You look as tired as I feel."

Tess shrugged. "Probably because neither of us got much sleep last night."

"I know you're worried about your friends and how my failure to tell them who I am and what I've done will hurt them. But I don't want you losing sleep over it. I'm going to tell them all. Today."

Tess pushed aside the woman's worry as if it were a weighted thing blocking her path. "I wasn't able to sleep because of Miriam—*both* Miriams."

"*Both* Miriams?"

"The one before you, and the one after you."

"I don't understand, child."

"*Before* you, Miriam was positively distraught, convinced there was something wrong with her that made David choose another girl to court. *After* you, and, really, *because* of you, Miriam was able to find comfort in knowing David wasn't the right one. That one day, when it's right, she'll meet someone who will truly see—*and treasure*—her as the special person you know her to be." Tess didn't mean for her words to pick up speed, or to have to practically gulp down breaths in order to keep up with them, but she couldn't help it, either. "The truth of what wasn't meant to be, and the truth of what's to come, helped Miriam forward yesterday. I saw that with my own two eyes. And it got me thinking about how the opposite can be true, too."

"The opposite?" Miss Lottie echoed.

"How the lack of truth and hope can make it so a person can't move forward, and how changing that might make all the difference in the world." She retrieved the card she'd tucked into her back pocket and glanced between it and Miss Lottie. "That's why I'd like to take you somewhere this morning if you'll let me."

Before the woman could inquire as to where, Tess held the card out for the taking and watched as the answer revealed itself by way of a furrowed brow, a pinched mouth, and, finally, an answering tear of understanding.

"Joe has spent too many years not knowing, Miss Lottie. So, tell him," Tess urged. "Let him listen the way you told Emma to listen. Let him figure out where he fits like you told Katie to do. And consider that there's a reason you're here, in this place, just like you told Danielle."

Somehow she wasn't surprised to see Jack's truck already in the driveway when she turned off Miss Lottie's car. Even though she'd requested ninety minutes, she knew he'd picked something up in her voice—something she'd explain when he drove her back home. For now, though, her focus was the woman seated beside her, quietly surveying the trappings of a life imagined a million times over.

"Are you ready?" Tess asked.

"I'm trying to be." Miss Lottie took the keys Tess held out to her and slipped them into the purse at her feet. "I *will* be."

"Just tell the truth. You've lived with it—and he's lived without it—for far too long."

"And if he doesn't let me finish?" Miss Lottie asked, hoisting her purse onto her lap with one hand and reaching for her cane with the other.

"He will."

"How do you know?

"Because the man inside that house"—Tess

nudged her chin toward the front porch—"wants nothing more than to know this truth."

Miss Lottie closed her eyes, drew in a breath, and then opened them in time with a deep exhale. "Okay. I'm ready."

Nodding, Tess stepped out of the car and made her way around to the passenger door in time to help Miss Lottie onto her feet. Together, they stepped onto the flagstone walkway as a steady *tap-tap* filled the air around them.

"It sounds like he's in his shop."

"He is." Startled, Tess turned back toward the house in time to see Jack emerging from the side door with a glass of lemonade in his hand. "Hey, Tess! Hey, Miss Lottie!"

"You know each other?" Tess asked as the two exchanged an embrace.

"We met through Emma, remember?"

"I didn't, but okay, it makes sense." She took in his button-down shirt and khakis and instinctively straightened her own shirt. "You're early."

"I know. But Brad and I finished with a meeting earlier than I expected so I just figured I'd head on over rather than wait."

His words pushed her back a step. "Oh, Jack, I'm so sorry. I wasn't even thinking about it being a workday when I called. If I had, I would've just called a cab or found another ride home."

"I'm glad you did. Though it looks like you've got a ride," he said, pointing to the driveway.

"That's Miss Lottie's car, and she'll be staying longer than me."

"You've got a big fix-it job for Joe?" he asked, smiling at Miss Lottie. "Because he can fix anything."

Looking in the direction of the tapping, Miss Lottie shook her head. "I only hope I can say the same thing."

"There's only one way to find out." Tess pointed the elderly woman toward the workshop. "So go find out."

Sensing Jack's forward motion, she stopped him with a gentle hand on his arm. "She's got this," Tess whispered.

"What am I missing?" he whispered back as Miss Lottie headed in the direction of the hammering.

She held her finger to her lips as Miss Lottie stopped at the partially opened door and knocked. "JJ? It's me—Dorothy."

They were barely in the truck before the questions started—one behind the other, in rapid succession.

"Dorothy? As in *the* Dorothy?"

Nodding, she looked back at the now-closed door of the workshop, her mind's eye replaying the hug that was sixty-four years in the making . . .

"But I thought her name was Miss Lottie and—wait! He called her his Lottie Dottie, didn't he?"

"Yes."

His mouth gaped, closed, and gaped again. "I can't believe this. I mean, she's been here for *how long* now?"

"Twenty-five years, I think."

"And she's just now coming to see him?"

"I'd say she didn't know, but I think it was more a case of being afraid to know," Tess said, resting her head against the seatback as he piloted the truck down the driveway and onto the road.

"Wow."

"I know. Trust me."

"How long have you known?" Jack asked.

"I didn't know for sure until we left Joe's on Sunday."

"Why didn't you say anything then?"

It was a good question—one she could finally answer thanks to Miss Lottie. "Because I was trying to guard my big story the way I've been trying to guard everything else in my life this past year."

She felt the truck slow, felt his eyes as they left the road in favor of her, but she wasn't ready to meet them. Not yet, anyway. "What you said on Sunday? What your grandfather said? You're both right. I've chosen to let two really bad apples sour me against living. Against trusting. Against . . . *myself*. And in the process of doing that, I have become bitter and prickly and not very likeable."

"My granddad would disagree with you, it seems."

She waved aside his words. "I think your granddad is just a really nice guy. Like Joe. And like you."

"I thought I was a jerk."

"A jerk who tried really hard to make a connection with someone who tried equally hard to brush him off. And still he jockeyed her around town on his day off, and gave up his lunch break to do it again today."

"Hmmm . . . So as far as jerks go, I could be worse?"

She smiled. "Most definitely."

Movement out of the corner of her eye had her looking toward the steering wheel in time to see him pump his hand in the air in victory. "So then maybe?"

"Maybe what?"

"Maybe I could talk you into a date sometime?"

She turned and looked out the window, her heart beginning to pound in her ears. "I-I don't think so. I'm only here for a little while longer."

"So? If it goes well, it's not like you live on the other side of the country. Three-plus hours is a more than doable drive."

She didn't need a mirror to know her smile had disappeared. She could feel its absence just as surely as she could the sudden misting in her eyes. "There's a lot I need to figure out—

to relearn—before I can even think about dating again."

"What do you have to relearn?"

"First and foremost, how to trust myself and my read on people. Because so far, I get a failing grade in both the friend *and* dating department."

"I'm pretty sure you're not the one who earned that grade."

"Maybe not. But I was too stupid to see it."

"Believing in people you care about doesn't make you stupid."

"It makes you vulnerable," she managed past the emotion building in her throat.

"You're right, it does. But in the chance you might find that perfect-for-you apple, it's so worth it."

"How do you know?"

"I watched it play out with my granddad and my grandmother right before my eyes. My parents, too. But just because they were lucky enough to find the right apple from the start doesn't mean you, or I, or anyone else should just give up if we don't."

Was he right? She didn't know.

"I'm willing to wait, Tess. Just so you know."

She turned to stare at him. "Wait for what?"

"For you to agree to a date."

"Why?" she asked. "You don't even know me. And what you *do* know of me has had me being bitter and prickly, to use your own words."

"*Reuben* thinks the world of you."

"Reuben is *four*."

"You know what they say about the mouths of babes . . ." He slowed as they approached a buggy, then carefully passed when it was clear to do so. "And it's not just Reuben, either. I was out at Emma's place with Brad and Levi when she got back from some gathering you were at together yesterday."

"Miss Lottie's birthday party," Tess said.

"Emma adores you."

Her answering laugh was shallow even to her own ears. "She wouldn't if she knew why I went to that party in the first place."

"Out of curiosity, why *did* you go?" he asked.

"To essentially blow up everything Naomi and Emma and Danielle and Katie thought they knew about Miss Lottie for"—she splayed her hands in the air—"my *big* story."

"I don't understand."

"Hello? Miss Lottie is Dorothy Miller? She disappeared after money was stolen from her father's house—money that was meant for a little boy's medical bills?"

He raked a hand across the top of his head. "Right. I forgot."

"Miss Lottie kept the truth of what she did from these women—women who adore her."

"Then why wasn't Emma upset when I saw her?"

"Because I didn't end up telling them right then and there."

"Why not?" he asked.

"Because I like these people." Tess looked down at her hands. "They've welcomed me into their lives—no questions asked."

"That's what friends do, Tess."

"Friends . . ." For the first time in far too long she didn't feel the desire to rail against that word. Instead, she let herself sit with its truth before continuing on with the story. "So I waited until everyone left to talk to Miss Lottie alone, fully intending to still tell them and to still write my story. But then, after hearing what really happened, I couldn't stop thinking about how she helped Naomi, and how she helped Emma, and how she helped Katie, and how she helped Danielle, and how she helped Miriam, and, really, what was in it for her? You could argue it was a way to clear her conscience, and maybe—just maybe—there was a small measure of that. But I don't think that's the overriding factor. I think, maybe it's . . ." Sinking down into her seat, Tess blew out a long, extended breath. "Long story short, I called you and asked you to pick me up."

"Why?" he asked.

"Why did I ask you to pick me up? Because you're the only person I know with a car around here."

He pulled a face. "No. I mean why did you bring her out to see Joe?"

Just like that, she was back at Naomi's, listening to words meant for someone else, yet they struck a chord deep inside her own heart.

"Don't cheat yourself of the one who is right because of one who wasn't."

Even now, the memory of that moment stirred something so strong inside her she had to hurry her answer before she got too emotional to speak. "For sixty-four years, Miss Lottie and Joe have been cheated out of their what-might-have-been because of *someone else's* deception. That's not okay."

"You're right, it's not okay." He pulled over onto the grassy shoulder and then guided her eyes onto his with the curve of his index finger. "It's not okay for them, and it's not okay for you."

CHAPTER 32

This time, when Tess sat at the kitchen table in the Grossdawdy Haus, she had everything arranged the way she did at the office. Her mug of coffee was to her left, her notebook and pen were to her right, and her fully charged (thanks to Jack) laptop was placed in just the right spot to make typing comfortable. But even without those things, she was finally ready to write.

It wasn't the big, splashy tale she'd imagined, nor was it anything that would necessarily cause a stampede in purchasing whatever issue Sam saw fit to place it, but it was the story most deserving of being told—a story of love and friendship and respect and . . . *hope*.

Hope that a better day would come.

Hope that truth really does matter in the end.

Hope that time does heal.

Hope that forgiveness is something worth giving.

Hope that kindness given will find its way back when it's needed most.

Hope that true friendship does exist.

And hope that love—real love—will always win in the end. For everyone.

Placing her fingers atop the keyboard, Tess

began to type, the opening coming as quickly and easily as her smile . . .

Nestled amid the farmland of Lancaster County's Amish, alongside crops of barley and wheat, something far more valuable and sustaining is being planted and grown: hope.

EPILOGUE

(Nine months later)

She was halfway across the conference center lobby when Murph stepped through the doors of the banquet room and halted her entrance with his hand and a less than subtle double take.

"Wow. You clean up really well, kid."

Glancing down at the lilac dress she'd finally decided on, Tess gave in to the smile her nerves had held at bay all afternoon. "You really think so?"

"I really *know* so." He swept his hands and her gaze toward the growing crowd. "So, what do you think? Is it what you thought?"

"I came to this last year, Murph. Remember?"

"As part of *my* cheering section, sure. But this time it's about you, and your story, and the fact it resonated with enough people that you just might end up getting that plaque you've been wanting before the night is over."

She took a moment to take it all in: the sea of faces making their way into the banquet room, the easel-topped placard announcing the annual top-story awards, her dress, and, finally, Murph in his once-a-year suit, the calm she felt hard-won but no less complete. "If it happens, great.

But I mean what I told you when the nominations were announced. Getting to write that story was better than any plaque could ever be."

Rocking back on the heels of his dress shoes, he studied her closely. "You ever wish Brian and Mandy could see you now—how far you've come, how happy you are, that"—he uncrossed his arms in favor of spreading them wide—"you made *this* happen?"

"If I thought about them, maybe I would. But I really don't. It's hard to move forward when you're looking backward all the time, you know? And besides, you're here for me tonight—that's so much more than enough."

"You sure about that last part?"

"About you being here for me tonight?" At his half shrug, half nod, she grabbed his hand. "I'm not sure when you became such a softy, but it becomes you."

He rolled his eyes. "And there you have it—my one and only positive for you leaving us behind for that rinky-dink paper in Pennsylvania. I can go back to being me, crusty and fear-inducing."

"As if." The people around them all but fell away as she waited for his full attention. When she had it, she held it fast. "And remember, just because I'm at that rinky-dink paper as you call it, I'm still reachable by phone, day or night. And when you feel like having a little Murph time, I'm only a few hours' drive away."

"But that would mean I had a life—with friends—outside of the office."

"We've got the friend part more than covered, Murph. My being in Pennsylvania just means you might finally have a reason to leave the office on occasion."

"You're a pill, kid."

"I know." Tightening her hold on his hand, Tess tugged him into the banquet room. "Now c'mon, we need to hurry or we might not be able to find two seats together."

"Oh, we've got seats—a whole table in fact, Miss Nominee."

She stopped, scanned the tables closest to where they were, and then looked back at Murph. "An eight-person table? For just you, me, and Sam?"

"And *them*."

Propelled forward by Murph's hand, she let her gaze skip ahead to Sam and—

"*Jack?*" she rasped.

"Nice guy, that one. I can see why you like spending time with him."

Her answering smile made her lips tremble as she picked up the pace, weaving her way between tables. "Oh, Murph, you have no idea. He's—"

She stopped as the misting in her eyes cleared enough to absorb the face next to Jack's. "Wait. *Tom* came, too?"

"That's Jack's grandfather, right?"

385

She was pretty sure she nodded or, at the very least, started to nod. But all she knew with absolute certainty was that she didn't need her name to be read in conjunction with an award for the waterworks to start flowing and—

"*Miss Lottie* and *Joe,* too?" she said as her gaze shifted still further around the table. "And . . . *Danielle?* I-I don't understand, Murph. Why are they all here?"

"It's easy, kid. You're loved."

Tess ran the rest of the way to the table and allowed herself to be swept up into hug after hug after hug, the reason for them being there—for *her* being there—paling against the fact that they *were* there. For her.

ACKNOWLEDGMENTS

I can't tell you how much I've enjoyed writing about Miss Lottie and the many Amish women she's taken under her wing in *Portrait of a Sister*, *A Daughter's Truth*, *Piece by Piece*, and, now, *Her New Story*. I've loved escaping into that world and seeing how each protagonist has maneuvered her way through life-altering moments and come out on the other side. Stronger than ever.

Life isn't easy. And sometimes it deals us the kind of heartache that is tough to come back from. But I believe we're all capable of doing just that. And if we have the right people in our lives cheering us on from the sidelines, even better.

My hope is that you all have people like that in your lives. And that you've been that for others, as well.

All problems are temporary. Remember that.

Thank you for making the choice to read this book. And if you enjoy it, please tell a friend about it so maybe they, too, will pick up a copy. And finally, if you like what you've read and are curious about what else I've written, please visit my website at laurabradford.com.

QUESTIONS
FOR DISCUSSION

1. Tess didn't see the betrayal from her husband and her best friend coming. Do you think being blindsided by betrayal makes it worse? Why or why not?

2. Murph is, in many ways, an unlikely person to offer a helping hand to Tess. But he does. Why do you think that is? Do you have a good and faithful friend like Murph that came from an unlikely place? Why do you think you two connected?

3. Tess hangs everything on her remote assignment. Why is that?

4. Murph tries to tell Tess to use her time while on assignment to get back on her feet. Tess is so blinded by hurt, she rebukes this idea. Do you think she knows, on some level, he's right, or do you think she truly believes she's okay?

5. Tess thinks trusting people can lead only to pain. Do you think it's better to be immediately trusting and risk being hurt, or to

keep people at a distance until they prove themselves?

6. Tess becomes so obsessed with finding a juicy story that she misses so much good that is happening around her. Have you ever found yourself in that same place?

7. When Tess tracks down the truth about Miss Lottie, she is determined to share it. She believes, that by doing so, she'll keep the women she's met from experiencing the same blindsided betrayal she has. Do you think that's her true intention or do you think—like Murph suggests—she's really going from betrayed to betrayer?

8. Tess has a change of heart where Miss Lottie is concerned. What do you think sparked that? Did you agree with her change of heart?

9. What one person got through to Tess most? Or, do you think it was a combination of people?

10. Was there a particular woman's story you identified with? Which one and why?

Books are produced in the United States using U.S.-based materials

Books are printed using a revolutionary new process called THINKtech™ that lowers energy usage by 70% and increases overall quality

Books are durable and flexible because of Smyth-sewing

Paper is sourced using environmentally responsible foresting methods and the paper is acid-free

Center Point Large Print
600 Brooks Road / PO Box 1
Thorndike, ME 04986-0001 USA

(207) 568-3717

US & Canada:
1 800 929-9108
www.centerpointlargeprint.com